FELL THE ANGELS

Charles Cranbrook collapses and dies a horrific death at The Priory, the neo-gothic house bought with his wealthy wife Cecilia's money. Was he murdered, or did he take his own life? In the course of the inquest, it emerges that beautiful Cecilia had been involved in a scandalous affair that is the talk of London.

FELL THE ANGELS

FELL THE
ANGELS

by

John Kerr

Magna Large Print Books
Long Preston, North Yorkshire,
BD23 4ND, England.

British Library Cataloguing in Publication Data.

Kerr, John
    Fell the angels.

    A catalogue record of this book is
    available from the British Library

    ISBN   978-0-7505-3730-8

First published in Great Britain in 2012 by Robert Hale Ltd.

Copyright © John Kerr 2012

Cover illustration © Clayton Bastiani by arrangement with
Arcangel Images

The right of John Kerr to be identified as the author of this work has
been asserted by him in accordance with the Copyright, Designs and
Patents Act, 1988

Published in Large Print 2013 by arrangement with
Robert Hale Ltd.

Magna Large Print is an imprint of Library Magna Books Ltd.

Printed and bound in Great Britain by
T.J. (International) Ltd., Cornwall, PL28 8RW

For Baine and Mildred Kerr

My dear father and mother

'I charge thee, fling away ambition

By that sin fell the angels'

Henry VIII Act 3 Scene ii

William Shakespeare

Prologue

A large orange cat, a male as its owner insisted that only males possessed the requisite temperament to share his lodgings, was curled on the grand piano, swishing its ringed tail slowly back and forth like a metronome. Its master, a tall man in early middle age, sat comfortably in his favourite armchair, imagining an invisible pianist playing a melody synchronized with the motion of the cat's tail. He gazed contentedly around the book-lined study, with its worn Persian carpet and eclectic works of art on the panelled walls and exotic objects from India and the West Indies. After a moment he lowered his eyes to the thick volume in his lap, titled *Principles of Toxicology*, consulted the index and located the entry he was seeking. With down-turned mouth, he grimly read the description of the properties of the powerful poison and its recommended uses, in extremely small doses, for the treatment of a host of human and veterinary maladies. Snapping the volume shut and putting it aside, he rose, walked to the coal scuttle, and used the tongs to place another lump on the grate, radiating warmth. With his back to the fire, he listened to the sound of the door in the hall and observed as a large man, wearing a heavy coat with fur collar, gloves, and astrakhan hat entered the study.

'Good evening, Cameron,' said the visitor, removing his hat and tossing it on a chair.

'Good evening, Clifton,' replied Duncan Cameron in a faint Scottish burr.

His visitor, obviously very much at home, stripped off his gloves and coat, which he folded over the back of the chair. Reaching for a crystal decanter on a trolley, he poured an inch of brandy in a tumbler and said, 'Wretched night out.'

Cameron straightened his waistcoat and gazed at James Clifton, a heavy-set man of similar age with dark sideburns and moustache in contrast to Cameron's clean-shaven face. 'You may pour me a glass,' Cameron said pleasantly.

Handing Cameron his brandy, Clifton said, 'Cheers,' and raised his glass. 'Who was the lady,' he asked, 'leaving in that elaborate coach as I was paying off the hansom?'

'A certain Lady Cranbrook,' said Cameron, swirling his brandy before taking a sip.

'Oh, really? Not the same Cranbrook in the newspapers...' said Clifton, his bushy eyebrows upraised.

'Precisely. The poor man's mother. Obviously, much distressed.'

Clifton took a step toward the door and removed a cavalry sabre from an umbrella stand. He briefly studied its fine tempered blade and tested its sharpness on his thumb. 'And so,' he said, 'did you agree to assist...?'

'Without hesitation.' Cameron sipped his brandy and smiled. 'The lady's prepared to pay a handsome fee.' He walked over to take the sabre from his friend and then suddenly lunged and thrust its tip into one of the pillows on the sofa. 'And I imagine,' he concluded, tossing the sabre back to Clifton, 'the case will prove to be a formidable, and exceptionally intriguing, challenge.'

Chapter One

Cecilia Castello sat in an over-stuffed mahogany chair in the large drawing-room at Buscot Park, her family's country house situated on 3000 acres of rolling parkland in Oxfordshire. Wearing a pink and burgundy silk gown and matching hat just acquired from her London dressmaker, she twisted her handkerchief into a knot as she waited nervously for her father, the wealthy industrialist Sir Richard Henderson. A servant opened a door, and Sir Richard strode in, finely polished boots tapping on the old parquet. 'There you are, dear,' he said, as he bowed at the waist and lightly kissed her hand. 'Feeling better?'

'I suppose so,' she replied with a wan smile and slight toss of her auburn curls.

'Now what is it you wished to discuss?' he asked, hooking his thumbs in his black waistcoat.

'Well, Father,' she said, 'I'd planned only to depart on Sunday, but I've been thinking of extending my stay. Perhaps through the summer.' She gazed absently at the tapestries and large oil portraits that adorned the pale-blue walls.

'I'm afraid that's out of the question,' said Henderson without hesitation. 'Your place is with your husband.'

'But Father.' She looked up at him pleadingly. 'I can't go back to him.'

'Nonsense,' he said. 'In marriage, you must learn to take the bad with the good, and besides, Captain Castello has provided very–'

'Don't say it,' interrupted Cecilia sharply. 'You've no idea what I've been through. I can't abide the man.'

Henderson began to speak but thought better of it, aware that his headstrong daughter, whom he was inclined to regard as a petulant child, was determined to have her say.

'Robert's a beast, Father,' she continued in a heated tone. 'He's constantly drinking, and he says and does the most unspeakable things. Ever since he resigned from his regiment, he has nothing to do but lie about the house and drink himself into a stupor.' She paused and then said, 'The other evening, following supper – during which Robert consumed an entire bottle of Madeira – I was reprimanding him for his shameful treatment of the scullery maid, when he flew into a violent rage. And he struck me.'

'Struck you?'

'Yes, three times, in the face. And then he overturned the furniture, shouting profanities, and when I struggled with him he hurled me to the floor. His manservant had to intervene or he might well have killed me.'

'Good heavens,' muttered Henderson.

'Would you care to see the bruises?' asked Cecilia, lifting the hem of her dress.

'No, dear.' Aware that his daughter was on the verge of nervous collapse, he said, 'I'm calling for the doctor. In the meantime you should go to your room and get plenty of rest.'

The following morning, when Cecilia was feeling well enough to dress and come down, she sat opposite her father at the breakfast-table in a sunlit alcove by the kitchen. Pouring each of them another cup of tea, Sir Richard said, 'It's your Christian duty, of course, to stand by your husband.'

She looked him in the eye and said, 'It's quite simple, Father: I refuse to go back to him.'

'Well, dear, you can't stay here. It wouldn't do. Despite what you say, your place is with Robert. Perhaps I could speak to him—'

'No!' she said fiercely.

'All right, then,' said Henderson, raising a placating hand. 'Your mother and I have been talking, and we have a suggestion.' Her features softened, and she took a sip of tea. 'Over lunch at White's last week,' he continued, 'I heard about a remarkable treatment developed by a physician named Gully. Doctor James Gully. Have you heard of him?' Cecilia shook her head. 'Very famous, who counts among his patients Dickens, Lord Tennyson, Charles Darwin, even the prime minister. I actually met the man, years ago...'

'Father, what can this possibly have to do with Robert?'

Unperturbed, Henderson said, 'Doctor Gully operates what is regarded as the finest hydro in the country. At Malvern. You're familiar with hydros?'

'Yes, I suppose. Where one goes for the water cure.'

'Precisely. Hydropathy, I believe they call it. Supposedly works wonders for all manner of maladies, not least mental and emotional exhaustion. All our Scottish cousins swear by it.' Henderson gazed at Cecilia and placed a hand on her arm. 'We can arrange for you to go to Dr Gully's sanatorium,' he suggested gently. 'Spend several weeks, a month.'

Cecilia shook her head and said, 'I'm not sure. It sounds rather dreadful, like going to hospital.'

'No, no,' said Henderson. 'Think of it as a holiday. An opportunity for rest and relaxation, and the curative effects of the famous Malvern waters.'

Cecilia nodded, and quietly said, 'All right.'

'And then,' he concluded, 'when you're rested and well, we can decide what's best for you and Robert.'

'Oh, Father,' she exclaimed. 'Thank you.'

Standing at the open window with her hands on the sill, Cecilia Castello gazed out on the nearby promenade garden, a densely wooded hillside and beyond, stretching to the far horizon, the gently rolling fields, a patchwork of green and straw in the bright May sunshine. Taking a deep breath of the pure country air, she turned and walked to the dresser, studying her reflection in the mirror. Wearing a simple, blue cotton shift and no jewellery, she turned her chin to examine her profile and smiled at herself in the glass. In truth, she was a vain and egotistical young woman, but she considered herself entitled to vanity, as she had been blessed with a petite and rounded figure and a

16

pretty face, with dimples that indented her cheeks when she smiled, bow lips, and auburn hair. Yet the simple, unadorned clothing made her feel drab and old. In the early morning light, she turned away from the mirror and surveyed her spacious room with its faintly striped wallpaper, a bright floral carpet, and comfortable bed with an eiderdown. She sat by the window and thought back to her arrival at the Great Malvern railway station, accompanied by one of the Buscot Park servants and two large trunks. They'd been met by a coach from the clinic, the driver of which eyed the heavy luggage sceptically as he helped the ladies up to their seat.

After a half-hour journey through the quaint village of Great Malvern with its fine Saxon priory to the adjoining town on the edge of the panoramic Malvern Hills, they arrived at the hydro, situated on the outskirts of town with unobstructed views of the rolling countryside to the west. The complex consisted of two large, adjoining but mismatched structures; a Tudor mansion of dark-red brick, replete with towers, turrets, and leaded glass, for the men, and a more conventional Victorian house for the women, connected by a whimsical, covered bridge on the second level. A severe-looking woman, who introduced herself as Mrs Pembroke, the ladies' 'matron', met them in the gravel drive. Taking one look at Cecilia's luggage, she said, 'Well, my dear, you shan't be needing all of *that*.' When Cecilia responded with a puzzled look, she added, 'I presume that trunk contains your trousseau.'

'M'lady's fine dresses and gowns,' said the

servant with a slight curtsy.

'You'll have no use for them, Mrs Castello,' said Mrs Pembroke, 'during your stay here. I suggest you return them to the station with your servant.' The servant, barely suppressing a smile, merely nodded.

Now, beginning her third day, Cecilia was becoming accustomed to the unvarying routines of the clinic, though less so to the dress code. The cotton smocks worn by the female 'guests' – the word 'patient' was frowned upon – without corsets and only the plainest undergarments, were far more comfortable than typical Victorian dresses and helped to promote the general atmosphere of restorative relaxation. She was beginning to enjoy the feel of the roughly woven cotton on her bare skin, so different from her usual organdie undergarments. The body, Cecilia learned on her first day, was to be purified, first through a strict dietary regimen, then with the water treatments in their varying forms, and lastly by regular exercise in the fresh, clean air of the Malvern Hills. Awakened at 6.00 a.m. by female attendants who wore not uniforms but simple black or brown dresses, they took the 'cold water treatment' at 6.30 followed by breakfast, which consisted of fresh fruit, perhaps a boiled egg, wheat toast, or porridge. At mid-morning they embarked on a brisk walk in the surrounding hills followed by a light lunch in the pump room, then, perhaps an afternoon nap. Guests were encouraged to avail themselves of the various hot and cold baths and to exercise outdoors in the manicured gardens, or on the many footpaths through the countryside. The women sat for dinner at seven, fish or boiled mutton with fresh vegetables, and then retired to bed promptly at nine. All of the so-called 'social poisons' were prohibited: sugar, salt, coffee, tea, or alcohol in any form, and the use of tobacco. Newspapers and all visitors were banned. The aim was not only rest and clarity of mind for those, like Cecilia, suffering from emotional or mental strain, but also a cure for sufferers of chronic digestive or respiratory ailments. Indeed they were often reminded of the remarkable cure Dr Gully had effected on the famous naturalist Charles Darwin, who theretofore suffered from severe dyspepsia.

Hearing a gentle tap on the door, Cecilia put on her house slippers and went to join the queue of identically dressed women, who ranged in age from their twenties, like Cecilia, to their sixties, for the morning session of Dr Gully's patented 'water-cure' in the lower-level baths. After dis-robing in the privacy of a dressing room, Cecilia nervously waited for the attendant, who soon appeared and tightly wrapped Cecilia, from her chest to her knees, in a sheet soaked in cold water. She then joined the other guests, similarly wrapped, in a large tiled enclosure which smelled of bath salts, where they were instructed to lie side-by-side on deck chairs and then covered in woollen blankets. During each of these sessions, Cecilia kept her eyes tightly shut and concen-trated her mind on keeping warm and avoiding all thoughts of her life outside the clinic. After a lapse of thirty minutes, the attendants reappeared, helped the women to stand and stripped off their blankets and sheets, now warm and dry. With the other shivering women, Cecilia was herded into a separate tiled enclosure and repeatedly doused by the attendants with buckets of ice-cold spring water. Perhaps it was the shock of this final phase of the treatment that drained her of the last vestige of modesty, standing naked and dripping wet among some twenty strangers of assorted ages, shapes, and sizes.

Having survived the early morning ordeal, Cecilia eagerly donned dry clothes and made her way to the dining-room, craving a cup of tea, which she was accustomed to taking with milk and several lumps of sugar. Instead, when her turn in line came, she stared at the unappetizing fare laid out on the sideboard and reluctantly selected a piece of dry toast, a soft boiled egg, and glass of tomato juice. Taking a seat midway down the long rectangular table, she smiled at the woman seated on her left, an attractive young woman perhaps in her early thirties, and said, 'I don't believe we've met. I'm Cecilia.'

'And I'm Agnes. My pleasure.'

Cecilia quickly ascertained that Agnes was married to a successful banker in London, lived in a fashionable neighbourhood in South Kensington, and had been dispatched to the clinic for the treatment of a persistent case of pleurisy. 'And,' said Cecilia between mouthfuls of egg and toast, 'have you found the water treatment to be helpful?'

'I've found it most disagreeable,' said Agnes, with a smile and toss of her dark-brown hair.

'Though in the week or so that I've been here my condition has improved considerably.'

Something about the slightly older woman's handsome looks and confident tone relaxed Cecilia and made her feel more self-assured. 'And why are you here?' asked Agnes.

'Well,' said Cecilia, 'my father and mother thought it best, as I've been under some ... well, emotional strain.' Agnes gave her a brief, searching look. 'In my marriage,' added Cecilia quietly.

'Frankly, dear,' said Agnes, 'I think Dr Gully's methods are better suited to cure a woman's nervous condition than her physical. Especially,' she added *sotto voce*, 'when there's a husband involved.'

'Speaking of Dr Gully, is the great man actually on the premises?'

'Evidently not,' said Agnes, after taking a sip of her juice. 'I'm told he's away, delivering a lecture somewhere on the Continent. I'm sure he'll return shortly.'

Somewhat impulsively, Cecilia decided they would become friends. 'Agnes,' she said, lightly placing a hand on her arm, 'would you mind if I walk with you on the constitutional?'

'I'd be delighted.'

The women assembled promptly at 10.30 in the rose garden, attired in the comfortable cotton dresses that covered them from neck to ankle, straw hats, and sturdy walking shoes. Mrs Pembroke, wearing an Alpine hat with a feather and matching green jacket, belted at the back, appeared in their midst. 'All right, ladies,' she said in

21

a firm voice, 'Mr McTavish' – she gestured to a middle-aged Scotsman wearing high laced boots, a kilt and Glengarry cap – 'will be our guide this morning on a five-mile trek to the North Hill and back. Each of you must take your alpenstock and Gräfenberg flask.'

'But, mum,' said a rather plump woman with a worried expression, 'what if we find it too strenuous?'

'Oh, ye'll be fine, ma'am,' said McTavish. 'We'll avoid the steeper braes, passing by St Anne's Well through the saddle between Worcestershire Beacon and North Hill. A loovely stroll on such a fine day.'

It certainly was that, considered Cecilia as she accepted her alpenstock, a long staff with an iron tip, and strapped her water flask over her shoulder, with a deep blue sky and puffy white clouds, abundant wildflowers, a gentle breeze, and temperatures rising to the 70s. The hydro was on the northern boundary of the Malverns, a picturesque and much frequented region of tall, limestone hills and wide, sweeping valleys, famous not only for its spectacular scenery but also for the quality of its spring-fed mineral water. Within five minutes, the ladies were embarked on a leisurely stroll along a grassy footpath, gently downhill in the direction of the eminence of Worcester Beacon that dominated the landscape. Feeling remarkably refreshed by the combination of pure air, warm May sunshine, and exertion, Cecilia turned to Agnes, walking beside her, and said, 'This is simply *marvellous*. I think I shall completely forget my troubles.'

Agnes responded with a smile and said, 'I'm curious about the way you speak. I can't quite place the accent.'

'I spent my childhood,' said Cecilia, digging into the soft turf with the tip of her staff, 'in Australia, near Adelaide. And grew up in Oxfordshire. My family are Scots. So there you have it. An Australian, English, Scottish blend.' Agnes smiled again, finding the obviously spoiled daughter of a wealthy family appealing in a way she couldn't name, compared to the generally older and dour female visitors to the clinic. 'Why do you suppose they call this a, ah … what did she call it?' said Cecilia, grasping her leather flask.

'Gräfenberg,' said Agnes. 'The name of a place in the Bavarian alps where people go for the water cure. They must have invented these.' Both women paused to uncork their flasks and take a swallow of cold spring water.

'Quite refreshing,' said Cecilia as they swung back into step. Reaching a swale at the foot of the rounded Beacon, the group crossed a footbridge over a meandering brook and then began a gradual uphill climb. The older and less robust soon languished, but Cecilia and Agnes quickened their pace, keeping up with the nimble Scotsman, breathing hard and with a sheen of perspiration on their brows. After climbing for perhaps a half-mile, McTavish halted abruptly and, leaning on his staff, said, 'Let's stop for a wee bit and let the stragglers catch up. Spectacular, isn't it?' The two women turned to look at a sweeping panorama of steep hills and wide valleys blanketed in yellow and blue wildflowers and bathed by a shaft of

23

golden light where the sun broke through a transient cloud.

'So beautiful,' said Cecilia as her breathing returned to normal. 'If I were an artist, I should paint it.'

Agnes carefully studied the landscape and then said, 'I am an artist. I think we should make a return visit, and I'll bring along my paints and brushes.'

'Are you really? How exceptional.' Cecilia gazed again at the panorama and then turned to observe Agnes kneeling on the grass, picking wildflowers.

'There,' said Agnes, rising and walking over to secure a spray of blue and lavender blossoms behind Cecilia's ear with a smile of satisfaction. 'We'll proceed ahead,' she said to Mr McTavish, who was lying comfortably on the grass staring up into the pale blue sky, 'while you wait for the others.' After the lapse of another hour, walking at a steady pace up and down the gentle slopes, the turrets of the clinic came into view on the hillside above the treetops.

'I feel wonderful,' said Cecilia, stopping to uncork her flask and drink the last of her water.

'And I feel starved,' said Agnes, doing the same. 'I only wish there was something beside fish and mutton.'

Later, following an indifferent lunch and short nap, the two new friends lounged side-by-side on chaises on the porch reading their novels, Thackery in the case of Cecilia and Trollope for Agnes. Putting her book aside, Cecilia dozed for several minutes and then opened her eyes and studied the arched bridge, constructed of brick with a tiled roof and leaded glass windows, that connected the women's building with the adjoining Tudor mansion. 'Is one allowed to cross over the bridge?' she asked.

'The Bridge of Sighs, you mean?' said Alice.

'As in Venice?'

Agnes nodded. 'According to one of the attendants,' she said, 'that's what they call it, as the ladies are forbidden to cross to the gentlemen on the other side.'

'How droll,' said Cecilia.

'The good doctor, of course, comes and goes as he wishes. In fact, if I'm not mistaken...'

A short, bald, white-haired gentleman wearing a black frockcoat with a cream-coloured waistcoat and charcoal trousers emerged on the ladies' end of the bridge, paused to take a quick look around, and then disappeared into the lobby.

'Is that...?' said Cecilia.

'Doctor Gully,' said Agnes with a nod. 'Returned from abroad.'

'He's very, well, genial-looking,' said Cecilia.

'Yes, and very amiable. Not at all severe. And he holds the most liberal views on the woman's place in society.'

'I see,' said Cecilia, frankly unacquainted with such views.

'I'm sure he'll want to schedule a consultation,' said Agnes, 'considering the nature of your, ah, malady.'

'In that case,' said Cecilia, swinging her legs around and sitting on the side of the chaise with a bright smile, 'I shall look forward to it.'

Chapter Two

Several days of the unvarying routine of early rising, the detested cold-water treatments, communal meals, and delightful walks through the
Malvern Hills passed, before Cecilia was informed, as she sat with her book in a wicker chair
on the porch, that Dr Gully would be pleased to
interview her at four o'clock in the afternoon. At
home she would have devoted at least an hour to
the selection of the proper dress and accessories
and putting up her hair, but in the relaxed
atmosphere of the hydro she merely arrived at the
appointed hour in her usual smock with her
auburn curls tied back with a black ribbon. 'You
may go in,' said a female attendant standing
outside the arched doorway to the clinic director's
study on the ground floor of the ladies' building.

Cecilia turned the handle and peered inside the
spacious office; Dr Gully sat at his walnut desk,
surrounded by bookshelves, before a tall window
with a view of the garden. With a benevolent
smile, he rose from his chair and said, 'Please have
a seat, Mrs Castello,' gesturing to one of the red
leather armchairs. Cecilia smiled nervously and
sat, quickly glancing around the room, illuminated by sunlight from the window in which motes
of dust were suspended, with a Persian carpet and
the pleasant aromas of pipe tobacco and abraded
leather. 'I've been acquainted with your family, of

course,' the doctor began in a conversational tone, 'for many years. Tell me, dear, the origin of the name Castello?'

'It's Portuguese,' replied Cecilia. 'My husband's family are British, but they came from Portugal, quite a long time ago.'

'I see. And I believe I detect an Australian accent.'

'Yes,' said Cecilia, feeling quite relaxed by the doctor's easy-going manner. 'I spent my early childhood there, though, as you know, my family's Scottish and we divide our time between London and Oxfordshire.'

Donning a pair of reading glasses, Gully opened a folder on his desk, turned several pages, and said, 'I gather your difficulties have arisen in relation to your husband?'

'Yes, but I...' Fighting back tears, she began again: 'After Richard resigned his commission, he seemed to undergo a change, and he, well, he began drinking rather too much, or too often...'

Reclining in his chair with his fingertips touching, and the same benevolent expression in his eyes, the doctor elicited a lengthy though at times halting narrative of the marital difficulties that had culminated in Cecilia's departure from home and decision to seek refuge at her parents' country estate. Occasionally jotting a note, Gully put his pen aside and said, 'Thank you, my dear, for confiding in me. I'm sure this has been terribly painful.' Cecilia nodded and dabbed at her eyes with her handkerchief. Rising abruptly, Gully hooked his thumbs in his waistcoat over his rounded belly and began to pace by the window.

'Women,' he said at length, 'are expected in our society to accept such behaviour in a marriage without complaint. To do their duty.'

He paused and looked Cecilia in the eye, who nodded glumly and said, 'Yes, Father insists I must return home.'

'Which,' Gully continued, 'in many instances, is a profound error. From all that you've told me, and much that I reckon you haven't, I believe that your husband, Mrs Castello, is an alcoholic and probably beyond redemption. And like many such men, especially coming from a military background, given to abusing his wife, even to violence.'

Cecilia raised her red-rimmed eyes and whispered, 'He struck me. In the face. Before the servants. And flung me to the ground, ruining the organdie roses in my sash!'

Gully leaned forward, resting his palms on his desk. 'May I call you Cecilia?' he asked.

'Of course.'

'I'm afraid, Cecilia,' he said gently, 'it would be hazardous in the extreme to return to your husband.'

'But Father insists...'

'I'm well acquainted with the attitude of men like your father. Tell me, Cecilia,' he said, folding his arms on his chest. 'Are there issues of infidelity?'

Blushing, Cecilia nodded.

'Have you confronted your husband?'

'Yes,' she replied softly, wiping away tears. 'After the, ah, the first woman. And of course he insisted ... it was a lapse in judgement, that it wouldn't...'

Dr Gully nodded and said, 'But then...'

'But then there were other liaisons, reported to me by the housemaids.'

'I'm afraid, Cecilia,' said Gully firmly, 'you have no choice. You must remain separated from your husband.'

'How can I? When my time here is finished, how could I possibly...?'

'Your father,' said Gully, sitting down and resting his elbows on his desk, 'has arranged for you to spend four weeks with us.' Cecilia nodded. 'I believe we should find a way to extend your stay. It will be midsummer, after all, the ideal season for the cure.'

Cecilia found that the doctor's mild yet firm tone and his attractive, though not handsome, looks for a man in his mid-sixties were not only comforting but also exerted a certain magnetic attraction. 'I should like that,' she said with a smile that dimpled her cheeks.

'Is your husband a man of means?' asked the doctor.

She nodded. 'Richard comes from a well-to-do family. His father is a Tory MP and the founder of the international telegraph company, and his mother is the sister of the Duke of Fife. They have a large house in Kensington.'

'I see,' said Gully, stroking his chin. 'Well, dear,' he concluded, rising from his chair, 'let me give this some thought, and we'll talk again in several days.'

Cecilia paused on the brick path to listen to a distant rumble. A mass of charcoal cloud billowed

29

above the horizon across the valley. 'I expect we're due for another downpour,' said Agnes, standing at Cecilia's elbow. The past several days had been marked by bright sunshine and warm temperatures through the early afternoon followed by rain showers. Cecilia strolled by the roses, inhaling the bouquet and listening to the buzz of insects and the songbirds in the tall oaks. 'I'm growing to like the hydro,' she said, 'notwithstanding the water treatments and the disagreeable old ladies we're thrown with.'

'And the wretched food,' said Agnes, leaning over to smell a bright pink rose. 'I'm craving a cup of tea and a biscuit.'

'Or a glass of wine,' said Cecilia. 'But you'll be leaving soon.'

'My time's almost up,' said Agnes. 'I must say it's done me a world of good. The pain in my side's completely gone.'

'I shall miss you.'

Giving her a sidelong glance, Agnes said, 'You'll make another friend. Tell me your impressions of Dr Gully.'

Rounding a corner, Cecilia sat on a wrought-iron bench, and Agnes dropped down beside her. 'Oh, he's a most remarkable man,' said Cecilia. 'I never imagined that someone of his reputation would take an interest in me.'

'Though it's none of my business,' said Agnes, glancing up at the darkening sky, 'what did he recommend?'

'Well,' said Cecilia, lowering her voice, 'he believes I must defy my father and remain separated from my husband. And extend my stay at the hydro.'

'I see. I think you should be very careful, as we have very little means of resisting our husbands, or fathers. I cautioned you that the doctor holds very liberal views on the place of women. Why, he even advocates the suffrage.'

'And I think he's quite correct,' said Cecilia, excited but puzzled by the impact of the suffrage, and hearing the first patter of raindrops on the leaves overhead. 'Oh my,' she exclaimed as the skies opened and both women leapt up and started for the building. 'We'll be drenched.'

Cecilia stood at the dresser brushing out her auburn hair and examining her reflection in the mirror. After weeks of warm sunshine, a cold, steady rain was falling, beading the window and obscuring her view of the nearby hillside. Putting the silver-handled hairbrush aside, she picked up a watercolour from the dresser and studied the landscape of the Malvern Hills blanketed in spring wildflowers, painted by Agnes on one of their outings and presented to Cecilia as a parting gift. At the sound of a gentle tap, she walked to the door, leaned her head close, and said, 'Yes? What is it?'

'A message from Dr Gully, mum,' replied an attendant. 'He wishes to see you in his study.'

Cecilia returned to the mirror, powdered her cheeks, added a touch of rouge, and put up her hair with pins and ribbons. Lastly, she applied a dab of perfume to her wrists from the vial she had secreted in the dresser drawer and hurried from the room. She found Dr Gully standing before his desk, wearing a pale-green waistcoat under his black frockcoat and the same genial expression as before. 'Hello, my dear,' he said, reaching out to take Cecilia's hands. 'You're looking well.'

'Thank you, Doctor.'

'Call me James.'

Taken aback, Cecilia said, 'Oh. Well, then, thank you, James. I'm feeling much better. The treatments have worked wonders.'

'I'm delighted to hear it. Ah, what an inviting fragrance.'

'From Paris.'

Gesturing to the settee and chairs arranged before the stone hearth, where a cheerful fire was burning, Gully said, 'Please sit down, my dear.'

Once he was seated facing her on the settee, Gully said, 'A dreary day, though I suppose we were overdue for a change.'

'Yes.'

'I've been giving considerable thought to your situation, Cecilia.' Gully spoke in an avuncular tone, crossing one polished boot over his knee. 'I remain convinced that it would be a grave mistake to return to your husband.'

'I should have explained,' said Cecilia, 'that Father is providing us with an annual allowance of a thousand pounds, which, if I go against his wishes...'

Raising a hand, Gully said, 'Never mind your father. I've decided to act as your legal representative and demand that your husband provide you with the support to which you're entitled. I'll arrange for you to remain here at the hydro. Free of charge, of course.'

'But Dr Gully ... James ... I couldn't possibly accept such an offer. It's far, far too generous.'

'I insist on it. My solicitor is drawing up the papers for my appointment as your guardian. In the interim, I've taken the liberty of drafting a letter for your signature advising Captain Castello of your decision and demanding suitable recompense.'

Conscious of her racing heart and a sensation of light-headedness – could he do this, what an astonishing idea? – Cecilia merely nodded and said, 'I see.'

Gully rose from his chair and went to his desk. 'Here it is,' he said, handing her a single sheet of bond. He stood with his back to the fire as she read it, advising her husband that as his behaviour toward her made life intolerable she was formally demanding a separation and the payment of alimony in an amount sufficient to provide for her living expenses. 'He'll protest, no doubt,' said Gully, as Cecilia looked up, 'but in the end he'll come round.'

Deliverance from her terrible dilemma, considered Cecilia, under the protection, the *guardianship,* of a great man like the doctor, was far more than she had ever imagined possible. And, it struck her with sudden clarity, a deliverance that her father would be powerless to prevent. Her father, after all, had authored the suggestion to place her under Dr Gully's care. 'Oh, James,' she exclaimed, rising from the settee and impulsively throwing her arms around him, 'how could I ever repay you?'

'Don't worry, dear,' he said, patting her back.

'It's nothing for a man of my means. Now,' he concluded, taking her gently by the shoulders, 'you must sign the letter and I must be off to my next appointment.'

Within days Cecilia received a reply in the form of a telegram demanding that she return home at once. This was followed by a long letter in her husband's hand expressing his sincere apology for his 'excesses' and 'maltreatment of my beloved wife', together with a pledge to reform his behaviour and 'begin anew their life together'. Though she answered neither the telegram nor the letter, she penned a note to her parents explaining the course of action she was taking and begging their acquiescence. Cecilia was, in fact, relishing her new-found and wholly unexpected liberation, free from her father, her husband, and yes – from her corsets – plunging into the therapeutic regimens of the hydro with the gusto of a recent convert and without the least concern or sympathy for her husband. She no longer missed the company of Agnes, or sought any other female companionship, as she was entirely absorbed with thoughts of the revered doctor ... of James. During the leisure hours of the afternoon she devoted herself to reading the great man's publications, gamely ploughing through the turgid prose of his treatise on hydropathy and academic writings on the virtues of homeopathic medicine. As she sat in her usual chair in the library with a thick medical text open in her lap she was approached by one of the female attendants who bowed and said, 'You have a letter, mum.'

'Thank you,' said Cecilia, accepting an envelope. Tearing it open, she read her father's neat cursive. *Your mother and I,* he wrote, *have endeavoured to conform to your stated desire that we accept your decision to separate from Capt. Castello, but are unable to do so.* She felt little emotion as she quickly finished the letter, in which her father, above all a man of business, advised that her *marital allowance could not be continued under the circumstances* yet acknowledged that she was free to accept the protection and generosity offered by the *estimable Dr Gully* and to remain under his care at the sanatorium, *as her return to Buscot Park would be unacceptable.* Refolding the letter in the envelope, Cecilia reflected with a sigh that the loss of her father's support was the price of her permanent separation from her husband. Exiting the library to return to her room, she observed Dr Gully as he emerged from the Bridge of Sighs and entered the lobby. Hurrying to him, she said, 'James ... is there any news?'

'In point of fact there is,' he said with a smile. 'I've just returned from an interview with my solicitor, who informs me that your husband has declined to file an objection to the guardianship.'

With a quick glance to make sure they were alone, Cecilia said, 'Thank heavens.'

'What's more,' said Gully cheerfully, 'he's indicated his willingness to negotiate an alimony settlement. It appears that he wishes to put the matter behind him.'

'Oh, James,' said Cecilia, clutching his arm. 'How can I ever thank you?'

'There is something that would please me very much.'

'And what is that?'

'As tomorrow is Sunday,' said Gully, placing his hand on her arm, pressing the cotton cloth against her, 'I intend to take my customary long walk in the hills. You could accompany me.'

A month had passed since Cecilia's arrival at the hydro, it was early summer, warm and verdant, and the quotidian customs of English country life in the thirty-fourth year of the reign of Victoria remained comfortingly traditional, circumspect, and solidly middle class. Never more so than on the Sabbath, with obligatory attendance of services at the parish church followed by a hearty repast, a nap, and, for those so inclined, an outing in the Malvern Hills. As it was generally understood among the staff and other female guests that Dr Gully had taken a 'special interest' in the young Mrs Castello – though his legal guardianship was a carefully kept secret – their departure together on the footpath attracted little notice from the women reclining on chaises or sitting in wicker on the porch overlooking the garden. The doctor was attired in an alpine hat and jacket, with tweed plus-fours, woollen socks, and laced-up boots. Cecilia wore her long cotton smock, belted at her slender waist, sturdy walking shoes and a wide-brimmed straw hat tied with a ribbon under her chin. Both carried alpenstocks and Gräfenberg flasks, and a rucksack was slung on the doctor's shoulders. 'A perfect afternoon,' he commented, as they started down the grassy path.

Cecilia nodded as she walked in his footsteps, glancing up the bright blue sky and cottony clouds that cast irregular shadows across the valley in the warm June sunshine.

Feeling utterly at ease as she strolled alongside him, Cecilia said, 'I never thought to ask, James, but is this your birthplace?'

'What, Worcestershire?' he said with a smile. 'Heavens no. I was born and brought up in Jamaica.' When she responded with a surprised look, he said, 'I grew up on a large coffee plantation owned by my father, rather like your experience growing up in Australia, I suppose.' Halting at a fork in the path, he briefly studied the signpost and said, 'To the left, toward Sugarloaf Hill.'

'Where are we going?'

'Willow Crescent,' said Gully. 'My favourite destination, with a view of the entire Malvern valley.' Leaning on his staff as they began a gentle ascent, he said, 'Yes, I fondly remember my early years in Jamaica. A life of luxury, in a large colonial villa on Blue Mountain, native servants attending to one's every need...'

'What happened?'

'I was sent to Britain, to study medicine at Edinburgh. It was while I was there, in 1833, that the Emancipation Act was passed, freeing the slaves in the West Indies. My father, of course, was ruined and, as a consequence, I learned my first truly important life lesson.' He stopped at a bend in the path and surveyed the hill above them on their left.

'Which was...?'

'To make my own way in life, relying on my own resources and ingenuity.'

Cecilia nodded and smiled, thinking, no man has ever spoken to me like this, as he might speak to his fellow man, even to his equal. 'Would you say,' she asked, 'that this lesson should be applied to a female?'

'I would indeed,' he said, starting off again. After the lapse of a quarter hour, walking in silence except for the doctor's occasional comments on the local flora and geologic conditions, the path turned steeply upward, a series of switchbacks in the final ascent to the shoulder of Sugarloaf Hill. Their exertions were rewarded with an exceptional vista: the whole of the broad Malvern valley ringed by pale-blue hills lay before them in bright sunshine. Willow Crescent was a treeless, rounded summit, with a smooth, lichen-covered outcropping of limestone that served as a natural resting place to picnic or merely take in the panoramic view. 'Magnificent,' said Gully, as he shrugged off his rucksack and patted his brow with his handkerchief.

Cecilia, breathing hard, uncorked her flask and took a long swallow of cold spring water. She stretched out beside Gully on the limestone ledge and rested on an elbow, the fabric of her wonderfully simple dress tucked about her ankles. 'I'm certain I've never seen anything so beautiful.' Shading her eyes with a hand, she said, 'Is that the hydro?'

Gully nodded, gazing at the turrets of the Tudor mansion on the distant ridgeline, and said, 'It is indeed.' He turned to Cecilia, smiled, and said, 'I've brought us a treat.' He carefully un-packed the contents of the rucksack: a tin of wheat biscuits, round of cheese, a ripe pear and two small cups. 'A good, aged Stilton,' he said, 'and, what's more,' – he paused to uncork his leather flask and pour each of them a cup of straw-coloured wine – 'a decent Moselle.'

'Mmm,' said Cecilia, taking a sip and enjoying the warmth of the sun on her face. 'The first wine I've tasted since leaving home.'

'Well,' said Gully with a chuckle, 'as we're out-side the jurisdiction of the clinic...' Taking a penknife from his pocket, he sliced the pear and spread cheese on several biscuits.

After sampling the fruit and cheese and taking another sip of wine, Cecilia said, 'James, I've been reading your publications on, ah, homeo-pathic medicine...'

'Excellent,' he said encouragingly.

'I was hoping you might elaborate.'

'Of course.'

Sitting up and crossing her legs beneath her skirt, Cecilia listened with rapt attention, moving her ankles a bit and occasionally helping herself to more wine and cheese, as Dr Gully propounded his controversial views on the importance of diet, certain foods in particular, fresh air and exercise, and cold water therapy in the treatment of a host of chronic ailments. 'And,' he concluded, 'in the *prevention* of any number of maladies that so often are the consequence of the propensity of our race to indulge in the consumption of rich food, ani-mal fats, tobacco, and' – he paused to take a sip of wine – 'alcohol in excess.'

39

Cecilia, feeling the unaccustomed, pleasurable effects of the wine, stared into Gully's lively, intelligent eyes, restraining the impulse to reach out and touch him, possibly just to run the tip of her fingers along the side of his face. 'James,' she said after a moment, 'I'm quite sure I've never been happier ... than when we're together.'

Chapter Three

Cecilia sat in a high-back upholstered chair, wearing pale-blue organdie with matching shoes and off-white stockings with the perfect shade of baby blue clocking, in place of the dowdy cotton smocks she'd been forced to wear at the hydro. She studied the handwriting on the cream-coloured envelope in her lap. Glancing around the snug parlour, with its floral carpet and striped wallpaper, she was beginning to feel at home in the small brick house in town which Dr Gully had arranged for her to let once the settlement with the Castello family had been agreed upon. With two small upstairs bedrooms, a parlour, dining-room, and kitchen, it was certainly modest in comparison to the elegant townhouse she'd shared with Richard in Knightsbridge or her family's estate at Buscot Park. But she'd happily traded luxury for independence and, more importantly, for proximity to the clinic – and to James Gully. Through the parlour window she glimpsed a passing coach drawn by a white mare and then lowered her eyes to the envelope. She recognized her husband's handwriting, though the script was uneven, as if penned with a trembling hand, and the stamp and postmark were from the German state of Westphalia.

Carefully opening the letter, she removed several sheets of bond and read:

1 August 1870
Cologne, Germany

My dear Cecilia
I am at present ensconced in a musty old hotel overlooking the Rhine with the avowed purpose of restoring my health. In truth, in my abject self-pity after you fled from me and refused my entreaties to reconcile, I was determined to get as far away as possible from memories of our life together in London. There are a number of former military men here, Germans, of course, with their absurd duelling scars, whose company I find tolerable over endless games of backgammon or whist.

Cecilia gazed at the penmanship, certain that it was deteriorating with each written word.

I am truly sorry for the pain I've caused you and hold you blameless for the dissolution of our marriage (though legally it remains intact). I trust that you are well, that the financial arrangements are satisfactory, and that perhaps, someday, in happier times I should see you again. I remain
Your devoted husband,
Richard

Tossing the letter aside with a sigh, Cecilia

41

reflected that it was truly a miracle she'd met Dr Gully and, thanks entirely to his intervention, escaped the horrors of her marriage, certain that Richard was drinking himself to oblivion or even to death. Lightly touching the wedding band on her finger, she thought back to their whirlwind courtship; the tall, handsome officer in his guards uniform with the exotic Iberian name and lineage – it was little wonder women threw themselves at him. And she, a spoiled, headstrong girl from an upper class family, had assumed that married life would simply be an endless succession of teas, balls, and dinner parties... It had never occurred to her, nor had her mother warned her, that once married she might be treated as an object of desire – what a shock that had been – or of scorn, or drink-induced violence. Cecilia rose and walked to the window, gazing absently at the row of identical brick houses on the opposite side of the street. Dr Gully had not only rescued her; he had taught her that the modern married woman need not submit to an abusive husband, that she was entitled to be free and to be happy.

But was James married? She'd assumed that he had no wife, as he was always unaccompanied and never spoke of a *Mrs* Gully. Surely, at his age and living alone, he must be a widower. Well, she insisted, she would have to get to the bottom of that. Hearing the chime of the clock on the mantel, she decided to go upstairs and change for a quick trip to the hydro, on the pretext of enjoying an afternoon bath but in the hopes of a chance encounter.

Unlike the early morning cold-water treatments, in which the women were herded like sheep and subjected to the humiliating ordeal of communal nudity, the hot baths were designed for soothing immersions in the restorative Malvern waters, in the privacy of large, individual tubs separated by canvas screens. Dressing in her simple smock following an indolent soak – the unadorned dresses were *de rigueur* even though she was no longer a guest at the hydro – she decided to take a turn in the promenade garden where she imagined she might find the good doctor. Instead, the neat brick pathways were trodden by various other female guests, primarily women in late middle-age, well-to-do, judging from their plump figures and the few articles of jewellery they were wearing, whom Cecilia condescendingly regarded as mere parvenus. After a while she sat down on a wrought iron bench, tilting back her head and closing her eyes in the warmth of the afternoon sun.

'Hallo, Mrs Castello.'

Cecilia glanced up at the imposing figure of Mrs Pembroke, standing over her with an expression of disapprobation. 'Hallo,' she said. 'Lovely day.'

Ignoring the comment, Mrs Pembroke said, 'As you've chosen to continue to patronize the hydro, it would be preferable if you adhered to our regimens.'

'Oh, the water treatments and diet, I suppose you mean. I'm no longer a guest here, madam, and I shall do as I please. I don't suppose Dr Gully is in the grounds?'

'I understand he's away on business. But he's

43

delivering a lecture in town this evening.'

'Oh, really? And where...'

'At the public library.'

'Why, thank you, Mrs Pembroke.' Rising from the bench, Cecilia said, 'May I ask you about a personal matter? Concerning Dr Gully?' Hearing no objection, she said, 'Is his wife with him here at the hydro?'

'His wife?'

'I presume he's married.'

'Yes, Mrs Castello,' said Mrs Pembroke with a frown. 'The doctor is married. To a much older woman who, frankly, is confined to an asylum for the mentally insane.'

'Good heavens,' said Cecilia, raising a hand to her mouth.

'The doctor hasn't spoken to her for some thirty years. Good day,' she concluded, turning to walk briskly down the garden path.

Cecilia sat in the high-ceilinged reading-room of the Malvern public library, intending to make eye contact with Dr Gully as he addressed the crowd of some forty or fifty townspeople, preponderantly middle-aged women, curious to hear the famous physician expound his controversial views on homeopathic medicine. She had chosen a black, decolletége silk gown with elaborate ruffles and a strand of South Seas pearls, having arranged for the trunk with her jewellery and gowns to be sent from Buscot Park. At the appointed hour the buzz of conversation abruptly died away as the short, rotund doctor with the wreath of white hair around his bald pate strode briskly to the lectern, donned his spectacles, and gazed out on his audience with a pleasant smile. Cecilia, returning the smile, would have wagered he looked briefly, knowingly, into her eyes.

'Good evening,' he began, adopting the stance of a lecturer with his hands on his hips. 'Tonight I intend to address not only the salutary effects of the water-cure as it is practised at the hydro, but more broadly the homeopathic approach to medicine. It was as a medical student in the late twenties, an *externe* at the École de Médecine in Paris, that I was first introduced to these principles.' So articulate, so self-assured in his knowledge of the subject, thought Cecilia, as she eagerly followed his words, delivered in a relaxed, conversational manner. 'Modern medicine,' continued Gully, 'concerns itself with surgery, the knife, and the apothecary. Pills, devised by chemists with as little understanding of their effects as alchemists purported to understand the transformation of lead to gold.' Gully paused to survey the audience, acknowledging Cecilia's presence with a momentary smile. 'In point of fact,' he declared, wagging an index finger, 'we have known since the days of the ancients, that human health is strongly influenced by the air we breathe, the food we ingest, liquids we drink, and the use to which we put our bodies.

'Would you administer poison to your child?' enquired Gully, searching the audience.

'Heavens no,' said an elderly woman in drab, faded bengaline who was perched in her many petticoats on the edge of a chair in the first row.

'Well, then,' said Gully, 'would you poison

45

yourself, madam, or see your husband poison himself, with tobacco or alcohol?' This elicited grumbles from several of the men in the audience. 'I assure you,' said Gully reprovingly, 'these are poisons.'

Listening to Gully's strong, mellifluous voice, observing his genial countenance, Cecilia was conscious of a quickening of her pulse, the feel of her silks against her bosom and a mild flush on the soft skin of her neck. Yes, she thought with a nod, poisons ... she understood all too well what alcohol could do to a man.

'Not that I'm a teetotaller, mind you,' continued Gully, raising a placating hand. 'I'm an advocate of temperance, not abstinence. In fact, it is well known that wine, consumed in moderation with the right foods, exerts a salubrious effect on the digestive system.' Gully paused to study the faces before him, clasping his hands on the lectern. 'The first principle of the water-cure,' he continued, 'is purification of the body. Elimination of the social vices, as we call them – tea, coffee, sugar, salt. In conjunction with the cold water treatments, administered daily, before partaking of food...' This, naturally, was what the audience had come for, paying rapt attention to the doctor's comprehensive description of the strict regimen practised at the hydro and its remarkable efficacy in the treatment of a host of chronic maladies, a *tour de force* performance that culminated in a standing ovation. Cecilia stood clapping with perhaps more vigour than anyone, fearing she might pop the buttons of her gown so great was the adulation she felt for the man she now regarded as her special, her secret, friend.

The following morning, after sleeping late and a breakfast of scones, jam, and sweetened tea, she penned a brief note and folded it in an envelope, which she addressed to *Dr J.M. Gully*. Determined to avoid another unpleasant encounter with the hydro staff, she selected green taffeta with a bustle and matching feathered hat and made the fifteen-minute walk to the clinic under the shade of a parasol. 'Morning, ma'am,' said the coachman, standing by the entrance to the ladies' wing.

'Good morning, Mr Percy,' said Cecilia, as she snapped shut her parasol. 'I wonder if you might do me a favour,' she said in a lowered voice.

'Yes, ma'am.'

She reached into her purse for a gold sovereign. Slipping it into his palm, she said, 'Would you get me a bottle of decent Madeira and bring it to my house? On the quiet, of course.'

'Of course, ma'am,' he replied with a smile.

Avoiding the inquisitive stares of the ladies in the parlour, Cecilia hurried through the dining-room to the wing where the doctor's office was located, where she found his secretary at her desk. 'Good morning, Miss Stokes,' she said. 'I have a private note for Dr Gully.' She reached into her purse for the envelope.

Aware of her employer's special regard for Cecilia, the secretary rose from her chair, smiled, and said, 'I'll see to it he receives it directly. At the moment he's in consultation.'

'Thank you.' Turning to go, Cecilia abruptly halted and, looking back, said, 'Oh, and you may tell the doctor that he can send his reply with Percy.'

James Gully walked to the window behind his desk, unfastened the latch, and lifted the sash, taking a deep breath of fresh air, scented with just mown grass. Lowering himself into his supple leather chair, he briefly considered the consultation he had just concluded with a married woman in her late forties, not yet in menopause, but complaining of the usual symptoms: headaches, insomnia, enervation, and anxiety, generally categorized as hysteria by the medical establishment. While he had no doubt she would profit from the water-cure and other regimens of the hydro, Gully was convinced that these symptoms were rooted in an absence of sexual gratification; upper middle-class Englishwomen, he believed, seldom engaged in sexual intercourse once beyond child-bearing and, if they did so, it was almost exclusively for the pleasure of their husbands. Glancing at the watch on the silver fob chain at his waistcoat, he decided it was time for the single smoke he permitted himself in the late morning. Removing the tobacco jar and curved briar from the shelf by his desk, he filled and tamped the pipe, struck a match and cupped it over the bowl, sucking in smoke from the curiously pleasant Balkan Sobranie blend of Virginia and Latakia leaf. Tilting back in his chair, he thoughtfully perused a medical journal and puffed on his pipe as he listened to the songbirds outside the window. After several minutes his concentration was interrupted by a tap on the door. 'Come in,' he called out.

'Pardon me, sir,' said Miss Stokes, standing diffidently in the doorway, 'but I have a note...'

'Yes, yes,' said Gully. 'You may come in.'

'From Mrs Castello.' She walked quickly to the desk and handed him an envelope.

'Thank you,' said Gully, as he briefly studied the inscription. Waiting for the door to close, he clenched the pipe in his teeth as he slit open the envelope and extracted a folded sheet. *Dear James,* Cecilia began in her flowery cursive. A smile spread over Gully's face as he read her extravagant praise for his public lecture and closed the brief note with an invitation to dinner at her *modest cottage* at *seven in the evening on Thursday,* the following night. Gully put the note aside with a contented expression, imagining Cecilia's pretty face as he took another draw on his pipe.

Arriving at the cottage precisely at seven, clutching a bouquet behind his back and with a rosebud in his lapel, Dr Gully reached out to give the brass knocker a sharp rap. After a moment, Cecilia appeared, wearing a low-cut gown of blue silk with a corset so tight Gully imagined he could encircle her waist with his hands. 'Good evening, my dear,' he said, as he stepped across the threshold and produced his bouquet, a half-dozen long-stem red and yellow roses.

'They're beautiful,' said Cecilia, accepting the flowers.

'Fresh from my garden,' said Gully, removing his top hat.

'Allow me,' she said taking his hat. 'Please sit

while I find a vase.' Gully sat in the sitting-room in one of two high-backed upholstered chairs with his legs crossed, smiling at the extravagance of Cecilia's blue silk bustle with its long, silvered blue fringe. 'There,' she said, placing the vase on a marble-topped table and taking the chair next to him.

'You look especially lovely, Cecilia,' said Gully. 'I'm so accustomed to middle-aged ladies in their plain cotton dresses.' She responded with a demure smile that accentuated her dimples, not daring to tell him that those cotton dresses were not without their comforts. 'You're finding these lodgings adequate?' he asked.

'Oh, yes,' she replied. 'To have a place of my own is quite wonderful, and such a short distance from the hydro.'

'Well, dear, you may remain here as long as you please.'

'Would you care for a glass of wine?' asked Cecilia.

'Well, customarily I ... but perhaps this once.'

She walked to the sideboard, poured each of them wine from a cut crystal decanter, and handed Gully a glass. 'It's Madeira,' she said. 'I hope you like it.'

Taking a sip, he said, 'It's quite good.' The unaccustomed effects of the alcohol, the fragrance of Cecilia's perfume, and the bouquet of the roses combined to melt Gully's usual reserve. 'Cecilia,' he said, after taking another swallow.

'Yes, James?'

'May I tell you how very fond I've grown of you?'

50

Blushing, she said, 'And I of you.'

'Not only as your physician,' he said, 'or as, say, a family friend but also ... as a man.' Cecilia reached over and placed a hand on his arm. 'Despite the obvious differences in our ages and circumstances...'

The cook, wearing a black silk dress and white cap and apron, appeared in the doorway and announced, 'Excuse me, mum, but dinner is served.'

At the conclusion of an indifferent supper of roast lamb with boiled potatoes and green beans, prepared, on Cecilia's instructions, without seasonings, sauces, or garnishes, and accompanied only by spring water, Cecilia suggested they repair to the parlour for a nightcap. In the soft yellow of the gaslights, Gully's eyes were drawn to Cecilia's sparkling amethyst ear-rings and around her slender neck the matching pendant on a gold chain that bounced occasionally and fetchingly on her bosom. 'This has been such a lovely evening,' he said as he sipped his Madeira. 'I daresay I can't recall the last time I felt so completely ... at ease.'

Seated beside him on a sofa, Cecilia smiled encouragingly and said, 'As you know, James, I remain a married woman, but in name only.'

'Quite so,' said Gully with a nod.

'Do I understand,' she said gently, 'that you, too, are in similar circumstances?'

With a faraway look, Gully put aside his wine-glass and said, 'Yes, dear, I'm afraid that is so. Trapped in marriage to a woman I haven't seen in decades.'

'Do you suppose,' she said, 'that between the two of us, we might pretend ... we were no longer married?'

Gully briefly searched her eyes, reflecting the flickering gaslights, and said, 'I'm not sure that's the wisest course, but ... I shall consider it.'

Over the following weeks Dr Gully was a regular visitor, dining alone with Cecilia with the knowledge of no one but the cook, a disagreeable woman who had no social interaction with the staff at the hydro. Departing at the conclusion of one such evening, Gully, standing at the door, lightly kissed Cecilia on the cheek and said, 'You know, my dear, I'm leaving shortly for Bavaria to deliver a lecture.'

'Yes, and I'll be terribly lonely.'

'I've been thinking,' said Gully, as he donned his hat, 'that perhaps you could come with me.'

'Oh, James,' said Cecilia, clutching his arm, 'do you really?'

'Why not? No one at the clinic will know. I'll see to the arrangements. We'll take the ten-fifteen on Friday.'

Travelling under her own name, in her separate railway compartment, Cecilia would have struck a casual observer as a mere passing acquaintance of the eminent Dr Gully, who frequently went abroad, to Germany in particular, to attend conferences on homeopathic medicine. Greeted at the station at Bad Kissingen by a delegation from the local medical society, Gully proceeded directly to a luncheon, while Cecilia, by prearrangement, hired a coach to transport her, and her large steamer trunk and numerous hat-boxes, to a luxurious hotel operated by Madame Manteuffel on a hillside overlooking the Bavarian village renowned for its mineral springs. As it was late August, the pinnacle of the season at the resort, frequented by European aristocracy, it was unusual but nevertheless unremarkable for an affluent, well-dressed Englishwoman, travelling alone, to take a room at the hotel. Cecilia occupied herself with late breakfasts in her room, leisurely strolls in the manicured grounds, and a visit to the celebrated public gardens in town while Gully attended the two-day medical conference. After delivering the keynote speech to a packed hall on the final day, Gully returned to Madame Manteuffel's, where he joined Cecilia for tea on the porch overlooking the village and surrounding countryside. With his white hair and short, rotund figure he could easily have passed as the grandfather of the pretty young woman with auburn curls seated next to him.

On their first morning together, Gully guided Cecilia on a vigorous two-hour walk up and down the nearby hills to the ruins of the twelfth-century castle at Bodenlaube, explaining along the way that an Austrian by the name of Priessnitz had invented the water-cure in the alpine village of Gräfenberg, which had then become widely popular at Bad Kissingen, known for centuries for the restorative powers of its baths. Following the bracing five-mile outing in warm sunshine, the pair lunched on Westphalian ham and boiled potatoes in the hotel's grand dining-room. Though

Gully demurred, Cecilia enjoyed two glasses of Moselle, whose effects emboldened her to place a hand on Gully's knee beneath the linen tablecloth.

'I'm feeling drowsy,' she said with a smile when the dishes were cleared away.

'From the exertion of our outing,' said Gully, 'and the soporific effect of the wine.'

'I believe I shall go to my room and lie down.' Gully held her chair and then took her by the arm as they walked from the dining-room to the wide stairs from the lobby. Arriving at her room on the second floor, Cecilia cast a furtive glance down the empty hallway and then took Gully's hand and said quietly, 'Will you read to me while I rest?'

'Of course.'

Taking the key from her purse, she hastily let them in. 'I'll just be a moment,' she said before disappearing into the bathroom. Gully walked to the window, glanced down on the lawn and then closed the heavy curtains. After a few minutes Cecilia appeared in the semi-darkness, barefoot and wearing a thin dressing gown so ruffled that it almost hid her charms, which she clutched to her neck. Turning down the covers, she slid under the linen sheets and eiderdown as Gully watched with his hands on the back of a chair. 'Sit closer,' she said, plumping the pillows and snuggling her toes against the linen, 'and read to me from my book of poems, will you please?'

Gully drew up the chair, picked up the slender volume of Elizabethan verse and briefly studied its contents. 'Ah, yes,' he said. 'Shakespeare's eighteenth sonnet. "Shall I compare thee to a summer's day? Thou art more lovely and more temperate".' Cecilia listened to Gully's strong, sonorous voice with an adoring expression, lying with her hair fanned out on the pillow and her gown partly open. '"So long as men can breathe",' Gully continued, '"or eyes can see, So long lives this and this gives life to thee".' He looked up into Cecilia's eyes and, conscious of her exotic perfume, stole a glance at her cleavage. 'Another?' he asked. She nodded, and Gully turned the pages and began to read:

They flee from me who sometime did me seek
With naked foot, stalking in my chamber.
I have seen them gentle, tame, and meek
That now are wild, and do not remember...

Thanked be fortune, it hath been otherwise,
Twenty times better; but once, in special,
In thin array, after a pleasant guise,
When her loose gown from her shoulders did fall,
And she caught me in her arms long and small,
Therewith all sweetly did me kiss And softly said,
"Dear heart, how like you this?"

'James,' murmured Cecilia.
Gully closed the volume and put it aside.
'Kiss me.'
He sat beside her, bent down and, as she folded him in her arms, kissed her, lightly at first but then with growing intensity. After a while he pulled back, searching her eyes in the dim light as she fumbled with the buttons of his waistcoat. 'Please,' she said urgently. 'Lie with me.'

55

Chapter Four

The cook was the first to go, for the simple reason that she knew too much and her silence could not, in Cecilia's opinion, be easily bought. Cecilia promptly engaged another domestic, a young woman from a nearby village who was just as promptly sacked when Cecilia discovered she was devoutly religious and attended services with several of the female employees at the hydro. At last Cecilia settled on an unmarried middle-aged servant whose own morals were lax and who eagerly accepted cash gratuities in return for her oath of silence regarding Dr Gully's comings and goings. Immediately upon their return from Bavaria, Cecilia became obsessed with arranging assignations with the doctor, at least thrice a week, either in the evenings after supper, first thing in the morning, or occasionally during the quiet of the afternoon. She was driven not so much by the infatuation she'd felt for Gully since her early days at the clinic, as by a newly awakened, voracious sexual appetite. Intercourse, in all of her previous experience, had been an utterly unrewarding and dismal affair, due in part to the disabling effects of alcohol on her husband. But to her amazement she had discovered those cotton frocks, all that silk and lace and ribbon, this whole new world, and in the hands, literally, of James Gully, despite his age and unimposing physique, she attained heights of passion and physical pleasure she'd never dreamt possible.

Lying contentedly spent on her pillows after an afternoon of prolonged lovemaking, with the pleasurably warm sensation of bare skin on skin, Cecilia drifted in and out of a dreamless sleep. When she awoke, drowsily rubbing her eyes, she looked up to observe Gully, clad in a silk dressing-gown, as he entered the upstairs bedroom, carrying a tray with a teapot, cups, and saucers. 'Ah, Cecilia,' he said as he lowered the tray to the surface of the dresser. 'I see you're awake.'

'Yes,' she said happily, sitting up on her pillows and drawing the covers up to her neck.

'Shall I pour your tea?' he asked.

'Thank you.'

Handing her a steaming cup before pouring his own, he said, 'And you also have a letter.'

'Oh, really? I wonder what it could be.'

'Postmarked London,' said Gully, lifting an envelope from the tray and holding it up for her inspection.

Placing her cup and saucer on the bedside table, Cecilia took the envelope from Gully, briefly studied the return address, and then slit it open. She removed a folded sheet, quickly read it, and said, 'Oh dear.'

'What is it? Nothing the matter...?'

'Richard's dead.' Cecilia looked around the room at the disordered bedcovers, and at Gully, who suddenly struck her as quite old with his silk robe, and was overwhelmed with a wave of shame and self-loathing. 'I must dress,' she said. 'Might I have some privacy?'

After a hot bath, Cecilia dressed in a black silk gown, found Gully in the parlour, who, wearing his usual frockcoat, waistcoat and striped trousers, resembled more a parson than a paramour. 'Do you know any of the details?' he asked, as he rose from his chair.

'Only that he died at his hotel in Germany.'

'Poor fellow,' said Gully, with a sad shake of his head.

'The letter,' said Cecilia, 'from Richard's solicitor, requests that I come to London as soon as possible, whereupon he promises to provide me with information concerning Richard's death and, I gather, his financial arrangements.'

'I see. When will you go?'

'First thing in the morning.' She walked over and lightly kissed Gully on the cheek. 'I should be back,' she said, 'by noon on Thursday.'

Alighting from a hansom cab before an imposing Georgian edifice on Chancery Lane, Cecilia, dripping with jet, in finest Battenberg lace and edged smooth wool, with a black shawl, hat, and veil, briefly studied the brass plaque by the double doors and then let herself into the foyer. She approached an elderly secretary seated at a writing desk, cleared her throat and said, 'I have an appointment with Mr Throckmorton.'

'And your name?'

'Mrs Richard Castello.'

'Excuse me, madam,' he said, as he rose from his desk and exited through a mahogany door. After a brief interval, he reappeared and said,

'This way, Mrs Castello,' ushering her into a nearby room, panelled in burl walnut, with a long table, Persian carpet, and red leather armchairs. Oliver Throckmorton, of the firm Throckmorton, Dewar, & Bell, stood with his hands on the back of a chair at the end of the table. A leather folder, tied with a black ribbon, lay before him on the gleaming table. Wearing the uniform of his profession, a black frockcoat, matching trousers and white shirt with a starched Piccadilly collar, he met Cecilia midway around the table, bowed stiffly and said, 'Good afternoon, Mrs Castello. Please sit.' Choosing a chair near the end of the table, she briefly studied the lawyer, whom she judged to be in his mid-forties, a tall, clean-shaven, and ascetic-looking man with an aquiline nose. 'Do you care for tea?' he asked.

'No.'

'Thank you, Higgins,' said Throckmorton to the secretary, who nodded and retired. 'Let me begin, Mrs Castello,' Throckmorton continued, 'by offering my deepest condolences on the untimely loss of your husband.'

'Thank you.' Cecilia was repelled by the lawyer's unctuous tone and odd manner of wringing his hands as he spoke.

'You are no doubt anxious to know the circumstances.' Cecilia nodded. 'I have in my possession,' said Throckmorton, 'a report from the coroner's office in the municipality of Cologne.' He paused to untie the ribbon and spread open the folder. 'In German, naturally, which we arranged to have translated.' Slipping on his spectacles, he extracted several sheets of paper from the folder. 'The

59

coroner's report on the autopsy,' he said as he glanced at the pages. 'The subject was discovered collapsed in his hotel room,' he read aloud, 'in a pool of dried blood. Pronounced dead at the scene. The immediate cause of death was haematemesis.' Throckmorton looked up at Cecilia with a frown and explained: 'The vomiting of blood.' She blanched and turned away. 'The post-mortem,' continued Throckmorton, 'revealed severe ulceration of the lining of the stomach and advanced cirrhosis of the liver as a result of alcoholism.' Returning the pages to the folder, Throckmorton took a linen square from his pocket and polished the lenses of his spectacles. 'I assume you were aware, Mrs Castello,' he said, 'that your husband was a heavy drinker.'

She nodded and said, 'I'm afraid he went to the Continent to drink himself to death. His drinking was the cause of our ... separation.'

'Yes,' said the solicitor with an inscrutable smile. 'In connection with your agreement to separate, I advised your husband to modify his will, as, to all intents and purposes, the marriage was at an end.'

'I see,' said Cecilia, dabbing at her eyes with her handkerchief. 'He never spoke to me about it.'

'At all events,' said Throckmorton, 'he was distracted and merely took my recommendation under advisement. Because he was preparing to go abroad for an extended stay, he instructed me to sell the Knightsbridge house you formerly occupied and to dispose of his shares in the international telegraph company.' Cecilia nodded. 'Richard's father was naturally willing to purchase the shares, considering the fragile state of his son's mind and health. Therefore,' summed up Throckmorton, as he turned to several long sheets of parchment affixed to a pale blue backing with a red seal, 'the estate was entirely liquid at the time of your husband's death.'

'Liquid...?'

'Consisting of cash, stocks, and bonds of the highest quality. This,' he said, handing Cecilia the parchment document, 'is your husband's last will and testament.' She briefly studied the elaborate blue-black script. 'Which he executed in October of '68, shortly after your wedding.' She turned to the final page and examined the signature and date.

'Under this will, Mrs Castello,' said Throckmorton, 'your husband has bequeathed his entire fortune to you. Consisting of some seven hundred and fifty thousand pounds.'

'What?' exclaimed Cecilia. 'Seven hundred and fifty thousand Surely, there's...'

'More or less,' said Throckmorton, 'depending on the value of certain securities.'

'How can it be?' said Cecilia softly, staring into her lap.

'You're a very wealthy woman, Mrs Castello,' said Throckmorton. 'Why, you could live very comfortably indeed on the interest alone from your property.'

'Is this ... has this become final?'

'The will has been admitted to probate. As there are no other heirs and no claims against the estate, I have applied to the court for leave to transfer the property to your name, which will be accomplished in a matter of weeks. I would naturally be pleased to assist you in the selection of a suitable banker. Personally, I would recommend Coutts on the Strand.'

'That would be most kind. May I ask you a legal question?'

'Of course.'

'Well,' began Cecilia, 'under my changed circumstances, not only Richard's death but my inheritance, it seems to me that I no longer have any need for a guardian.'

'I recall that Dr Gully was appointed your guardian,' said the solicitor with a scratch of his chin, 'for the limited purpose of managing the separation from your late husband.' Cecilia nodded. 'I'm reasonably confident the appointment lapsed with Richard's death, but I shall make certain.'

'Thank you.' Cecilia rose from her chair.

'Now, may I be of assistance in arranging a hansom?'

Over the course of the three-hour journey from London's Paddington station to Great Malvern, Cecilia's emotions ran the gamut as the train lurched and clattered along, ranging from horror at the grotesque manner of Richard's death, to disbelief that he was possessed of £750,000, and elation at the thought of her unexpected independence. By the time the train crossed the Severn at Worcester, her feelings were as composed as the placid river flowing beneath the railway trestle. By all rights, she'd decided, she was *entitled* to her inheritance. It was no fault of hers that Richard had ignored her pleas and chosen his self-destructive path; to whom else should he have left his estate? The sheer size of the inheritance at first troubled her, as though the solicitor had made some mistake, but, as the carriage rattled and the telegraph wires dipped outside the window, the reality sank in and with it the breathtaking implications of so vast a fortune. With the stroke of a pen on a sheet of parchment, she was utterly free to do as she chose, to *own* what she desired, without the sanction of her wealthy father or the approval of a husband ... or guardian, a realization that filled her with joy.

And so it was a delighted, confident, self-satisfied young woman in widow's weeds who alighted from the carriage on the station platform. She had half expected that Gully would be there to meet her and experienced a fleeting moment of resentment when she realized he hadn't come. It was just as well, she considered, as she tipped a porter to see to her valise and arrange for her transportation to the nearby village of Malvern. She imagined the look of amazement on the doctor's kindly face when she told him the news of her changed circumstances, or at least so much of her news as she decided would be prudent.

Arriving by early afternoon on a dreary, overcast day, Cecilia decided to meet Gully in his office at the hydro rather than arrange another discreet encounter at the college. As the weather had turned cold and wet, she took a carriage to the clinic, wearing her same widow's costume but with the addition of some of her finest jewellery, an exquisite baroque black pearl brooch with

63

matching ear-rings and a carved gutta-percha ring. As it was late afternoon, the women guests in their dowdy best were gathered in the parlour, reading or playing cards, forbidden to take tea and unable to exercise in the outdoors.

'I'm here to see the doctor,' Cecilia announced to Mrs Pembroke, who met her at the entrance. With a look that clearly signified her disapproval of Cecilia's appearance as well as her relationship with the doctor, Mrs Pembroke instructed Cecilia to wait while she determined if Dr Gully were available. After a few minutes she returned and wordlessly beckoned to Cecilia with a bony forefinger.

'Hallo, Miss Stokes,' said Cecilia with a pretty smile to Gully's secretary when they arrived outside his office. Turning to Mrs Pembroke, she said, 'Thank you, madam,' reached for the doorknob, and let herself in.

Gully was standing before his desk with an expectant expression. 'Come in, Cecilia, my poor dear,' he said with outstretched arms.

Affecting an air of mourning, she walked up and briefly took his hands. 'Hallo, James,' she said simply. 'May we sit?'

'Of course.' He helped her into one of the armchairs by the warming fire and sat near her on the sofa. 'Were you successful,' he asked, 'in arranging an interview with the solicitor?'

Cecilia nodded and said, 'Yes. It was quite a shock.'

'No doubt.'

'Quite dreadful what happened to poor Richard.' She took a handkerchief from her handbag

64

and dabbed at her eyes. 'He was found,' she began again, 'dead in his hotel room, lying in a pool of his own blood...'

'Oh dear. Was there foul play?'

'No. A haemorrhage, from his diseased liver, according to the coroner's report.'

'Cirrhosis,' said Gully with a nod, 'which destroys the lining of the stomach. A consequence of alcoholism.'

Cecilia bit her lower lip and stared at Gully. 'The solicitor,' she said, 'a rather cold fish by the name of Throckmorton, informed me that he advised Richard to change his will – following our separation.'

'I see,' said Gully. 'As he was a man of means.'

'But Richard refused. He loved me too much and felt a deep responsibility to provide for me, knowing, as I'm sure he must, that his days on earth were numbered.'

Gully nodded, thinking back to the contentious negotiations over the alimony he was willing to provide for Cecilia's support. 'Very honourable,' he said. 'I assume he made some allowance for you in his will? An annuity perhaps?'

'Annuity?' said Cecilia with a short laugh. 'Richard left his entire estate to me.'

'Good heavens. His entire estate?'

Cecilia smiled inwardly. 'Yes, a rather substantial estate.'

Gully rose and stood with his back to the fire. 'All of this must have come as quite a shock, my dear. The news of Richard's sudden death and now this unexpected inheritance.'

'Unexpected? I should say not. He loved me a

65

great deal. To whom else—'

'I meant nothing,' said Gully with a placating gesture. 'I merely was concerned about your feelings. You will undoubtedly need help in managing your affairs.'

'Mr Throckmorton recommended Coutts on the Strand. He's written a letter of introduction.'

'I see.'

'And he informs me that with Richard's death the guardianship is terminated.'

Gully smiled pleasantly and said, 'The guardianship was merely a device to allow me to act on your behalf in the negotiations with your husband. I quite agree that there is no longer any need for it. I shall be happy to assist you, my dear, in any way that may be helpful.'

'Thank you, James,' said Cecilia, rising from her chair and approaching him, her silk rustling. Putting her arms around him, she kissed him lightly. 'You may help me,' she murmured, 'just as you have done. By making me happy.'

Gully sat on the side of Cecilia's bed, lacing up his shoes as he listened to the water splashing in a basin from the adjoining bathroom. A shrewd and practised observer of humanity, he detected a subtle but profound change in Cecilia, who was every bit as passionate as before but displayed a new confidence, almost, he considered as he stood up and studied his reflection, a haughtiness, a far cry from the hysterical young woman who had arrived at the hydro months earlier. He buttoned his waistcoat and then deftly knotted his black silk tie in the stiff collar. Taking a step closer to the mirror, he examined the lines on his face and the smooth baldness of his pate. An old man, he considered, in love with a pretty, head-strong girl. No, not girl. A woman, with property, who in time, he feared, would grow tired of him and seek some new adventure.

Emerging from the bath wearing yet another new silk robe with her cheeks rouged and auburn hair put up, Cecilia glanced at Gully and said, 'As you're dressed, darling, would you go down and pour me a glass of wine? Then you must take me to dinner.'

Briefly consulting his watch, Gully said, 'It's a little early for wine, dear. Perhaps you should wait until dinner.'

'I always crave wine after you make love to me,' she said. 'To calm the palpitations of my heart.'

'Very well,' he said with a smile. When he returned after a moment with a glass of sherry, she admonished him for failing to bring the carafe and another glass, which he rectified without argument. Seated in a chair by the chest of drawers, Gully sipped his sherry as he watched Cecilia, wearing bloomers and a camisole, step into her long dress, sewn of what she called tulle in a lovely pale green, and stretch her arms into the sleeves.

'Now,' she said, 'you must do up my buttons.' Standing behind her, Gully inhaled her expensive perfume as he somewhat awkwardly fastened the long row of buttons at the back of her dress.

'There,' he said, holding her slender waist and leaning down to kiss the nape of her neck.

'Mmm,' she said, turning to face him. 'Naughty

boy.' She softly kissed him on the lips and then finished her sherry. Putting the glass aside, she said, 'I'm famished.'

Seated at their usual corner table in the quiet back room of the restaurant, which had few other patrons now that the long, warm days of summer in the Malvern Hills had turned to autumn's cold and damp, Cecilia stared into Gully's eyes as she took another sip of claret.

'Are you finished with your chop, my dear?' he asked, maintaining pressure of his knee against hers under the table. 'You shouldn't neglect your vegetables, particularly the leafy greens.'

'I dislike greens,' she said. 'Besides, I don't intend to get fat like all the old biddies at the hydro.'

'Vegetables will never make you fat, dear, whereas wine–'

'James.' She reached across the table and took his hand. 'I've made up my mind.'

Gully, casting a furtive glance around the room, said, 'To do what?'

'To move to London.'

Gully waited for the waiter to clear the dishes from a nearby table and then squeezed Cecilia's hand and said quietly, 'This doesn't mean you no longer desire–'

'Of course not. It's just that there's nothing for me to do here. And now that I'm free to do as I please...'

'Cecilia,' said Gully in a low, urgent tone, 'I want to marry you. As soon, of course, as my wife is deceased. But she's very elderly and infirm.'

A tear appeared in the corner of Cecilia's eye. 'That's very sweet, darling,' she said. 'But for now simply come with me to London.'

Chapter Five

Having lived in London with her husband in Knightsbridge, and earlier with her family in Belgravia, Cecilia was well acquainted with the city's attractions, in particular the fine shops in Mayfair, evenings at the theatre and dining afterward in the West End, the hurly-burly of Piccadilly, and yet with her newly acquired wealth she aspired to something grander than a typical terraced house, a mansion in its own grounds where she could keep a stable, and yet close enough to the metropolis to meet friends for lunch or dinner. The bankers at Coutts had proved to be most accommodating, arranging to invest her assets in a portfolio of the highest quality bonds, notes, and shares that would produce an income far in excess of her needs. When she explained that she was interested in acquiring an estate, possibly on the outskirts of the city, they were pleased to refer her to a property agent by the name of Osgood Sneed, a man 'of the utmost discretion'.

Seated opposite Sneed, a short, middle-aged man wearing a heather-mixture jacket and puffing on a meerschaum pipe, in his cramped office in Baker Street, Cecilia explained her requirements – at least five bedrooms, quarters for a cook and maids, and a stable, situated in an acre or more of land but within an hour's trip by coach or rail from central London. 'What you've described,' said Sneed, 'Mrs, ah–'

'*Miss* Henderson,' said Cecilia, having decided to revert to her maiden name within weeks of her husband's death.

'Yes, thank you. You've described a country estate, but cheek-by-jowl with the city.' He rose from his chair and walked over to a map of London mounted on the wall. Slipping on a pair of spectacles, he leaned over and studied it. 'Do you know Balham?' he asked, looking at Cecilia over his shoulder. Cecilia shook her head. 'Tooting Bec, perhaps?' He sucked on his pipe and expelled an aromatic cloud.

'I know the name.'

'To the south,' said Sneed. 'Near Streatham. A very lovely area, quite rustic, but within easy access to London by train and not more than a forty-five minute journey by coach.'

'Very well, Mr Sneed,' said Cecilia, rising from her chair and walking over to give him a businesslike handshake. 'Please let me know if you find anything suitable. You may contact me at the Langham.'

'Excellent, Miss Henderson,' said Sneed. 'I'll be in touch within the week.'

Sneed was as good as his word, sending a note to Cecilia at her hotel within three days advising that 'a very fine property' in Balham was for sale and suggesting that she accompany him to inspect it 'on the morrow'. Within thirty minutes of

70

departing from the Langham, their carriage left the factory chimneys and rows of identical brick terraced houses behind and entered upon a semi-rural district with cultivated fields, barns and hedgerows interspersed with some of the capital's oldest outlying villages, with public houses, town halls, and church spires dating from the Middle Ages.

'The property in question,' said Sneed, delicately eyeing Cecilia, elaborately draped in many shades of black, grey, and lavender, as the carriage rattled along in bright sunshine, 'is known as The Priory, though I am advised it was built in the last century as a residence and has never housed monks or clergymen of any sort.'

'The Priory,' said Cecilia. 'I rather fancy the name.'

'Coming up on Bedford Hill Road, guv'nor,' called the driver from his seat.

'Turn right,' instructed Sneed. 'We'll be there shortly,' he added to Cecilia. She gazed out on a row of redbrick houses with neatly tended gardens and further in the distance at green fields and stately oaks and elms, where Old England, she imagined, merged with the great modern city. 'Just before the common,' said Sneed to the driver, 'you'll see a gravel drive on the left. Our destination.'

The driver turned the carriage on to a drive leading to an imposing white stone house, built in the style of a Gothic Revival castle, with casement windows and faux battlements along the roofline studded with numerous chimneys designed to resemble medieval turrets. To the left of the house was an apple orchard and to the right a stable; just beyond, the emerald sward of Tooting Bec Common. When the driver brought the carriage to a halt, Sneed alighted and helped Cecilia to step down, her grey and lavender silk-shod feet hitting precisely the middle of the unsteady step. For a moment she stared at the house, by far the most impressive in the neighbourhood, thrilled by the realization that it might actually be hers. 'Shall we have a look round?' said Sneed, trying to keep from adding up the shades of grey in Cecilia's dress and cloak. He walked with her to the entrance beneath a stone arch, took a key from his pocket and unlocked the door. They entered a high-ceilinged drawing-room with a crystal chandelier and marble fireplace, whose walls and parquet floor were bare, as the previous occupant had vacated. Listening to the echo of their footsteps, Cecilia imagined how the room would look with fine carpets, antique furnishings and works of art on the walls, as grand as the main hall at Buscot Park. What, she considered, would her father think of *that?*

Following a leisurely inspection of the mansion, with four bedrooms and baths on the second floor, servants' quarters on the third, and a library, dining-room, solarium, and modern kitchen in addition to the drawing-room on the ground floor, Sneed accompanied Cecilia on a tour of the coach house, with its rooms for the coachman, and adjoining stables, with stalls for three horses, concluding the visit with a stroll through the orchard, planted in neat rows of apple trees. As they returned to the carriage, Sneed said,

'Well, Miss Henderson, a very fine property, I'm sure you'd agree.'

'Oh, yes,' she said, admiring the white stone façade. 'Very fine.'

'And, as it's adjacent to the common, it has rather the feel of a country estate, though it only occupies two acres.'

'How much?' said Cecilia, turning to Sneed.

'Beg pardon?'

'What price is the seller asking?'

Unaccustomed to doing business with a woman, Sneed appeared to have been struck by a sudden nervous affliction. 'Er, ah,' he stammered. 'I'm not sure I...' He halted, staring at Cecilia with a perplexed expression.

'Come now, Mr Sneed,' she said. 'Surely the seller is demanding a price.'

'Why, yes,' agreed Sneed, recovering his senses. 'Yes, of course. Perhaps I, ah, could speak to your banker.'

'Don't be absurd,' said Cecilia, with a small stamp of her foot.

'Well, ah, Miss Henderson,' said Sneed in a low, conspiratorial tone, 'the seller is asking a price of fifteen thousand.'

She considered. 'You may advise the seller,' she said after a moment, 'that I'm prepared to pay twelve.'

In a matter of days Sneed negotiated a final price of £12,500 for the property, and Cecilia promptly directed the solicitor Throckmorton to draw up the necessary legal papers. In a single visit to the offices of her banker on the Strand she arranged to liquidate sufficient securities to effect the purchase, and, within a fortnight of her conversation at dinner with Dr Gully, she was, in the words of her lawyer, 'the fee simple owner of The Priory, free of all mortgages, liens, or encumbrances'. At the small writing-desk in her room at the Langham, Cecilia dipped her quill in an inkpot and composed a note to Dr Gully:

5 November 1870
Dear James
I have just returned from the offices of my solicitor where I was shown the deed to the property I have purchased, a comfortably large house known as The Priory located in Balham, a short drive from central London. While it doesn't compare to the beauty of the Malvern Hills, it is a quaint village in a rustic setting, with a common adjoining my house, where I intend to keep horses. I must now set about the tasks of acquiring furniture and artworks and employing household staff.
   You must come as soon as your affairs at the hydro permit and see my new home and hopefully look for something suitable for yourself. Please don't tarry as I have longed to see you.
   Your beloved darling,
   Cecilia

She blew softly on the stationery, folded it in an envelope and, after addressing it to the doctor, hurried to the front desk to post it. She filled the intervening days as she awaited Gully's reply in the company of another individual recommended by her banker, a dandy by the name of String-

74

fellow who dealt in furnishings and works of art and was pleased to accompany Cecilia to the finest shops and galleries in Mayfair. Returning to her hotel at the end of a long day of shopping for extravagant furnishings, carpets, paintings, and bronzes, Cecilia was handed a letter by the desk clerk, an envelope addressed in familiar hand. Returning to her room, she sat by the window, slit open the envelope and quickly read Gully's letter. *My dear Cecilia,* he began, *I confess I was somewhat startled to learn that you have already acquired a household in the vicinity of London. Are you not,* he wondered, *proceeding with undue haste?* Gully assured Cecilia that he *respected her judgement and assumed her financial resources were sufficient,* professed that he *loved her dearly* and closed with a promise to travel to London as soon as it could be arranged. She stared out the window at the busy street below, resentful of the patronizing, almost parental, tone of Gully's letter and yet excited by the prospect of seeing him after weeks of separation.

After the lapse of two days a telegram arrived, delivered to Cecilia's room by a page as she was breakfasting on poached eggs with kippers. Tearing open the envelope, she read:

ARRIVE SATURDAY 3:15 PADDINGTON STOP WILL PROCEED TO LANGHAM STOP J M GULLY

What shall I wear, she wondered aloud? Pushing aside her breakfast, she rushed to the shops and bought an array of gowns and shoes dyed to

75

match. Returning to her room, she sat, sipping a glass of wine and trying to decide which of the gowns to wear.

She chose to wait in the hotel's elegant lobby, seated beneath a crystal chandelier, wearing the dark-green dress with silk ruffles and collar and matching hat and her finest jewellery. She observed Gully as he entered the lobby, attired as usual in a top hat, black wool frockcoat and silk waistcoat. and immediately accosted by another hotel guest, a distinguished-looking gentlemen who shook his hand and said, 'Ah, Dr Gully, how are you, sir?' in a voice loud enough for Cecilia to overhear. Eyeing Cecilia, Gully walked quickly to her and lightly kissed her hand as she rose to greet him. 'Hallo, my dear,' he said with a smile. 'What a beautiful dress.'

'The latest Paris fashion.'

'Shall we have tea?' said Gully, noticing the waiters serving hotel guests in the far corner of the spacious lobby where a string quartet was playing.

Seated together on a sofa with their tea, and, in the case of Cecilia, a plate of pastries, Gully smiled and said, 'You appear to be in rosy good health, my dear. London must agree with you.'

'I wish you wouldn't say *my dear*,' said Cecilia, delicately holding her teacup. 'It sounds as if you are speaking to your niece.'

'Well, then,' said Gully affably, 'I shall address you as my darling.' He took a sip of chamomile tea as Cecilia nibbled a petit four. 'I see you've succumbed to bad habits,' he observed.

'Eating pastries?' she said with a toss of her auburn curls. Gully nodded. 'Well, James, this is not the hydro and, as I'm completely cured, I shall do as I please.'

'I'm glad to hear it, though as your physician I'd advise you to refrain from these social vices and take plenty of exercise out-of-doors.'

Finishing her tea, Cecilia put her cup aside and said, 'I'll have ample opportunity for exercise at my new home.' He responded with an expectant look. 'The Priory,' she added. 'We're going to see it in the morning.'

'I do worry, my dear – my darling – that you've acted impulsively on a matter of such importance.' Cecilia merely smiled and sampled another pastry.

It was a bright, cold autumn day with a dusting of frost on the fallow fields as the four-in-hand rumbled along the thoroughfare. Cecilia sat close beside Gully on the upholstered seat, warmed by her rabbit-fur collar and hat and the cashmere blanket spread over their laps. 'Do you know Balham?' she asked.

'I once gave a lecture there,' said Gully with a nod. 'Charming village as I recall.'

'Quite,' agreed Cecilia, 'with a common called Tooting Bec, a rather humorous name.'

Gully smiled as he gazed out at the trees and open fields. Patting her knee under the blanket, he said, 'You've no idea how happy I am. I missed you terribly.'

'And I you.' She leaned over and kissed him lightly on the lips. After a few minutes, he noticed a signpost for Balham, 1½ miles, and watched as the steeples and rooftops of the town came into view. Sliding open the small rectangular box above them, Cecilia called to the driver, 'Turn right on Bedford Hill Road, toward the common.'

'Aye, ma'am.'

Cecilia wore a prideful, confident expression as the driver brought the coach to a halt in front of The Priory. 'My goodness,' said Gully, peering out the window at the large stone house. Cecilia smiled briefly and then took the coachman's hand as he opened the door and helped her down. 'I had no idea,' said Gully, as he climbed down after her somewhat stiffly, 'that you had acquired such a ... well, something so *grand*.'

'Oh, pshaw,' said Cecilia with a girlish laugh. 'It's merely a country house. And' – she paused to look him in the eye – 'what's expected of someone in my position.'

'I see,' said Gully, clasping his hands behind his back as he walked with her to the imposing entrance.

Taking a key from her purse, Cecilia unlocked the door and led the way through the hall into the drawing-room. 'The furniture,' she said, 'at least the first of it, should be delivered in the morning.' Walking to the centre of the empty room, which seemed even larger than its actual dimensions, she turned again to Gully and said, 'Well, James? What do you think?'

Gully looked carefully around the room and then walked over to examine the intricately carved marble fireplace. 'It's ... it's very fine, Cecilia,' he said at length in an uncharacteristically low tone of voice. 'Very fine indeed.'

After taking Gully on a tour of the house, outbuildings, and orchard, she held his hand as they walked to the carriage. 'We should go into the town,' she said, as he held open the door, 'and have a look round.' Once Gully was seated beside her, she instructed the driver to take them to Balham, turned to Gully with a smile and said, 'We must find you suitable lodgings.'

Gully knitted his brow and said, 'I worry about neglecting my duties at the hydro. After all, darling, I've spent the last twenty-five years—'

'You needn't neglect your duties. What about Dr Wilson? Surely he can look after things in your absence.'

'But with patients like Lord Tennyson and Gladstone,' said Gully with some exasperation, 'I'm expected to be on hand. For private consultations.'

'You shall divide your time,' said Cecilia sharply, 'between Malvern and Balham. I *insist* you find lodgings here.'

'But, darling...'

'Let's not have a row.' Having settled the matter, Cecilia called to the driver, 'Take us to the hotel, if you please.' Gully stared sullenly out the window, observing the shops, churches, and public houses as the carriage creaked along the cobblestone streets of the village and came to a stop before the three-storey Bedford Hotel. Alighting from the carriage, Cecilia instructed the driver to wait and then set off down Baiham High Street with Gully at her side. Within minutes they turned on Bedford Hill Road and entered a quiet residential neighbourhood comprised of sturdy

79

brick and stone cottages. At the end of the block they halted at a wrought-iron gate before an attractive redbrick house with a sign in the front window that read: *To Let – Contact Jno. Smyth & Sons, High Street, Balham*. Cecilia briefly studied the building and then turned to Gully. 'It's just right,' she said. 'No more than a five minute walk from The Priory.'

'Perhaps,' said Gully, standing with his hands on the gate. 'Depending, of course, on the cost.'

'Don't worry about the cost,' said Cecilia. 'If need be, I shall pay the rent.'

'You'll do no such thing. If it suits, I'm perfectly prepared to absorb the expense.'

'Oh, James,' said Cecilia with a happy smile, clutching his arm. 'Let's call on the agent.'

Within the hour, Gully, introducing himself to the property agent as Cecilia's uncle, arranged to tour the cottage, known as Orwell Lodge, which had two upstairs bedrooms and a comfortable parlour and study, and negotiated satisfactory terms for a one-year rental. 'As the landlord has supplied the furnishings,' he said, as he returned with Cecilia to the hotel, 'I should be in a position to settle in as soon as I fetch my belongings from the hydro.'

'And I shall be moving to The Priory,' said Cecilia, walking beside him arm-in-arm, 'by the middle of next week.'

After days supervising large numbers of workmen – housepainters, plumbers, and handymen – readying the house for occupancy and overseeing the delivery of furniture, carpets, artworks, mirrors to be hung in every room and hallway, household necessities, not to mention her extensive wardrobe, Cecilia prepared to spend her first night at The Priory. For the occasion, the newly hired cook was roasting a leg of lamb for a sumptuous dinner Cecilia would share with Dr Gully, just returned from the hydro. At the appointed hour, he appeared at the front door, gave the brass knocker a sharp rap and was greeted by a servant in a black dress and starched white cap. 'Good evening,' she said with slight bow. 'The missus will be down shortly.' Gully hung up his hat and worsted cloak and walked into the drawing-room, illuminated by gaslights, his tread muffled by a thick Persian carpet. He stared at a large oil landscape over the mantel and then looked around the spacious room, richly appointed with fine English furniture: a Chippendale secretary and writing desk, a rosewood settee and matching armchairs facing the marble fireplace, and a Broadwood walnut piano in the corner. Lightly running his hand over the back of the settee, Gully studied the painting and then turned as Cecilia, wearing a low-cut, red silk dress with a strand of pearls at her neck, descended the elegant curved staircase.

'What an extraordinary transformation,' he said, as she walked up and took his hands.

'Do you like it?'

'It's exceptional.' He paused to give her a kiss and said, 'One might imagine you've lived here for some time. How did you manage it?'

'Oh, I've found a very efficient assistant – Mrs Clark – who's been most helpful overseeing the workmen. And Mr Stringfellow, of course, was invaluable when it came to the selection of furnishings and fine art.'

'Speaking of art,' said Gully, approaching the fireplace, 'tell me about this painting.'

'A Gainsborough. Do you like it?'

'An actual Gainsborough?'

'Of course.'

'Well, I must say,' he said, walking over and taking her hand, 'you've outdone yourself. On the whole, as fine a drawing-room as any in Mayfair or Belgravia.'

'And,' she said with a suggestive look, 'you've yet to see my bedroom.'

'Beg pardon,' said the parlourmaid, standing in the entrance to the dining-room.

Gully sat next to Cecilia at one end of the long mahogany table, which accommodated twelve chairs upholstered in red leather, dabbing at his chin with a napkin following roast beef accompanied by gravy, Yorkshire pudding, and haricots. Pouring the last of the wine, a French claret, in her goblet, Cecilia said, 'You'll be pleased to know, James, that I've dispensed with dessert.'

'After an over-abundance of food and wine,' said Gully with a pleasant smile, 'I'm quite sure I'd have no room for it.' He gazed at her in the flickering light from an elaborate, gold candelabrum, admiring her rosebud lips and the soft white skin of her neck, exposed by her up-combed hair. Sipping her wine, she lightly rubbed her knee against his under the table. 'Listen,' she said. 'Can you hear my petticoats rustle?'

'Do the servants,' he asked quietly, leaning closer to her, 'live in the house?'

'Several have quarters in the coach-house, other than Mrs Clark, who has her own room upstairs.' In response to Gully's concerned look, she added, 'Don't worry, darling. I'm sure she's retired for the evening.' Finishing her wine, Cecilia rose from the table, took Gully by the hand and wordlessly led him up the staircase. Quietly entering the master bedroom, panelled in oak, with a four-poster bed, she locked the door and removed the key and then closed the heavy curtains. Gully took her in his arms and kissed her, softly at first but with growing intensity as his hands explored the soft curves of her back and hips beneath the silk.

'Mmm,' she murmured, as he ran his hand lightly across her breasts. 'Undress while I go to my boudoir. I'll just be a minute.'

Emerging from her boudoir, Cecilia observed Gully lying in the four-poster bed with his head propped up on pillows, in the dim light of a single candle on the chest of drawers. Walking to the bedside, she glanced at his bare shoulders and chest and then untied the sash of her silk robe and let it fall to the floor. For a moment he stared at her breasts, her slender waist and the curves of her hips and then silently drew back the covers.

Chapter Six

Seated on a cushioned stool before the oval mirror in her boudoir, Cecilia, in her newest embroidered silk dressing-gown, combed out her auburn hair. Turning to the side, she examined her profile and then powdered her nose, rouged her cheeks, and lastly painted her lips a deep red gloss. At the sound of footsteps, she observed the reflection of Mrs Clark, standing in the doorway.

'Let me help you with your hair,' said Mrs Clark, a petite woman in her mid-forties who wore her dark hair in a bun and almost always dressed in black. She stood behind Cecilia, who sat motionless as Mrs Clark adroitly combed and pinned up her hair. 'There,' said Mrs Clark, lightly placing her hands on Cecilia's shoulders. 'You look quite beautiful, Cissie, as always.'

'Don't flatter me, Janie,' said Cecilia, turning to look up at her friend with a smile.

'The truth is not flattery,' replied Mrs Clark, well aware that the vain young woman delighted in flattery.

Cecilia rose and walked into the sunlit bedroom. 'What a lovely spring day,' she remarked, unlatching and throwing open the casement window. 'We should take a long drive on the common.'

'I shall tell Mr Griffiths to bring round the carriage,' said Mrs Clark in a businesslike tone. 'Will you have breakfast?'

'Have the cook poach an egg,' said Cecilia, as she slipped off her robe and tossed it on the bed, revealing her chemise and petticoat. 'With a rasher of bacon.' Gazing briefly at Cecilia, Mrs Clark smiled and walked briskly from the room.

Wearing a double-breasted dark-blue coat with a sable collar, matching hat, and navy kid gloves, Cecilia stood on the gravel drive admiring the matched pair of white horses coupled to the open-top coach, painted a glossy green with red wheel-rims and seats upholstered in supple cowhide. 'A very fine carriage, ma'am,' said the coachman Griffiths, running a hand over the fender. 'And well sprung.'

'It should be,' said Cecilia. 'It cost me a pretty penny.' Taking Griffiths' hand, she put a petite foot on the running board and climbed in, choosing the front-facing seat and admiring her navy, gold-trimmed boots. After a moment Mrs Clark emerged from the house, wearing a hat and wool shawl. She sat beside Cecilia, clapped her hands, and said, 'What a perfect day for an outing.' Griffiths climbed up on the driver's seat, unlooped the reins, and started the horses into a trot. Turning from the drive on Bedford Hill Road, they entered Tooting Bec Common, an expanse of some 300 acres with stands of oak and bright green fields dotted with daffodils waving in the gentle breeze. The driver turned on a track that encircled the Common, where a number of children, under the supervision of their teachers or nannies, were playing, including a group of schoolgirls in matching white dresses and beribboned straw boaters. 'To be a child again,' said Cecilia happily, placing a gloved hand on her companion's knee. Mrs Clark merely smiled, thinking back to her own miserable childhood in a Liverpool slum. Reaching the far end of the Common, Cecilia leaned forward and instructed the driver, 'Take us to Streatham. A turn around the common there and we'll be ready for home.'

By the time they returned to The Priory, Cecilia had regaled Mrs Clark with descriptions of her time at the hydro – 'showered with buckets of ice water, *in the nude,*' she whispered – the communal meals and outings in the countryside, eliciting polite smiles and an occasional soft laugh from her reticent companion. 'I trust,' said Mrs Clark as the carriage came to a halt on the gravel drive, 'that the regimen is beneficial to one's health.'

'Oh, James – Dr Gully – swears by it,' said Cecilia, as the coachman opened the door and helped her down. Mrs Clark betrayed no emotion at the mention of the doctor, though she had long since deduced that he was a regular visitor to her employer's bedroom. 'And I suppose,' Cecilia added, 'it did me some good, though the food was wretched and I was forced to abstain from wine and tea.' Mrs Clark responded with a hint of a smile and followed Cecilia up the flag-stones and into the house. With a glance at the grandfather clock in the hall, Cecilia said, 'Tell the cook to have lunch ready at half past the hour. I'm going up to my bath.'

'Yes, madam.'

Cecilia dried herself with a soft towel as the water

noisily drained from the claw-foot bath. Folding the towel on a rack, she started for the adjoining boudoir when she perceived someone standing just outside the door. 'Oh,' she said, instinctively crossing her arms over her bare breasts.

'It's only me,' said Mrs Clark, emerging from the shadows. 'Shall I get your robe?'

For a moment Cecilia stared in the older woman's dark eyes, feeling a blush on her neck, and then said, 'Yes, what is it?'

'I merely wanted to tell you,' said Mrs Clark, as she took one of Cecilia's silk dressing-gowns from the closet and helped her to slip it on, 'that a boy from the telegraph office delivered a telegram.' She produced an envelope from her pocket and handed it to Cecilia.

'I see,' said Cecilia, studying the address as she tied the sash. Looking up, she said, 'You may tell cook that as soon as I'm dressed I'll be ready for lunch.' As Mrs Clark turned to go, Cecilia closed the doors to her boudoir and fastened the latch.

Wearing her latest silk undergarments, she sat before the mirror and studied her reflection. The telegram, crumpled into a ball, was on the dresser beside her silver hairbrush. As she'd expected, it was from James, informing her that he'd returned from his sojourn in Europe and would arrive in Balham on the 6.00 p.m. train. Though the thought of an evening with her lover, after an absence of some three weeks, evoked pleasurable feelings of anticipation, and though he was still capable of arousing her to sexual fulfilment, her ardour had dimmed and the trysts no longer had the dangerous, illicit quality that had thrilled her in Malvern. And, as a consequence, she had grown careless in her precautions to hide her scandalous secret from prying eyes. Taking the old, pale-pink organdie from the closet, she thought about Mrs Clark, about Janie, as she fastened the buttons. There was something, she considered with a shiver, about the way the older woman looked at her, or touched her, that was disturbing and yet exciting in a way she couldn't explain.

As usual, Cecilia's place was set at the head of the dining-room table; the good silver and bone china were laid out on linen beside a silver water goblet and crystal wineglass. As soon as she was seated, the parlourmaid appeared, serving her a bowl of vichyssoise and a selection of finger sandwiches. Once she was alone, Cecilia took a sip of water and then poured herself a full glass of straw-coloured wine from the decanter at her elbow. 'I always take wine with my meals,' she had once advised the disapproving maid, 'to improve my digestion.' As she was enjoying her soup, Mrs Clark appeared in the passageway holding a clutch of letters.

'I've sorted your mail, Cissie,' she said. 'Shall we go over it now, or would you prefer to wait?'

'Now would be fine. Please join me.'

'A letter from Mr Taylor, at Coutts,' Mrs Clark began, as she sat in the chair next to Cecilia, 'enclosing a statement of your accounts, which of course, I did not open.'

'Of course.'

'And an invoice from Madame Rousseau, the dressmaker on Bond Street–'

'I'm sending the dress back,' interrupted Cecilia.

'It isn't right for me. Don't pay the invoice. We'll also return the slippers.'

'But, Cissie? The poor woman...'

'Why should I keep them?'

'Very well.' After reviewing the usual assortment of bills, social invitations, and correspondence, including a rather stiff letter from Cecilia's mother, Mrs Clark held up a pale-blue envelope and said, 'And finally, an invitation from Mr Throckmorton, your solicitor.'

'Oh, really?'

'To lunch, on Saturday the 24th, at his house in Surrey.' She extracted the neatly lettered invitation from the envelope and handed it to Cecilia.

Cecilia smiled as she glanced at the invitation, surprised that the dour solicitor would reach out to someone of her social position. 'Send him a reply,' she said, as she handed the invitation to Mrs Clark, 'advising that I accept and that I shall be accompanied by my friend Dr Gully.'

The doctor arrived at The Priory at half past seven, weary from the day's journey and aggravated by a delay in departing from Waterloo. Shown by the parlourmaid to the drawing-room, he walked slowly, leaning heavily on a silver-handled cane, and seemed to Cecilia, seated by the fire, to have aged during his brief absence. Rising to greet him, she gave him a kiss on the cheek and said, 'My goodness, James, whatever is the matter?'

'Oh, it's nothing,' he said with a grimace, slumping heavily on the settee facing the fire. 'I took a tumble while on a walk outside Gräfenberg and sprained my knee.' He reached down to massage the limb.

'Poor dear,' said Cecilia. 'Let me get you a glass of wine.'

'No, thankee,' said Gully. 'Bad for my gout.'

'Your visit was a success?' Cecilia lifted her wineglass from the table and took a sip.

'Oh, yes. An excellent opportunity to visit my Continental colleagues, all homeopathic men, of course. And the wildflowers were exceptional.' Cecilia nodded politely, noticing the whiteness of Gully's hair, the lines on his face, and the blue veins on the back of his hands. 'Lots of discussion about the slanderous attacks from our medical colleagues.'

'Attacks?' said Cecilia with a puzzled expression.

'Calls for a ban on homeopathic medicine,' said Gully, thumping his cane on the floor. 'Decrying the water-cure as quackery. Humbug!'

'Oh, dear.'

'Well, Cecilia my dear, they have *my* answer!'

'Are you sure you won't have a glass of wine?'

'Perhaps with dinner.' Gully reached into his waistcoat and produced a folded page torn from a medical gazette. Slipping on his spectacles, he said, 'I wrote a letter to the editors of the medical journal answering these slanderous attacks, which they've published. Shall I read it to you?' Cecilia nodded. 'The fetor of servility,' he began, in a stentorian voice, 'which exhales from minds putrescent with sordid calculations, may be sweet incense to the nostrils of the low-minded members of the medical profession....'

90

'My goodness,' said Cecilia.

Gully smiled and continued to read. 'I will not believe that the great mass of medical gentlemen will reverence any *confrère* who crawls at their feet or licks their saliva. Impertinent statements regarding my financial position, offscourings of gossip about my patients, such a farrago of vulgarities, of shoppishness, and snobbishment on which no gentleman would undertake to pass a comment. And so forth and so on,' concluded Gully, refolding the page in his waistcoat.

'You write so beautifully,' said Cecilia, 'though I'm not sure I fully understand...'

'No matter. Shall we repair to the table? I confess I'm famished.'

Following a supper of roast beef and parsleyed potatoes, during which Gully amused Cecilia with anecdotes from his travels, including an evening at the Folies Bergère in Paris – 'very naughty,' he assured her – Cecilia suggested they take the last of their wine to the drawing-room. Seated in one of the upholstered armchairs, she studied Gully, relaxing beside her on the settee with his usual genial expression, but looking older and frailer than the vigorous man who'd led her on many a strenuous walk in the Malvern Hills. 'We have an invitation,' she said after finishing her wine and putting the glass aside, 'to visit my solicitor, Mr Throckmorton.'

'An invitation...' said Gully.

'To lunch at his country house in Surrey.'

'Are you socially acquainted with the man?'

'No, but I thought it would be impolite to

decline, considering all that he's done to help me.'

'Well, dear, you may go without me,' said Gully. 'I recall that he was somewhat disagreeable.'

'No, James, you shall go with me. I insist. On Saturday next.'

Gully listened to the chimes from the grandfather clock in the hall and then said, 'Very well.' Leaning closer to Cecilia, he whispered, 'Shall we retire to your room?'

'Not tonight, darling,' said Cecilia, with a patronizing smile. 'It's the wrong time of the month.'

'Well, then,' said Gully, rising painfully from the settee, 'I should be going home.'

Sharing a railway compartment with a dozing Anglican priest, Gully and Cecilia sat facing one another by the window, gazing out on lush green fields and sturdy oaks in the bright sunshine of a glorious May morning. 'At least,' said Gully, putting aside his medical journal, 'we have a nice day in case our host should care to take us on a ramble.'

'But what about your knee?' said Cecilia, glancing at Gully's cane. 'And besides, I doubt Mr Throckmorton spends much time in the out of doors.'

'We shall see,' said Gully cheerfully. Within an hour of their departure, the train slowed at the approach to a station, and the conductor, standing in the corridor, sang out: 'Reigate!' When the train came to a halt with a hiss of escaping steam, Gully donned his top hat, offered his arm to

Cecilia and escorted her from the carriage. 'We may have a devil of a time hiring a coach,' he said, looking around the virtually empty platform. A short young man wearing high boots, a rough jacket, and soft wool cap emerged from the station and began walking toward them. 'Miss Henderson?' he said, approaching Cecilia.

'Yes,' she replied. 'You must be...'

'Mr Throckmorton's driver. How dy'do,' he added, tipping his hat to the doctor.

'Hallo, my good man,' said Gully. 'Let's be on our way.'

Fortunately, the railway station was only a few miles from The Bellows, Oliver Throckmorton's country estate, as the road was badly rutted and the springs on his carriage were sorely in need of replacement. Cecilia peered out the window as they turned on to a gravel drive and approached a redbrick house the walls of which were overgrown with ivy and climbing roses. With a final jolt, the driver brought the carriage to a stop, leapt down and held open the door. Gully awkwardly stepped down after Cecilia and, leaning on his cane, walked with her up the flagstone path. After giving the door knocker a rap, a girl wearing a gingham dress and prim, stiff apron appeared with a diffident smile and directed the couple to the parlour, a cosy room with wide plank floors, worn carpets and exposed beams. Oliver Throckmorton, wearing a green sporting jacket with a plaid waistcoat and cream-coloured trousers, stood with his arm on the mantelpiece.

'Good day, Miss Henderson,' he said, as cheerfully as he was able.

Walking up, Cecilia said, 'Let me introduce–'

'The esteemed Dr Gully,' said Throckmorton, reaching out to shake hands. 'A privilege to make your acquaintance.'

'The pleasure is mine,' said Gully. Turning to two middle-aged ladies who entered from the passageway, he bowed slightly and said, 'How do you do...'

'My wife Florence,' said Throckmorton. 'And my sister Violet. Doctor Gully and Miss Henderson.'

'Cecilia.'

'*Doctor* Gully,' said Mrs Throckmorton, a full-figured woman with a florid face. 'I've heard so many wonderful things about you. Doctor Gully,' she added, in an aside to her sister-in-law, 'is the personal physician to Lord Tennyson, Charles Darwin *and* Mr Gladstone.'

'Shall we sit?' suggested Throckmorton, gesturing to the chairs and horsehair sofa arranged before the fireplace. Gully seated Cecilia, waited for the other ladies to sit and then lowered himself into an armchair. 'Would you care for tea?' said Mrs Throckmorton.

'Dr Gully doesn't approve of tea,' said Violet, who, like her brother, was tall and thin, with an aquiline nose.

'Doesn't approve of tea?' said Throckmorton with a querulous expression.

'Or sugar,' said Violet, 'from what I've read.'

'At the hydro,' said Gully equably, 'as part of the water-cure, the consumption of tea is prohibited, as well as sugar, salt, coffee, alcoholic beverages and the use of tobacco.'

'And what, may I ask,' said Throckmorton, 'is the water treatment intended to cure?'

'Ah,' said Gully, delighted by the opportunity to expound his unorthodox views. As Cecilia listened with a bored expression, he recited the many virtues of hydropathy, its salubrious effects on a host of maladies, not least respiratory ailments, digestive difficulties, and general hysteria, to the evident approbation of Violet and scepticism of her brother, concluding with a disdainful critique of the 'shibboleths' of conventional medical practice with its heavy reliance on opiates and other 'noxious chemicals'.

'Do you not approve of laudanum?' enquired Mrs Throckmorton. 'I know of many women–'

'I condemn all use of opium,' said Gully, with a thump of his cane on the floor, 'including laudanum, which merely dulls the senses and, of course, is habit forming.'

'Pardon me,' said the girl who'd greeted Gully and Cecilia at the door. 'But luncheon is served.'

Seated around a long walnut dining table with matching sideboard in a room with a view of the nearby flower garden and verdant countryside, Cecilia picked at her lunch of mutton chops with stewed vegetables and buttered rolls, as she listened to the desultory conversation, which ranged from politics – Throckmorton's strong preference for Disraeli, notwithstanding his Jewishness', over Gladstone – the delightful spring weather, to Violet's deep religious convictions. Gully, who had deduced that the woman was both a spinster and a teetotaller, said, 'I, for one, am a believer in spiritualism.'

Violet gazed at him with a reverential expression. 'Have you communicated with the dearly departed?' she asked after a moment.

'Indeed,' replied Gully. 'On several occasions.'

'And how,' said Throckmorton with a sceptical scowl, 'does a man of science, a medical doctor...'

'Through a medium, of course,' said Gully pleasantly. 'The proper medium is essential.'

'Do you care for dessert?' asked Mrs Throckmorton. 'The cook baked a pie.'

When at last the dessert plates had been cleared away, Throckmorton looked to his guests and said, 'It's such delightful weather, I believe I'll take a stroll. Who would care to join me?' Cecilia turned to Gully, inwardly pleading with him to decline.

'Perhaps another time,' said Gully. 'The repast was excellent, but its effects were somewhat soporific.'

'I'll come along,' said Violet.

'As will I,' announced Mrs Throckmorton.

'And I,' said Cecilia, 'shall keep the doctor company.' Once the Throckmortons were out of the door and a safe distance down the drive, Cecilia settled on the sofa in the parlour, kicked off her shoes and said, 'That woman Violet is a frightful bore.'

'So much so,' said Gully, as he sat beside her, 'that I'd forego a walk in the country on a beautiful day.' He smiled at Cecilia and patted her knee. She snuggled against him, and, placing an arm around her shoulder, he leaned down to kiss her.

'Mmm,' she said after a moment. 'We shouldn't.'

'We're all alone,' said Gully. 'They won't return for at least three-quarters of an hour.' Drawing her even closer, he kissed her again, running his hand over the outline of her breasts.

'I say the man's a damned fool,' said Throckmorton, walking between his wife and sister.

'Don't swear,' said Violet. 'He's regarded as a genius by the most eminent men of the day.'

'Damn,' said Throckmorton again, glancing up at a transient dark cloud. 'Looks like rain.'

'Don't worry,' said Violet. 'I'll run back for an umbrella.' Arriving at the front door, it occurred to her that the esteemed doctor, judging from his remark, might be taking a nap, so she entered the house covertly, walking on tiptoe as she moved from the door toward the umbrella stand in the hall. Approaching the arched entrance to the parlour, she heard a peculiar grunting sound. She glanced at the mirror on the far side of the room and, for a split second, an image of snow-white buttocks, thrusting pelvis, and entangled limbs was indelibly imprinted on the poor woman's mind. Clasping her hands to her eyes, she shrieked loudly and fainted dead away.

Hearing a woman's cry, Throckmorton raced back to the house and bolted into the hallway, where Violet lay crumpled on the carpet. Turning toward the parlour, he observed Gully furiously fumbling with his fly, his shirttail untucked, and Cecilia standing beside him with a wild expression and her dress partly unbuttoned. 'What!' exclaimed Throckmorton. 'What in heaven's name!'

Violet groaned, rose to an elbow, and then

shrieked again. 'Now, now,' said Throckmorton, helping her to her feet. 'Let's get you upstairs,' he said, taking her by the arm. By the time he returned, Gully had recovered his dignity and Cecilia occupied a chair at the end of the room, gazing out the window.

'You, sir,' said Throckmorton in a low, threatening voice, 'shall answer for this.'

'I have no idea what you're talking about,' said Gully calmly.

Pointing a bony finger at Gully, Throckmorton said, 'You know very well what I'm talking about. My poor sister, who is utterly beside herself, observed the two of you...' – he lowered his voice to a whisper – '*in flagrante delicto.*'

'That's absurd,' said Gully. 'The woman is obviously delusional. Not entirely uncommon among women of her age and, ah, proclivities.'

'Get out!' growled Throckmorton.

'Cecilia,' said Gully sharply.

'I'm sending for my driver,' said Throckmorton. 'And *you* shall be hearing from my barrister.'

Gully turned his back, walked slowly to Cecilia, took her by the arm and escorted her to the front door.

Chapter Seven

'I'm ruined,' said Cecilia, propped up on pillows. 'Utterly ruined.'

'Remarkable,' said Mrs Clark, who was seated in a chair at her employer's bedside, 'that an old man, even one so old as Dr Gully, can impregnate a woman. But a scientific fact.'

Cecilia nodded bleakly. 'One would have thought that wretched, rumour-mongering Throckmorton was misfortune enough,' she said, 'but now *this*.' Suppressing a sob, she dabbed at her eyes with a handkerchief.

'Poor Cissie,' said Mrs Clark. 'You're quite sure?'

'I think so, but as it's never happened before... In any case, the doctor's coming later this morning to examine me.'

'You should rest,' said Mrs Clark, rising from her chair.

When Gully appeared – a kindly looking older gentleman holding a black medical bag – the casual observer would have assumed it was merely the doctor calling on a patient rather than a lover calling on his mistress. And so it seemed to Cecilia when he was shown into her bedroom by the efficient Mrs Clark; the affair had ended, had ended very badly, and her relationship to Gully from that moment on would be purely a

99

professional one.

'Good morning, dear,' said Gully, placing his bag on the bedside table.

'Hallo,' said Cecilia softly.

'Have you been feeling ill?' She nodded. Removing his stethoscope from his bag, Gully slipped it on, leaned down, and gently placed its silver disk on Cecilia's abdomen through the thin fabric of her nightgown. Closing his eyes in concentration, he listened through the instrument, removed its earpieces, and then gently probed her abdomen with his fingertips. Standing upright, he looked her in the eye and said, 'How long has it been since you missed your period?'

'Three weeks,' she replied. 'Or a bit more.'

Nodding solemnly, Gully said, 'It's as we feared. And all my fault. How could I possibly have been so reckless...'

'No,' said Cecilia in a stronger voice. 'It was *my* fault. I'd had too much wine at dinner and thought, perhaps this once I could do without...' Her shoulders shaking, she burst into tears.

Gully sat beside her and gently placed a hand on her shoulder. 'There, there,' he said. 'You know how much I love you.' She nodded. 'And that I intend to marry you.'

'If it becomes known,' said Cecilia, wiping her eyes, 'that I'm expecting, after everything else I've endured...'

'As far as these vicious rumours are concerned,' said Gully irritably, 'I believe I've succeeded in silencing Throckmorton. After he threatened an action for damages, I instructed my lawyers to prepare a counter-suit for slander and serve

100

notice that I intend to go through with it.'

'Oh, well,' said Cecilia. 'The damage has been done. There's nothing left of my reputation.'

Nor mine, reflected Gully dismally.

'Why, some of the tradesmen in the village refuse to do business with me, and my own parents won't answer my letters.'

'What will you do,' asked Gully, 'in light of this new development?'

'I don't know,' said Cecilia, fighting back another wave of tears. 'Leave the country, I suppose. Emigrate to Australia.'

Gully nodded and said, 'And I may be forced to remove my practice to the Continent. To Bavaria.'

'That would be terrible. After all you've accomplished at the hydro.'

'But if you bear the child... And I not in a position to marry you.'

'Is there any alternative?'

Gully rose from the bedside and began to pace, his hands clasped behind his back. 'Speaking as your physician,' he said at length, 'considering that it's only been five weeks since, ah, conception...' Cecilia stared at him expectantly. He halted and looked her in the eye. 'You might choose,' he said, 'not to have the baby.'

Cecilia closed her eyes, lightly running her hand over her belly. After a moment she opened them and said, 'Do you know someone, a surgeon, to whom I...?'

'I would have to perform the procedure,' said Gully. 'I believe that I'm competent. Otherwise, we would be risking...'

'Yes,' said Cecilia, closing her eyes again. 'Yes,

of course.'

Gully sat beside her again and gently stroked her hair. Looking up at him, she said, 'How soon can this be arranged?'

'I must return to Malvern this afternoon,' said Gully. 'I'm scheduled to consultations with patients in the morning. I shall return on the following day, and we can...' He thoughtfully bit his lower lip. 'We can see to it then.'

Doctor Gully chose to walk from his cottage on Bedford Hill Road, carrying his medical bag in one hand and an umbrella in the other. The June morning was unseasonably warm and sultry, the sky a billow of dark clouds and the still air charged with electricity. Hurrying along the cobblestones, Gully considered that a year had passed since he first met Cecilia, an emotionally fragile young woman suffering at the hands of an alcoholic husband. He'd merely wanted to help her, to enable her to escape an abusive marriage in which she believed she was hopelessly trapped. And yet ... he'd permitted himself to fall in love with her – no, he had *seduced* her. As images of the picnic at Willow Crescent, the hotel room at Madame Manteuffel's, and Cecilia's bedroom at her house in Malvern filled his mind, he was startled by a loud clap of thunder and snapped open his umbrella just as the skies opened. In the pouring rain, Gully hurried the final hundred yards to the imposing Gothic edifice of The Priory.

When the maid answered his knock, he stepped quickly into the hall, put the umbrella in the stand and hung up his hat and frock-coat. 'Would

102

you be so kind,' he said, 'as to tell Mrs Clark I'd like a word with her?'

Mrs Clark found Gully in the drawing-room, standing before the fireplace admiring the Gainsborough over the mantel and listening to the downpour outside the windows. Wearing her usual black dress, she walked up to him and said, 'Good morning, Doctor.'

'Good morning, madam,' he replied. 'I trust Miss Henderson is upstairs...'

'She's resting in her room.'

'Very well.' Glancing around the large room to ensure they were alone, he said, 'I presume you are aware of her condition?'

Mrs Clark looked at him pointedly and said, 'That she's pregnant?'

Gully arched his silver eyebrows, shocked at her choice of words, as the condition was almost always referred to euphemistically. 'I understand from Cecilia,' he said after a moment, adopting his well-practised conversational tone, 'that you spent a portion of your adult life in Jamaica?'

'That is correct. When my husband was living and my children were young.'

'I spent my first twenty-one years in Jamaica,' said Gully. 'My father was a coffee planter.'

'I see.'

'I would imagine, therefore,' said Gully, 'that you know something of the ways of the world.' Mrs Clark nodded. 'More so than the typical Englishwoman.'

'Doctor Gully,' said Mrs Clark, 'if you would get to the point...'

103

'The point, madam, is that Miss Henderson desires not to have the baby. After today, no one, absolutely *no one*, will ever know that she was expecting.'

'I see.' Mrs Clark glanced uneasily at the doctor's bag.

'However, I shall need your assistance.'

'Very well. I consider it my duty to attend to Miss Henderson in every way she desires.'

'The procedure,' said Gully, 'carries certain risks, which we must do our best to minimize. In particular, the risks of bleeding and postoperative infection.' She nodded. 'The other members of the household staff,' he continued, 'are to know nothing about this. They are merely to be told that Miss Henderson is unwell and confined to bed for several days.'

'I understand.'

'Before I proceed, she must have freshly laundered sheets, and a supply of clean towels, cotton wool, and denatured alcohol.'

'I'll see to it myself.'

'Mrs Clark,' said Gully. 'Do you have the fortitude to assist me in the procedure?'

'Yes.'

Gully, seated in the drawing-room with a surgical text open in his lap, glanced up as Mrs Clark appeared, clutching a stack of towels. Putting the book aside, he stood up and straightened the front of his waistcoat. 'Everything's in order?' he asked.

'Yes, sir.'

'I would suggest that you take her a glass of

Madeira. To calm her nerves. I'll be up shortly.'

When Gully appeared, Cecilia was lying in the four-poster under the counterpane, her auburn hair fanned out on the pillow and her face pale and drawn. Mrs Clark stood by the window, the heavy curtains of which were drawn. Gully, who had rolled his shirtsleeves up to the elbow, approached Cecilia and placed his leather bag on the bedside table next to an empty wineglass. 'Are you comfortable, my dear?' he asked. She merely nodded. Adjusting the gas-lit lamp to its brightest, he opened his bag and removed a dropper, a small metal frame, and a glass vial containing a clear liquid. 'I'm going to put you to sleep,' Gully explained, 'using chloroform.' He held up the vial for her inspection. 'Entirely safe, I assure you, and you won't feel a thing.' He carefully folded a square of cloth in the frame and used the dropper to wet it liberally with the anaesthetic. 'Simply breathe normally,' he said as he placed the mask over her nose and mouth, 'and close your eyes. You'll be fast asleep in no time.' Gully consulted his pocket watch and, after the lapse of thirty seconds, he removed the mask. 'Now,' he said, turning to Mrs Clark, who was watching impassively, 'we may proceed.'

Half an hour later, Gully stood over the washbasin in the adjoining bathroom vigorously scrubbing his hands and forearms with soap and hot water. Gazing at his reflection in the mirror over the basin, he muttered, 'A terrible business. But it had to be done.' He dried his hands and returned to the bedroom, where Mrs Clark was standing by the bed, her face a blank mask. Walking up to her, Gully briefly studied Cecilia. 'She'll be waking up shortly,' he said. 'Look after her while I dispose of these, ah, linens.' They both looked down on the bloodied sheets and towels heaped on the floor. In response to Mrs Clark's questioning look, he added, 'Don't worry. I've brought along this.' He reached into his medical bag for a folded canvas sack with a drawstring. 'I'll be back in half an hour,' he said after stuffing the bloodied linens in the sack. 'She'll be very weak when she awakens,' he added as he gazed down on Cecilia, who was beginning to stir. 'As she's lost a pint or so of blood.'

When Gully returned, having disposed of the evidence – *criminal* evidence, as he well knew – in a waste receptacle at his own house, Cecilia was conscious but suffering from nausea, enervation, and the twin sensations of grief and guilt. She said nothing and averted her eyes when Gully approached her bedside and lightly placed his hand on her forehead. 'Cool and clammy,' he intoned, 'as one would expect in a mild case of shock.' He turned to Mrs Clark and said, 'You must be vigilant for the first signs of infection. Her skin hot and dry to the touch, a certain pinkness to her complexion.'

'Yes, Doctor.'

Gully reached for Cecilia's hand, lying limp on the coverlet, and gave it a gentle squeeze. 'I know,' he said, 'that this has been terribly difficult. What matters now is that you rest and recover your strength.' She nodded weakly. Turning back to

Mrs Clark, he said, 'She may have a cup of clear broth and dry toast for supper, if she's able to keep it down.'

'Yes, Doctor.'

'I shall return in the morning. Send for me at once if there should be a problem of any kind.'

By midnight, Cecilia was running a fever, sleeping fitfully at intervals and trembling under an extra blanket as Mrs Clark hovered over her, wringing out cold washcloths and holding them to Cecilia's brow and periodically checking for signs of more bleeding. 'There, now,' she said in a soothing tone, brushing back a strand of damp hair from Cecilia's face, 'try to sleep.' When at last she quieted, Mrs Clark dimmed the light and curled up in an armchair at the foot of the bed, dozing lightly as she remained alert for sounds of distress. After an hour or so of peace, she was awakened by a loud groan and sprang up. 'Ohh,' said Cecilia, running a hand over her face. 'I'm going to be sick.' Mrs Clark hurried to the bathroom for a towel and then supported Cecilia as she violently retched. Her face wan and lips colourless, she slumped back on her pillows with another groan. After checking Cecilia's faint pulse and determining that the fever, for now, had abated, Mrs Clark drew the chair close, dimmed the light, and endured the remainder of the long night with her eyes open, waiting for the first hint of dawn at the windows.

By morning Cecilia had at last fallen into a deep sleep. Mrs Clark noiselessly slipped out and went to her room to bathe and change her clothes. She summoned the maids, cook, and butler to the kitchen and informed them, 'Miss Henderson is unwell. I am personally looking after her. If Dr Gully should arrive, notify me at once.'

'Yes, mum,' they answered in unison.

'And Florence – would you be so kind as to bring me a boiled egg with toast and tea. I'll be in m'lady's bedroom.'

As the grandfather clock in the hall chimed nine times, Mrs Clark looked up from her chair in Cecilia's room at the sound of a soft tap on the door. Opening it a crack, she peered out at Mary Ann, the upstairs maid, who whispered, 'Doctor Gully is here. Shall I show him up?'

'No. Show him to the drawing-room. I'll be there directly.'

She found Gully, wearing his usual black frock-coat and charcoal trousers, standing by the piano at the far end of the room. 'How is my patient?' he asked, as she walked up to him.

Mrs Clark glared at him briefly and then said, 'Not well. She developed a fever during the night and appeared to be in some discomfort. And then she became sick at her stomach.'

'Vomiting?'

'Yes. But her fever seems to have gone and she's sleeping soundly.'

'Has she had anything to eat?'

'No.'

'Naturally, I intend to examine her,' said Gully, 'But I'd prefer not to wake her. I'll wait here until you send for me.'

'As you wish.' She turned away and walked

quickly from the room.

At midmorning Mrs Clark reappeared in the drawing-room where she found Gully seated in an armchair reading the newspaper. 'You may see Miss Henderson now,' she said as he rose to greet her. 'But I caution you to be careful, as she's very weak and emotionally distraught.'

'I see,' said Gully with a frown, unaccustomed to being lectured in this way, especially by a woman even without training as a nurse.

He found Cecilia resting in bed. With Mrs Clark's help, she'd managed to change into a fresh nightgown, wash her face and comb out her hair. 'Good morning, Cecilia,' he said. 'I understand you had a difficult night.' She merely nodded as Gully placed a hand at her wrist and checked her pulse. 'Let's take your temperature,' he said, removing a thermometer from his bag and placing it in her mouth. Removing it after several minutes, he held it up and said, 'Ninety-nine point eight. Are you in any pain?'

'A little,' she said, gently placing a hand over her abdomen.

'Pardon me, madam,' said Gully to Mrs Clark, 'while I examine her.' Once he had concluded his pelvic examination, Gully removed his stethoscope and looked Cecilia in the eye. 'The fever you're running,' he said in a calm voice, 'is consistent with a low-grade post-operative infection. The nausea in the night was likely the result of the anaesthetic. You're feeling better now?'

'Yes,' she said softly. 'I'd like something to eat.'

'The good news,' continued Gully, 'is that

109

there's no sign of haemorrhage. The important thing, my dear, is to fight the infection, with plenty of rest and wholesome food and drink.' Turning to Mrs Clark, who was standing at the foot of the bed with a severe expression, he said, 'She may start with a breakfast of unsweetened tea with dry toast and a boiled egg. Later on she may have consommé.' Mrs Clark nodded. 'You must take her temperature each hour,' he continued. 'Send for me at once if it rises above 100° or if she becomes sick again.' He leaned down, kissed Cecilia on the forehead, and said, 'I'm leaving now, but I'll be nearby. You should try to rest.' He turned for a moment to the inscrutable Mrs Clark and then let himself out.

In the days that followed, Mrs Clark was constantly at Cecilia's side, serving her meals in bed, helping her to bathe and change clothes and, when the fever subsided at last and she regained much of her strength, to take strolls in the orchard, filled with ripening apples. The name of Doctor Gully was almost never mentioned, except when Mrs Clark reported that he had dropped in each morning, asked to see Cecilia, and had been firmly told that she was recuperating in a satisfactory fashion and did not wish to be disturbed. Late one afternoon, almost a week following the 'procedure', Cecilia, clad in an elaborately embroidered blue silk robe with matching slippers, was enjoying tea with Mrs Clark in the drawing-room. 'I've made up my mind,' said Cecilia betweens bites of scone, 'to speak to James.'

'I see,' said Mrs Clark. 'And what do you intend

to tell him?'

'That I do not wish to see him again.' The faintest suggestion of a smile curled Mrs Clark's lips. 'I'm determined to regain my reputation,' said Cecilia. 'I mustn't have anything further to do with him.' Mrs Clark took a sip of tea and nodded. 'Please send Griffiths to the doctor's cottage with the message I desire to see him.'

Having been turned away on each of his previous attempts to visit Cecilia, Gully was taken aback by the invitation delivered by the coachman and made the five-minute walk with something like foreboding. Entering the mansion, he was escorted by the parlourmaid to the drawing-room, where he found Cecilia seated in one of the rosewood armchairs. Rather than rise to greet him, she extended her hand and allowed him to kiss it. 'Hallo, darling,' he said with a smile.

'Hallo, James. Thank you for coming.'

'Of course.' He settled on the settee beside her. 'You're looking well,' he said, noticing that the rosy colour had returned to her complexion.

'I'm feeling much better.'

'I came earlier, to look in on you—'

'I was in no condition to receive visitors.'

'But as your physician—'

'James ... let's not quarrel.'

'All right, dear. Is there something you wished to tell me?'

'Yes. I've made the decision...' She paused to clear her throat and brush back a strand of hair from her face. 'The decision to end our affair.'

'I see,' said Gully softly. 'As I feared.'

'You see,' said Cecilia calmly, 'under the

111

present circumstances, with all the talk, we can ill afford to be seen–'

'I know.'

'–in public.' She reached over and placed a hand on his. 'You understand.'

'Yes, I understand,' he said with a grim expression. He looked in her eyes and said, 'I had hoped to marry you. Or at least to continue to see you in private.'

'Oh, James, who knows how long that wife of yours will continue living? I can't go on like this. My good friend insists that I–'

'Your good friend?'

'Yes; Janie. Mrs Clark. She insists that I must enter society with persons of my own age, and standing.'

Gully shook his head and stared at the geometrical pattern of the Persian carpet. Looking up at Cecilia, he said, 'It was a mistake from the very beginning. An old man like me, falling in love with someone less than half my age. I should never have–'

'Don't say it,' said Cecilia, giving his hand a squeeze. 'You saved me from a terrible predicament. You taught me that I could be happy and be free. Why, you're the finest man I've ever known, and I shall always love you.'

Reflecting that it was Cecilia who insisted that he move from Malvern to Balham, that he take his own lodgings, *and* that he accompany her on the ill-fated outing to Throckmorton's, he said, 'I'm sorry. I don't know what more there is for me to say. Of course, I shall respect your decision.'

'What will you do?' she asked, rising from her

112

chair. 'Return to Malvern?'

'I'm not sure,' he replied, as he rose stiffly from the settee. 'Goodbye, darling,' he said, leaning over to kiss her.

'Goodbye, James.'

Gully turned and walked slowly toward the hall, eyed wistfully by Cecilia, standing with her hands on the back of the chair, and by Mrs Clark, concealed in the shadows of the adjoining dining-room.

Chapter Eight

Mrs Jane Clark, the highly efficient keeper of the household, supervising a large staff of maids, cooks, gardeners, and stablemen, though Cecilia's constant companion she remained something of a mystery. What adjectives would Cecilia have chosen to describe her? Loyal, capable, discreet, reticent; though others would have been less charitable: severe, humourless, even malevolent. Though little was known of her past, her references had been excellent, and Cecilia had gradually educed the salient details of her life story: that she was of indeterminate middle age, a widow, the mother of a son and daughter in school in the south of England, that her childhood had been spent unhappily in Liverpool, and that she had lived with her late husband for a number of years in Jamaica. Now that Dr Gully had passed out of Cecilia's orbit, Mrs Clark occupied an increasingly central place in the life of the vain, self-indulgent, wealthy young widow.

'Ahh,' murmured Cecilia, sinking up to her chin in the steaming hot water of her claw-foot bath. She closed her eyes and inhaled the pleasant bouquet of the expensive French bath crystals. Sponging her neck and shoulders, she stirred the surface of the sudsy water with her toes, and said, 'Read me another poem, Janie.'

'Very well,' said Mrs Clark, seated on a stool just outside the tiled enclosure of Cecilia's bath. She turned to the fly page of the blue volume, an anthology of Elizabethan verse, and glanced at the inscription: *To Cecilia with much love, James*. 'Shall I read a sonnet?' she asked.

'Yes,' said Cecilia. 'The one that begins with ... *"sweet silent thought"*.'

Locating the poem, Mrs Clark read:

'When to the sessions of sweet silent thought
I summon up remembrance of things past,
I sigh the lack of many a thing I sought
And with old woe new wail my dear time's waste.'

'Old woe ... new wail,' said Cecilia. 'That's very good.'

'Yes,' said Mrs Clark, 'Shakespeare was quite clever with words.'

Grasping the sides of the bath, Cecilia lifted herself up and said, 'Bring me a towel, dear.'

Putting the book aside, Mrs Clark took a thick towel from the rack and handed it to Cecilia who stood dripping on the tiles, her soft skin a healthy pink. She ran the towel over her face, shoulders, and arms, untroubled by nudity before another woman after her weeks of communal bathing at the hydro, and said, 'There's nothing more refreshing than a good, hot soak.'

Mrs Clark made no comment, but watched Cecilia with a detached, critical expression. 'You should eat more, Cissie,' she said at length. 'You're too thin.'

'I prefer to be thin,' said Cecilia, dropping the towel on the floor and walking past Mrs Clark into her boudoir. 'It's the new fashion. I think I must have some new clothes to match.' After a few minutes she emerged from her dressing-room, wearing a sleeveless cotton bodice and frilly knickers that reached below her knees, and sat before the mirror. 'After you've done up my hair,' she said, as she powdered her cheeks, 'tell the cook I'm ready for breakfast. And then I'm taking the 10.40 into the city.'

In the months since Cecilia had severed her relationship with Gully, her efforts to re-enter polite society had availed her little. Though the gossip surrounding her scandalous affair had died away, and she was no longer treated as a pariah in the village, her mother and father would not consent to see her and she had no friends, apart, of course, from Mrs Clark. Much to Cecilia's surprise, Gully continued to divide his time between Orwell Lodge, his cottage in Balham, and the hydro, presumably, she considered, in the hope that she would relent and see him again. On one occasion she had passed him on the pavement in town, though he merely tipped his hat as she waved and drove by in the carriage. Living alone in the large house, surrounded by servants, without a single invitation to tea or dinner, or even to meet an acquaintance over lunch, Cecilia grew increasingly withdrawn and melancholy as autumn gave way to the cold, dark, and damp of December and the approach of Christmas and its society balls and dances, where she would be unwelcome. Fearing that Cecilia would fall deeper into despair, and in her despair turn back to Gully, Mrs Clark intruded on her one evening at supper, seated alone at the long dining-room table with a bowl of soup and carafe of wine. 'May I join you, Cissie?' she said as she drew back a chair.

'Of course. Would you care for a glass of Madeira?' Cecilia summoned a servant with a small silver bell, who promptly returned with another wineglass.

'Do you recall,' said Mrs Clark as Cecilia poured each of them a glass of the garnet-coloured wine, 'that my late husband was employed in Jamaica?'

'You've mentioned it.'

'He was the supervisor of a large coffee plantation–'

'Doctor Gully was brought up on a Jamaica coffee plantation,' interjected Cecilia.

'Yes,' said Mrs Clark. 'On one occasion we conversed about our experiences in the colony. At all events, the plantation owner who employed my husband is a wealthy man named Cranbrook. Sir Harry Cranbrook.' Cecilia sipped her wine and dabbed at her lips with her napkin. 'I made his acquaintance, of course,' continued Mrs Clark, 'and his wife. As one does with fellow Britishers on an island populated by black Africans.'

'So I imagine,' said Cecilia, taking a spoonful of soup.

'The Cranbrooks have a very fine house in London,' continued Mrs Clark, 'on Palace Green, in Kensington.'

'Good heavens,' said Cecilia. 'On Palace Green? Very fine indeed.'

'Yes,' added Mrs Clark with a smile. 'And Sir Harry has a stepson by the name of Charles, a barrister in the Temple, whom I'm told is very well bred and quite handsome.'

'I see,' said Cecilia, helping herself to more Madeira.

'A young man of your age,' said Mrs Clark. 'And a bachelor. With your permission,' she concluded, 'I can arrange a social call on the Cranbrooks. I should like you to meet them.'

'You're such a dear, Janie,' said Cecilia, running a finger nervously along the edge of the soutache on her sleeve.' Of course you have my permission.'

After the hectic social calendar of the Christmas season, Mrs Clark's efforts to arrange a visit to the Cranbrook home finally met with success: an invitation to tea, early in the new year. At Victoria Station, the two women shared a hansom cab, passing along the streets of Belgravia and Knightsbridge to Kensington Road on a clear, cold January day. With a fur over their laps, Cecilia pointed out familiar sights along their route: the imposing town house she'd once shared with Captain Castello, the art gallery on the Brompton Road where she'd acquired her Gainsborough, and the broad expanse of Hyde Park, blanketed in snow. Turning on Palace Green, they rode past Kensington Palace in a clattering of hoofs on cobblestones and arrived at the imposing Cranbrook mansion punctually at half past three. Before exiting the hansom, Cecilia looked Mrs Clark in the eye and said, 'I appreciate what you're trying to do.' Mrs Clark responded with a thin smile. 'To help restore my reputation,' said Cecilia. Mrs Clark nodded.

'Mind your step, ladies,' said the driver, opening the door and extending a gloved hand. 'It's a bit icy.'

Cecilia stood at the tall iron gate and studied the brick and stone façade of the house, one of the grandest in London, with a flutter in her chest. Mrs Clark held open the gate and escorted Cecilia up the walk to the varnished mahogany door, the bell of which was answered by a butler in a black cutaway and starched bib. Ushering the visitors into a sky-lit entrance hall, crowded with potted ferns and marble statuary, he said, 'I'll take those,' helping Cecilia out of her dark-blue coat with the sable collar. 'M'lord and M'lady are expecting you in the drawing-room.'

Cecilia had taken care to dress for the occasion, choosing an expensive blue gown from her dressmaker on Bond Street, with flounces at the skirt, an elaborate, diaphanous sash at her slender waist, a double row of buttons in front, long sleeves with white cuffs, and a matching blue hat.

118

With her porcelain complexion, red lips, and auburn curls, the overall impression combined beauty with wealth and high fashion, precisely what she intended. Sir Harry and Lady Cranbrook stood with their backs to the fire blazing in the marble fireplace when Cecilia and Mrs Clark entered the high-ceilinged room, decorated with worn Persian rugs on the parquet floors and an arrangement of oil portraits of the Cranbrook ancestors hanging on the pale-green walls.

'Come in, come in,' said Sir Harry cheerfully. As Cecilia walked confidently up to him, he added, 'My dear Mrs Clark. How good to see you again.'

With a slight bow, Mrs Clark said, 'Let me introduce Miss Cecilia Henderson. Sir Harry and Lady Cranbrook.'

Extending her hand to Sir Harry, Cecilia said, 'How do you do.'

'My goodness, what a beautiful dress,' remarked Lady Cranbrook, a short, stout woman with greying hair and rouged cheeks who Cecilia judged to be in her fifties.

'Why, thank you,' said Cecilia, confident that her clothing was the very best in the room.

'Let's sit,' said Sir Harry, motioning to a grouping of armchairs and a sofa upholstered in pale-blue silk, 'and I'll ring for tea.'

Once they were seated, Lady Cranbrook turned to Cecilia and said, 'Miss Henderson, I understand you live in Balham.'

'Yes,' said Cecilia, who sat with her hands folded in her lap, 'after the death of my husband...'

'Your husband?' said Sir Harry.

'Henderson's my maiden name. I was married

to Richard Castello.'

'Castello?' said Sir Harry. 'Of the international telegraph?'

'Yes,' said Cecilia. 'Richard's father. And after my husband's untimely death, I acquired a property in Balham adjoining Tooting Bec Common. It's country living, really, yet close enough to the city.'

'And,' said Sir Harry affably, 'you have the capable Mrs Clark to manage your affairs. Ah, here's tea.' Two servants appeared bearing silver trays, one with a bone china tea service and the other with an assortment of pastries and finger sandwiches, which they carefully lowered to the butler's tray table in front of the sofa. As the servants poured, Sir Harry, a short, sturdy man with a shiny bald pate, tufts of white hair at his temples, and a ruddy complexion, reminisced with Mrs Clark about their years in Jamaica: '...so dreadfully hot and humid ... yet exceptionally beautiful ... nothing to equal Blue Mountain coffee.'

Putting aside her teacup, Cecilia turned to Sir Harry and said, 'Do you have family living here with you?'

'Our daughter Martha is married,' he said, 'and lives with her husband in Birmingham, and our boy Charles, a barrister, has rooms in Knightsbridge and, of course, his chambers at Gray's Inn.'

'I see,' said Cecilia, reaching for a scone, which she liberally smeared with clotted cream.

'But he's home for a visit,' said Sir Harry amiably. 'Tell me, Mrs Clark, are your children well?'

'William's in school at Brighton, and Florence – do you remember Florence?'

'I seem to recall a small sprout of a girl.'

'Yes, well, she's all of fourteen now–'

'My, my.'

'Away at school in Tunbridge Wells.'

Munching her scone, Cecilia considered Sir Harry's reference to Charles as 'our boy', deducing he regarded him as an adopted son.

'I understand that your father,' said Lady Cranbrook between bites of a cucumber sandwich, 'has an estate in Oxfordshire?'

'Yes,' said Cecilia. 'Buscot Park. My parents divide their time between the country and their house in Belgravia.'

'More tea, miss?' asked a servant.

'Please.' At the sound of footfalls, Cecilia turned toward the hallway just as a young man strode into the room.

'Sorry to interrupt,' he said. 'Just searching for my dashed tobacco.'

'Come in, Charles,' said Sir Harry, 'and meet our guests.'

Charles Cranbrook, a 30-year-old man-about-town with sandy brown hair and neatly trimmed side-whiskers wearing a dark-brown jacket and charcoal trousers with boots polished to a high gloss, walked up to Cecilia, bowed at the waist, and said, 'How do you do.'

With a pretty smile, Cecilia said, 'Very well, thank you. I'm Cecilia Henderson and this is my estate manager, Mrs Jane Clark.'

'Whose late husband,' interjected Sir Harry, 'managed one of our plantations in Jamaica.'

Turning to Mrs Clark, Charles smiled and said, 'I seem to recall Mrs Clark.'

'Ahem,' said one of the servants, standing inconspicuously beside a marble-top table against the wall. 'I believe this is the master's tobacco.'

'Why, thank you, my good man,' said Charles, walking over to accept a leather pouch. Turning to Cecilia, he said, 'I'm afraid I must be going, but I'm delighted to have made your acquaintance.' He paused, looking for a moment in her eyes. 'Goodbye, Mother,' he concluded, and then walked briskly from the room.

'Youth,' commented Sir Harry.

Goodbye, said Cecilia inwardly, retaining a mental image of Charles's interesting, if not especially handsome face.

Putting her teacup aside, Mrs Clark turned to Sir Harry and said, 'We, too, must be going, before it grows dark.'

'Are you staying over in the city?'

'No,' said Cecilia as she rose from her chair. 'Returning to The Priory, my house in Balham.'

'I hope we shall see you again before long,' said Lady Cranbrook.

'You're very kind,' said Cecilia. 'Nothing would please me more.'

'Do you have a coach?' asked Sir Harry.

'We instructed our driver to wait,' replied Mrs Clark.

Escorted to the door by their hosts, Cecilia offered her profuse thanks for their hospitality, donned her hat, coat, and gloves, and followed Mrs Clark to the cab waiting at the pavement. With a final wave to the Cranbrooks standing in the doorway, the two women climbed up onto the seat and, with a snap of the whip at the horse's ears, the hansom was on its way in the fading light of the midwinter afternoon.

'Well, Cissie,' said Mrs Clark, seated opposite in the half-empty railway carriage, 'what did you think?' Both women had spent most of the thirty-minute trip from Palace Green to Victoria Station in silent introspection, listening to the creaking wheels and hoofbeats as the hansom rolled along in the gathering dusk.

'Think?' said Cecilia. 'Of the Cranbrook mansion? Very grand, even more so than our own house in Belgravia—'

'No. About Charles. When I last saw him, he was a youth, quite bright but a bit of a cad.'

'I thought him, well, rather interesting. Not unattractive. Well dressed but not a dandy. I suppose he has money?'

'Perhaps,' said Mrs Clark. 'His stepfather certainly has riches. But Charles' mother – Lady Cranbrook – married Sir Harry when Charles was virtually a grown man. So one doesn't know.'

Appearing in the swaying doorway, the conductor called out, 'Next stop, Balham.'

'All in all,' said Cecilia with a smile, 'a very successful outing. And who knows? Perhaps I may see Charles again.'

As Mrs Clark had her own room on the second floor of The Priory, down the passage from Cecilia, took all of her meals there, and led an otherwise parsimonious lifestyle, her savings were

123

sufficient to enrol her son and daughter in mediocre schools in the south of England, where she hoped they would acquire enough of an education and polish to rise above tradesman status. On a clear, mild April morning, Mrs Clark, accompanied by Cecilia, boarded the train at the Balham station *en route* to Brighton to attend sports day at her son's school, St Anne's Asylum for the Children of Distressed Gentlefolk. Sharing a first-class compartment, Cecilia put aside her novel and said, 'Tell me, Janie, what does one do at a sports day?'

'Well,' said Mrs Clark, who for a change was wearing a plum-coloured dress, 'all the boys are required to participate in athletics – team sports, cricket, rugby, that sort of thing.' Cecilia nodded. 'And each term the parents are invited to attend an exhibition. Hence, sports day.'

'I see. Will we observe a match?'

'I should think so. William plays on the older boys' cricket team.'

To Mrs Clark's mild surprise, Cecilia had never witnessed a cricket match and consequently sat amid the visiting parents, resting her chin on her fists, utterly fascinated yet baffled by the crack of the bat on the bounding ball and dash of the boys to the wickets, invigorated by the salt-laden Channel breeze across the broad, emerald expanse. 'Look, Cissie,' said Mrs Clark, pointing, 'William's coming up to bat.' Cecilia watched as a gangly youth, clad in white, strode to the pitch to face the bowler, a tall, muscular boy who with a hop, skip, and windmill motion of his arm.

hurled a ball that bounced at the feet of the batsman. 'Swing, Willie!' cried Mrs Clark. 'You can do it!' On the next toss, William swung clumsily, driving the ball high in the air and deep into the outfield. 'Run, Willie!' exhorted his mother, restraining the impulse to leap up from her seat.

As the boy loped to the wicket, Cecilia turned to Mrs Clark with a smile. 'Jolly well done,' she said, with a clap of her hands. Heedless of the score, or the innings, or which of the sides had the advantage, Cecilia was content to observe the action and listen to the cheers of the boys and their families until the sun sank low in the western sky and the umpire at last announced that the game was suspended for the evening, to be resumed in the morning. Having met William, a thin, awkward boy with a shock of dark hair, Cecilia advised that she intended to return to the hotel, where they would meet for dinner, while Mrs Clark had the rare opportunity to see her son privately. As the setting sun tinged the horizon with a band of mauve, Cecilia strolled from the school grounds into the seaside town, oppressed by thoughts of Dr Gully and her deepening isolation. 'Without a friend in the world,' she muttered to herself, as she approached the old hotel on the promenade, 'apart from dear Jane.'

Cecilia sat at a banquette facing the bevelled-glass doors, observing the men and women, some accompanied by children, who crowded into the hotel lobby, noticing in particular the ladies' hats, decorated with plumage with absurdly wide brims, resolved that she must have one, or two, just possibly three. At length Mrs Clark appeared, looking wan from the long afternoon, and somewhat gloomy, perhaps due to her simple dress and comparative lack of ornamentation. 'Over here, Jane,' said Cecilia, as Mrs Clark walked by.

'Oh,' said Mrs Clark. 'I didn't see you.'

Cecilia rose and placed a hand on Mrs Clark's arm. 'Let's take a turn on the promenade, shall we?' she said. 'I could use a breath of fresh air before dinner.'

After walking arm-in-arm several blocks from the sea-front hotel, the two women halted at the entrance to the long, covered pier, festooned with Japanese lanterns and packed with visitors. 'The penny arcade,' said Mrs Clark. 'Reminds me of my childhood, when my father would give a shilling each to my brother and me to wager.' Cecilia smiled, thinking back to the lavish entertainments on the grounds at Buscot Park to which she and her sisters had been treated by their over-indulgent parents.

'Let's return to the hotel,' said Cecilia, fighting another wave of melancholy. 'I'm ready for dinner.'

Strolling past The Crown, a popular public house whose patrons spilled out on the pavement, Mrs Clark almost collided with an impeccably dressed young man. 'Beg pardon,' he said as he tipped his silk top hat. 'Oh,' he added with a look of surprise, 'it's Miss Henderson.'

'Mr Cranbrook,' said Cecilia, with a happy smile that dimpled her cheeks. 'What a coincidence.'

'Indeed,' he said, 'and a happy one at that.'

'We were just returning to our hotel for dinner,' said Cecilia. 'Would you care to join us?'

'I'd be delighted, as I'm at loose ends this evening.'

Seated across from Cecilia and Mrs Clark, Charles Cranbrook ordered a bottle of claret and then resumed a humorous account of his reason for visiting Brighton. 'One of the chief disadvantages,' he said, 'of being admitted to the Inns of Court, is the requirement to argue cases before our circuit judges. Here, we're in Quarter Sessions.' Cecilia nodded politely. 'Nothing very exciting, I assure you. The usual action for trespass, that sort of thing. Ah, here's our wine.' After allowing the waiter to pour each of them a glass, he said, 'I understand, Mrs Clark, you're visiting your son in school?'

'Yes, at St. Anne's. Today was the boys' spring sports day.'

'Ah,' said Charles after sampling the wine. 'The sports day with its athletic exhibitions. I always loathed it.'

Smiling pleasantly, Cecilia studied his face; his neatly brushed, light-brown hair, trimmed side-whiskers, penetrating, intelligent eyes and something almost cruel about his mouth. Making eye contact with her, Charles said, 'Miss Henderson...'

'Cecilia.'

'Cecilia, you have no children of your own?'

'No. My late husband and I were not blessed with children.'

'Someday,' said Charles, 'I intend to have a large brood of them.'

Cecilia sipped her wine, ran a finger along the edge of her decorated cuff, smiled, and said, 'But first you shall have to find a wife.'

Chapter Nine

Walking quickly along the flagstone path on a warm May morning, Cecilia halted at the entrance to the stables and called out, 'Griffiths?'

'Yes, ma'am?' replied the stableman, emerging from the nearest stall.

'Have you groomed and saddled Bluebell?'

'Yes, ma'am. And the gelding.' He looked approvingly at his wealthy employer; what a show she made of it, as she was clad in a green redingote riding habit, a double-breasted tailored jacket over her dress and boots, with a white silk scarf knotted at her neck and tiny hat pinned to her auburn hair.

'I'm riding alone today,' said Cecilia, as she strolled into the enclosure, redolent of straw and horse manure. Emerging at the far end in bright sunshine, she smiled at Griffiths and said, 'Help me up, if you please.' Placing one finely polished boot in the stirrup, she grasped the pommel as he lifted her by the waist onto the side-saddle on the bay mare. 'Thank you, Griffiths,' she said, slipping a half-crown into his hand. 'Advise Mrs Clark that I'll return by midday.'

'Yes, ma'am.'

'And remind her I'm expecting company for lunch.' With the reins in her left hand, Cecilia slapped the mare's haunch with her crop and cantered along the gravel path through the alley of oaks, emerging on Tooting Bec Common, the open fields of which were blanketed with bright yellow and blue wildflowers. An accomplished horsewoman, she turned the mare onto the dusty track through the common, slowing to a trot as she bypassed several nannies pushing prams and then returning to a canter. 'Good girl,' said Cecilia with a reassuring pat on the mare's neck, thinking that the strong, spirited animal might have been taught to jump but for the absence of fences or hedges. At the far end of the common she slowed the horse to a walk, traversed the streets of the village and then entered the some-what smaller Streatham Common, where she skilfully put the mare through her gaits, from a trot to a canter and a final gallop across a quarter-mile of soft turf. 'Whoa,' she called, with a tug on the reins at the approach of the woods that bordered the common, halting the mare to water at a public trough before heading home. Almost an hour had passed when she turned on the gravel drive to the Priory stables where Griffiths was waiting with his arms crossed at his chest. Taking Cecilia's hand and helping her down, he said, 'She's had her exercise, from the look of her', noting the mare's sleek, lathered neck and haunches.

'She's had water,' said Cecilia as she straight-ened the front of her jacket, 'but I've no doubt she could use more.' Unknotting the scarf at her neck, she walked quickly along the path to the door at the rear of the house, glancing up at the noonday sun and wondering with a quickening of her pulse if her visitor had arrived. Entering the kitchen, with its exposed beams and array of gleaming copper pots and pans, she walked over to the stove where the cook stood over a cauldron of simmering soup. Bending down to inhale its inviting aroma, Cecilia asked, 'Has Mrs Clark specified the hour lunch is to be served?'

'Yes, mum,' replied the cook as another servant entered the kitchen. 'At one o'clock sharp.'

'Very well,' said Cecilia as she turned to go.

As Cecilia entered the central passageway, Mrs Clark rose from her desk beneath the stairs, smiled briefly and said, 'Your guest has arrived. I showed him into the drawing-room.'

Charles Cranbrook stood beside the Broadwood grand piano in the corner of the drawing-room, lightly running a finger over its gleaming walnut finish. During his five minutes alone he had carefully examined Cecilia's collection of fine art and furnishings: the Gainsborough over the mantel, a fine bronze figure of winged Mercury, a large Meissen urn, and the expensively upholstered rosewood chairs and settee. The piano alone, he reckoned, must have cost a thousand quid, and he seriously doubted Cecilia could play it. Hearing footsteps, he turned as Cecilia appeared in the arched entrance from the passageway. 'Hallo,' he called out in a cheerful voice.

'I'm going up to change,' she said with a smile. 'I'll just be a minute. Have the maid fetch you

130

something to drink.'

'Right-ho.' As the hem of Cecilia's dress disappeared up the stairs, a maid wearing a black dress with starched white apron arrived from the kitchen. 'I say,' said Charles, moving in her direction, 'is there a chilled bottle of champagne to hand?'

'Yes, sir.'

'Bring it along,' instructed Charles, resting his arm on the back of the rosewood settee, 'with two glasses.'

By the time Cecilia descended the staircase, wearing pale-pink organdie with a scarlet sash and matching shoes peeking from beneath the cloud of flounce, Charles had consumed the better part of a flute of fine champagne and made up his mind that life in The Priory would suit someone of his expensive tastes very nicely indeed. He reached for the bottle in the silver bucket, poured a second glass, and walked up to Cecilia. 'You look smashing,' he said, as he handed it to her. 'I hope you don't mind, but I've raided your supply of champagne.'

'Mind?' she said before taking a sip. 'It's there to be drunk.'

'Cheers,' said Charles, reaching out to touch glasses. 'I understand you've been out riding.'

'A wonderful ride on the common,' said Cecilia, 'and then over to Streatham and back.'

'How very convenient, to have your own stable, and adjacent to Tooting Bec.'

'It's why I chose to live here. To be able to take advantage of a day like today, yet close enough to the city for shopping and the theatre.'

'Why, I suppose,' said Charles, as he strolled with Cecilia back into the drawing-room, 'a man might even take the train to work in the City.'

'It's frequently done,' said Cecilia, as she sat in one of the plush armchairs. 'Or so I'm told.'

Charles sat facing her, with one neatly creased charcoal trouser and polished boot crossed over his knee, interlacing his fingers. 'I spoke to Mrs Clark,' he said, 'on my way in. I gather she looks after the household.'

'Jane sees to everything,' said Cecilia. 'Apart from my financial affairs, of course, which are managed by my banker at Coutts.'

'Coutts on the Strand,' repeated Charles, 'a very reputable establishment.' And, he considered, a bank that catered almost exclusively to the very rich and powerful. 'I suppose your late husband chose to bank there...'

'My late husband was a military man who knew nothing of investments. But he had the good fortune,' added Cecilia with a smile, 'to be the only son of Sir Alfred Castello.'

'The Tory MP...'

'And founder of the international telegraph company. It was my solicitor who recommended Coutts, after my husband's death.'

'I see.'

'Excuse me, mum.'

Cecilia and Charles turned to the maid standing in the archway. 'Luncheon is served,' she said with a diffident smile.

Following an elaborate repast which featured more champagne, Yorkshire pudding to accompany the roast beef, and a raspberry tart, Cecilia

132

invited Charles to take a walk with her in the orchard. As the day was warm, he left his coat in the drawing-room and strolled in shirtsleeves rolled up to the elbow. Bending down to inspect a primrose, Cecilia snapped off the blossom and held it to her nose. 'Pretty,' she said, 'but with little scent.'

'Like some girls I know,' said Charles with a half smile. 'Pretty, but with little *sense*.'

'Oh, that's good,' said Cecilia with a laugh. 'You're very clever.'

'Do you think so?'

'Of course. Though I know so little about you.'

'What would you like to know?'

'Well, about your upbringing, your schooling, what you intend to do with your life.'

'Oh, is that all?' said Charles with another of his crooked smiles.

Reaching the end of the orchard, Cecilia sat on a wooden bench facing the green expanse of the common and listened as Charles gave a succinct account of his childhood, the only son of a prosperous but not wealthy businessman in Manchester named Turner, who died when Charles was twelve. 'After Mother remarried,' he said, 'I decided to take my stepfather's name.'

'When was this?' asked Cecilia.

'In '62, when I was eighteen. My first year at King's College, in London. I made up my mind to study law and went on to Oxford – I was a Magdalen man.'

'King's College and Oxford,' said Cecilia with a smile. 'You're certainly well educated.'

'True,' said Charles. 'I have a keen interest in

133

the classics and in English poetry. And to sum things up, after Oxford I returned to London and the Temple Bar. Admitted to Gray's Inn four years ago.'

'I should imagine,' said Cecilia, 'you look quite imposing in your wig and gown.'

'Perhaps.' He sat beside her on the bench and stretched out his legs. 'I enjoy my profession, though it's certainly not the path to riches.'

'But you needn't worry about that.' He gave her a brief, questioning look. 'Considering your stepfather's position,' she explained.

'True,' said Charles with a nod. 'Now that you've heard my life story, my dear Cecilia, perhaps you should tell me yours.'

'Well,' she began, resisting the impulse to run her finger along the edge of her cuff, 'I spent my childhood, with my two sisters, in Australia, near Adelaide.'

'I thought I detected an accent.'

'My father is in the mining industry. We moved back to the family estate, Buscot Park in Oxfordshire, when I was eleven, and divided our time between the country and our house in Belgravia.'

'I see. And your marriage to Captain–'

'Castello. We met at a ball when Richard was serving in the army and, well, fell in love and were married.' Cecilia paused, feigning a faraway look. 'But sadly,' she continued, 'Richard died after a brief illness, while touring in Germany. Just over a year ago.'

'How tragic.'

'Yes, very. And in my mourning I'm afraid I've become a bit of a recluse, choosing to live alone

here and only recently accepting social invitations.'

'Well, we shall have to rectify that,' said Charles.
He stood up and reached out to take Cecilia's
hand. Helping her to her feet, he leaned over and
kissed her cheek. 'I would very much hope,' he
said, looking in her eyes, 'that you'll consent to
see me again.'

'You have my word,' said Cecilia, gently squeez-
ing his hand.

In a silk dressing-gown, seated in her boudoir
facing the mirror, Cecilia applied rouge to her
cheeks and painted her lips as Mrs Clark pinned
up her hair. 'I presume you understand,' said Mrs
Clark, as she thoughtfully studied Cecilia's
reflection, 'that marriage to a man like Charles
Cranbrook is the only realistic means of restoring
your reputation.'

'A man *like* Mr Cranbrook?'

'Perhaps Mr Cranbrook,' said Mrs Clark,
gently placing her hands on Cecilia's shoulders.

'I'm not ready for marriage,' said Cecilia. 'Not
after everything I've been through. Charles
seems, well, respectable, and he's certainly intelligent, but I hardly know him. I should think that
merely accompanying him to the theatre and the
right social occasions–'

'No, Cissie. You must listen to me. The *only* thing
that will stop them talking behind your back is to
marry the right sort of man from the right element
of London society. The right clubs, the right
schools, the right friends. Charles is the stepson of
a wealthy businessman, an Oxford man, Magdalen

135

College, and a member of Boodle's and White's.'

'True,' said Cecilia glumly.

'And, what's more,' said Mrs Clark, as she fastened a necklace at the nape of Cecilia's neck, 'he's utterly smitten with you.' Stepping around to look Cecilia in the face, she said, 'If not Charles Cranbrook, I don't know who. You must use all of your feminine wiles to bring him to his knees with a marriage proposal.'

In the weeks that followed it seemed to Cecilia that Mrs Clark had overestimated the difficulty of attracting the attention of Charles Cranbrook, who clearly had succumbed to her beauty, the sensuality that had blossomed during her affair with Dr Gully, and the irresistible allure of her fortune. Invitations abounded, to the theatre and dinner, the regatta at Henley, Sunday lunch at Brown's, and a lawn tennis exhibition at the new All England Club at nearby Wimbledon. Discovering that Charles shared her passion for riding, he eagerly joined her on weekend jaunts through the common on her spirited horses, followed by lunch or tea at The Priory. The notion of marriage was gradually becoming more acceptable to her; he was handsome in a way, very bright and well read, a sportsman, and always impeccably dressed if somewhat old-fashioned. Yet she couldn't help comparing him to James Gully, who was infinitely more astute and kind and gentle in a way she was certain Charles would never be. In fact, she was sure a man like Charles would loathe Dr Gully, with his beliefs in homeopathic medicine, nature and the outdoors, and spiritualism. Yes, she considered with a sigh, as she awaited Cranbrook's arrival for dinner, he was condescending and narrow ... a snob. Well, perhaps she could accept being married to a snob.

A frequent visitor to The Priory, Cranbrook ignored the servant who answered the door, hung his coat and top hat in the hall, and strolled into the drawing-room with the air of a man who was at home. As Cecilia had yet to make her usual theatrical appearance, with a swish of petticoats and always a new skirt, on the staircase, Cranbrook stood before the empty fireplace with hands clasped behind his back, unknowingly under the observant eye of Jane Clark, concealed in the shadows of the dining-room.

'There you are,' he exclaimed, as Cecilia descended the stairs with a hand on the curved banister. 'My, what a beautiful gown.' She walked up, and he kissed her lightly on the lips with one hand at her slender waist.

'Lovely, isn't it?' she said, swirling the elaborate folds of the skirt and extending her right arm as if to show off the ruffle at her wrist and the large emerald and diamond ring on her finger. 'It was delivered only today from my favourite dress-maker on Bruton Street.'

'I should think it cost a small fortune,' he said, as he studied the dress's fine embroidery and the large bow on the bustle.

'Not really,' said Cecilia. 'Only thirty pounds.'

'I see that your charming little boots match perfectly.'

'I can't abide boots that don't match.' Reaching for a silver bell on a side table and giving it a sharp ring, she said, 'I presume you're ready for your drink?'

The butler appeared after a moment and said, 'Yes, madam?'

'Champagne, Sawyers,' said Cecilia. 'Pink champagne.'

'Sir?'

'Brandy and soda.'

After the butler returned with their drinks, Cecilia settled on the sofa and patted the cushion for Charles to sit next to her. Taking a sip of champagne, she said, 'I have a little surprise for you.'

'Oh, really?' Charles took a swallow of brandy from his crystal tumbler.

'Yes. An invitation.'

'I see.'

'As the weather's turned wet and cold, to stay the night.'

The merest smile curled his lip. 'I have a court appearance in the morning,' he said with a rub of his chin. 'At ten o'clock. But I reckon I can catch the early train.' He leaned over to give her a gentle kiss, to which she responded with a passion that nearly caused him to drop his glass. Putting it aside, he reached an arm around her, pulled her to him and kissed her again, a long, sensuous kiss as he allowed his free hand to roam over the curve of her hip.

'Mmm,' she murmured, lying against his chest. 'You're not going to ravish me before dinner?'

'Good heavens, no,' he said, aware of a flush on his cheeks and pounding of his heart.

'Very well,' she said with a smile, as she sat up

138

and inched away from him. She reached for her glass and took another sip of champagne as Cranbrook, regaining his composure, took a large gulp of his drink.

'Do you love me?' she asked, looking him in the eye.

'Why, ah, yes. Yes, I believe I do.' Taking another swallow, he added, 'Sometimes you quite take me aback.'

'Pardon me, madam.' Cranbrook shot a wild look at the young parlourmaid who had appeared in the archway, as though she'd wandered into the room while he was taking his bath. 'Dinner,' she announced, 'is served.'

'Very well,' said Cecilia calmly. 'Don't worry about your drink,' she said to Charles as she rose from the settee. 'There'll be time for more brandy after we have dined.'

A bottle of fine Chablis accompanied dinner – roast squab with peas and Lyonnaise potatoes – though the lion's share was consumed by Cecilia, as Charles expressed his general dislike of all things French and drank only a glass. Following dessert of chocolate cake with ice cream, they repaired to the drawing-room for coffee or, 'if you prefer,' said Cecilia, 'brandy, though I forbid the smoking of cigars.'

'Very well,' said Charles as he walked to the sideboard where he found a crystal decanter of cognac and several glasses, 'as I prefer a pipe to a cigar.' As he poured a glass, the maid entered with a small silver tray and wine goblet, which she served to Cecilia.

'Anything else, mum?'

'No, Florence. You and the others are free to go for the evening.'

When they were alone, Charles sat in a chair facing Cecilia on the sofa, sipping his brandy with his legs crossed. 'Does it concern you,' he asked, 'that the servants might discover I've stayed the night?'

After taking a swallow of Madeira, Cecilia said, 'No. How could they? There's only Mrs Clark, and she retires early to her own room.' She looked at him suggestively and took another sip of wine.

'If you're certain,' he groused, 'though I'm not sure I'd trust a servant to be discreet.'

'Jane is my friend,' said Cecilia a bit unevenly. 'My very dear friend.' With a slight lascivious wink, she finished her wine and said, 'I'm going up to get ready for bed. The guest bedroom is at the top of the stairs.'

Casting a furtive glance down the darkened passageway, Cranbrook silently crept on tiptoe and bare feet to Cecilia's bedroom. He gave the door a gentle tap and, after a moment, she opened it a crack. With a soft giggle, she let him in and turned the key in the lock. He studied her briefly in the dim light and then slipped off his shirt and folded it over a chair. With his hands on her bare shoulders he bent down and kissed her hard on the mouth, running his hands over the curve of her breasts under her diaphanous nightgown. 'Mmm,' she murmured as she moved backward toward her bed. Holding her slender waist, he lifted her up and pushed her back on the

140

mattress, falling heavily on top of her. He kissed her neck and then lifted up her nightgown and roughly, almost brutally, made love to her.

'Ohh,' she muttered. 'That hurts. Don't ... please... Ohh, be gentle.'

Ignoring her entreaties, he quickly reached a climax, grunting through clenched teeth. 'There,' he said with a groan, pinning down her shoulders and staring for a moment at her frightened face before rolling over on his side. He lay beside her for another five minutes, while his breathing returned to normal, and then silently got up, slipped on his shirt and let himself out.

Chapter Ten

Adjusting her hat in the mirror above the coat stand in the hall, Cecilia slipped on her kid gloves and started for the door. 'Where are you going?' asked Mrs Clark, standing in the entrance to the drawing-room with her hands on her hips.

'Out. There are several things in town I must attend to.'

'You know how much I disapprove–'

'It's none of your affair,' said Cecilia with asperity, scolding herself for telling a lie and for allowing her employee to attain the status of a virtual equal.

'I'm aware that you've been seeing the doctor.' As Cecilia's private secretary, Mrs Clark saw, even if she left unopened, all of Cecilia's private correspondence, including the envelopes with the return address 'Orwell Lodge, 21 Bedford Hill Rd, Balham.'

Cecilia eyed her coldly. 'If it's Mr Cranbrook you're worried about,' she said, 'you needn't. I fully expect a marriage proposal any day.' Mrs Clark responded with a dispassionate stare. 'And, frankly,' said Cecilia, 'it's partly why I want to see the doctor. To seek his advice.' With that, she turned, let herself out and started out on a brisk, five-minute walk into the village. She arrived before noon on a fine midsummer day, and stood for a moment at the iron railing, studying the ivy-covered cottage with the profusion of day lilies in the neatly tended flowerbed and bright red geraniums in the window-box, wondering if she might have found true happiness in a simpler life with the genial doctor – if only it weren't for his elderly, estranged wife. Walking up to the door, she gave the brass knocker a rap. After a moment Gully appeared and, with a kind smile, welcomed her inside.

A tea tray sat on a table in the parlour before a sofa and two armchairs. Cecilia chose the sofa and Gully, pouring their tea, sat in a chair alongside her. 'You're looking very well,' he began, as he handed her a cup. 'Though perhaps a bit too thin.'

'That's what Jane always says.'

'Jane?'

'Mrs Clark.'

'Oh, yes,' said Gully with a frown. 'In any case, what matters is your diet, dear. Plenty of fresh fruit and vegetables, especially leafy greens, fish,

142

and the avoidance of sugar and fats, including butter.'

Cecilia looked briefly at the tea tray, noting the absence of pastries, sugar, or jam. 'And you're looking well,' she said. 'How was your trip abroad?'

'Wonderful,' said Gully, after taking a sip of tea. 'The July weather was perfect in the Alps, so many opportunities for long, strenuous walks. Do you recall Bodenlaube Castle in the hills outside Bad Kissingen?'

'Yes,' said Cecilia, thinking back to their trip to Bavaria, when Gully first made love to her. As he continued to talk, she thought about how, after the frustrations of love-making with her husband, Gully had awakened her to sexual fulfilment she'd never imagined possible, an experience that now she expected would be exclusively reserved for the male of the species.

'I say,' said Gully. 'Cecilia?'

'Oh, sorry,' she said. 'My mind wandered.'

'I was merely enquiring about your father,' he said. 'Whether you've seen him.'

'No. He still won't answer my letters.'

'What a pity,' said Gully with a shake of his head. 'Some men.'

'If I were to remarry,' said Cecilia, putting her cup and saucer aside. 'The right sort of man, of course, I expect I would be welcomed back into the bosom of the family.'

'You're probably correct,' said Gully, reaching for the pot to pour each of them more tea. 'Is such a prospect in the offing? Is that what you've come to discuss?'

'No,' said Cecilia. 'I mean, it ... that isn't why I wanted to see you, though I do very much want your advice, James, dear.'

'Very well.'

'Frankly, I miss you very much. I expected, after everything that happened, that you would have gone back to Malvern and I'd never see you again.' Looking her in the eye, Gully nodded gravely. 'But as you're here,' she continued, 'so close by, of course I desire to see you. I only wish–'

'Don't say it,' said Gully. 'We both know it can't be.'

Cecilia nodded. 'But to answer your question,' she said, 'I have been seeing someone. A man my age, a barrister at Gray's Inn who's the stepson of a wealthy man named Cranbrook. Sir Harry Cranbrook. Mrs Clark's late husband was employed at his coffee plantation in Jamaica.'

'Oh, yes,' said Gully. 'I recall Cranbrook from my days in the colony. One of the more successful planters.'

'How ironic,' said Cecilia. 'That you should know the family of the man I may–' Halting, she looked at Gully with a trembling lower lip.

'That you may marry,' he said.

Nodding, she softly said, 'Yes. I expect he's going to propose.'

'I believe I understand,' said Gully, looking her sternly in the eye.

'You do?' she said doubtfully.

'Mrs Clark,' said Gully with a frown, 'that mischievous woman, having persuaded you to sever all relations with *me,* has now cleverly arranged for you to marry the stepson of her former employer in Jamaica.'

'That's not so...'

'It patently is so.' Gully glared at Cecilia. 'Well?' he demanded. 'Do you love him?'

'I'm not sure romantic love,' she answered, 'is necessary to be married. I like Charles, he amuses me, and he's, well, from the proper social background.'

'I see,' said Gully. 'You regard marriage as a means of restoring your sullied reputation; I see it as a highly perilous experiment.'

'But how could you, James, when you don't even know the man.'

'Because I know *you*, my dear. I know that you need to be loved. And I fear with your great riches, there are many men who would–'

'What? Marry me for my money?'

Looking her in the eye, Gully nodded and said, 'Yes, Cecilia. Marry you for your money.'

'But Charles,' she said, nervously wringing her hands, 'comes from a very wealthy family. He studied at King's College and Oxford, is a member of Boodle's and White's. Why, he doesn't need my money. He's a very attractive, eligible man-about-town. Why shouldn't I want to be married to him?'

'You mentioned that Harry Cranbrook, the Jamaican planter, is his stepfather.'

'Yes, Charles's mother married him after the death of Charles's father.'

'Well,' said Gully with a shrug, 'one never knows. But there are plenty of young men about London with an Oxford pedigree but hardly a sovereign to their name. And while I appreciate your beauty and charms as well as any man, it would be a grave error to underestimate the importance of your wealth to a man considering marriage.'

'Very well,' said Cecilia. 'A point well taken. But that's not what I came to discuss.' Gully smiled in his well-practised, encouraging way and sipped his tea. 'Assuming Charles asks for my hand,' she began, 'what should I disclose to him? About us?'

'Hmm,' said Gully, putting his cup aside and scratching his chin. 'A moral as well as a practical dilemma.'

'I'm inclined to say nothing, of course. But with all the vituperative gossip-mongers about, in particular that wretched sister of Throckmorton, there's always the risk...'

At the mention of the solicitor, Gully swallowed hard with the expression of someone who's taken a bite of rotten fish. 'Well,' he said after a moment, 'I think it almost inevitable that after the announcement of your betrothal, which will no doubt be widely reported in the society pages, someone or other will come forward and inform Cranbrook of our affair in the most scandalous terms, intending, of course, to destroy your engagement.'

'Oh, it's too dreadful,' said Cecilia with a groan. 'If I tell him about us he's almost certain to reject me.'

'Perhaps,' said Gully with a nod, considering that such an outcome would suit his own interests very well. 'But better to take that chance, my dear, than to run the risk that he discovers it *after* you are married.'

That eventuality had not occurred to Cecilia. 'Oh,' she said, placing a hand on her brow. 'I suppose he would be quite spiteful.'

'True,' said Gully, 'though I have no idea whether he's a harsh or a gentle man.'

Harsh, considered Cecilia. Very harsh.

'In our society,' continued Gully with the air of a distinguished lecturer, 'there are public mores and private mores, and especially among the upper classes, the two are frequently in conflict.'

'How so?'

'The gentleman would no doubt react to news of our affair with shock and censure, whereas privately he may very well have engaged in such conduct himself.'

This was the second possibility that had not occurred to Cecilia. 'How very wise of you,' she said. 'I knew I could depend on your sagacity. My mind is made up. If Charles should propose, and I should accept, I shall make a clean breast of it and inform him of our affair, that it's a thing of the past.'

'The soundest course,' said Gully with a nod. 'However, I must repeat my deep reservations, Cecilia, about entering into a marriage to a man who doesn't truly love you and whose motives may be largely pecuniary.'

Seated in an armchair in her bedroom with her feet on a footstool, Cecilia gazed down at her fancy mauve satin boots, tightly laced up to mid-calf, with patent leather toes and one-inch heels. Intended to distract men's attention from a lady's comely ankles, she considered with a smile that they had the opposite effect. Returning to the sheets of stationery in her lap – the latest letter from Charles – she reread his humorous description of a lawn tennis match and his boasts of triumphing in the weekly chess tournament at White's, the venerable gentlemen's club on St James's, closing with professions of love for his 'dearest Cissie'. Did he love her, and what, exactly, was love? Something more than physical attraction or mere affection, she was sure of that. She'd never loved her husband, nor had she really been in *love* with James but rather had deeply revered him and found his physical, sexual qualities irresistibly seductive. Putting the letter aside, she picked up her pocket calendar and turned to the month of January, the date of her visit with Mrs Clark to the Cranbrook mansion on Palace Green. Almost eight months had passed since she first met Charles. Eight months and tonight she expected matters would come to a head. What should she wear?

Arriving at The Priory punctually at seven o'clock, Charles Cranbrook was welcomed by the butler and shown into the drawing-room, where Cecilia was seated in one of the rosewood armchairs. 'Hallo, darling,' he said as he walked up to her. Rising, she took his hand and turned her cheek for a kiss.

'How pretty,' she said, glancing at the nosegay he was clutching.

'You're the pretty one,' said Charles, looking admiringly at her décolletage, tightly corseted red dress and the spectacular sapphire pendant at her throat and matching ear-rings.

'Sawyers,' said Cecilia, 'would you bring us two glasses of champagne?'

Cranbrook, who as usual was impeccably dressed in a black frockcoat, cream-coloured waistcoat, and dove-grey trousers, waited for Cecilia to sit and then settled comfortably on the settee. Crossing one leg over his knee, he said, 'I came directly from Gray's Inn, without stopping at my flat. A journey of precisely forty-six minutes.'

'Not so long, really,' said Cecilia.

'Not at all,' said Charles. 'One could easily become accustomed to it.' The butler reappeared and served their champagne from a salver. Holding up his glass, Charles said, 'Cheers', and took a sip. After waiting for Cecilia to sample her drink, he said, 'I believe the time has come, darling, to discuss our plans.'

'Not now,' said Cecilia. 'But after dinner. For now, I'd like you to finish that amusing story about the judge who fell asleep in the middle of the trial.'

Cecilia had arranged a sumptuous, three-course dinner of vichyssoise, stuffed goose with French beans, and a chocolate soufflé, accompanied by more champagne and a bottle of vintage claret. She was careful to steer the conversation to banalities during the drawn-out affair, so that when dessert was served, the mood was pregnant with anticipation of the unspoken topic of their future. Pushing back from the table, Cecilia said, 'Let's take our coffee or liqueur in the drawing-room.' Helping her up, Charles walked wordlessly with her to the adjoining room, illuminated by flicker-

149

ing gaslights on sconces, and helped himself to a glass of brandy as Cecilia sat in her favourite chair.

Standing before her, he said, 'I feel as I often do when making a closing argument to a jury.' Cecilia smiled encouragingly. 'Having rehearsed all the things I want to say,' he continued, 'at least a dozen times.' Taking a sip of brandy, he began to pace. 'You may recall,' he said, 'when we were first together in Brighton, I expressed my desire one day to have children.'

'A brood of them,' said Cecilia.

'Yes,' said Charles, halting with a crooked smile. 'And you said, "but first you must find a wife".' She nodded. 'My dear Cecilia,' he said, looking her in the eye. 'I want you for my wife.' Dropping to one knee, he said, 'Will you be mine?'

'Oh, Charles,' said Cecilia, rising from her chair. 'Nothing would make me happier.'

Standing, he put his hands on her shoulders and then kissed her and held her close. 'Charles,' she said softly after a moment.

'Yes, dear?'

Pulling away, she took his hands and said, 'There's something you must know.' He gave her a puzzled look. 'About my past ...'

'Your previous marriage–'

'No. Something that may cause you to change your mind.'

'Don't be foolish,' he said. 'Nothing could cause me to change my mind. I'm quite in love with you.'

'Oh, Charles,' she said in an anguished voice, slumping back down in her chair and moving her knees against the silks of her petticoat. 'If only I could spare you.'

'What? Spare me?'

Cecilia nodded, wiping away a tear. 'Please sit,' she said. Once he was seated on the sofa, she said, 'I was involved in ... well, in a love affair. With an older man.'

'I see,' said Charles with a frown. 'But I don't see the point...'

'A man named Dr James Gully. A very distinguished man. The personal physician to Lord Tennyson and Charles Darwin.'

'Gully,' repeated Cranbrook. 'I seem to have heard of him.'

'It was during the time I was separated from my husband.'

'Separated?'

'Yes. Robert suffered terribly from alcoholism. Life became unbearable; we separated, and I was sent by my father to Dr Gully's hydro for treatment. And then Robert died.' Though determined to confess her transgression, she saw no point in admitting to adultery.

'I see,' said Cranbrook with a shake of his head. He took a large swallow of brandy.

'Doctor Gully was exceptionally kind to me,' explained Cecilia. 'And I was very, well, vulnerable, I suppose. We had an affair.'

'Well, damn it all,' said Cranbrook, suddenly rising from the settee. 'Damn it all to hell.'

'There's more,' said Cecilia quietly. 'Doctor Gully, you see, is in his mid-sixties. And married.'

'What?' Cranbrook's eyes flashed with anger.

'His wife is quite elderly and confined to an

151

insane asylum. He hasn't seen her for years.'

'Good God,' said Cranbrook, downing his drink and walking over to the sideboard to pour another.

'We tried to be very discreet, of course,' said Cecilia, fidgeting with her cuffs. 'But my solicitor found out, and has spread the most vicious rumours. All lies, of course,' she said looking up into Cranbrook's eyes. Suddenly bursting into tears, she muttered, 'It's over now, I swear it.'

'An affair with an old man,' Cranbrook muttered. 'And word of the scandal spread around town. *Damn.*'

Cecilia wiped the tears from her eyes, rose from her chair and took a step toward Cranbrook, who eyed her warily. 'I think I should leave you alone to your thoughts,' she said calmly, obviously having anticipated his surprise and outrage. 'You may help yourself to another drink, or coffee, if you prefer. In a while I shall return, and you may give me your decision.'

Cranbrook nodded, sipped his drink, and said, 'All right.'

Cecilia went to her bedroom to undress, satisfied that Mrs Clark had retired for the evening. Half an hour had elapsed when she emerged from her boudoir, wearing an elaborately embroidered silk dressing-gown and slippers. With a final, resigned glance at her reflection in the mirror over the dressing-table, she left the room and quietly descended the staircase. She found Charles where she had left him, standing before the fireplace with a glass in his hand, his face a blank mask. 'Well,' she said as she walked up to him. 'Have you reached a decision?'

Cranbrook placed his glass on the table at the end of the sofa, raised his chin, and said, 'Yes, I have. The fact of the matter, Cecilia, is that I too have been guilty of this sin.' Cecilia responded with a searching look. 'In my anger, or jealousy, regarding your affair with this man Gully, I very nearly failed to consider my own past.'

'I see,' said Cecilia, lowering herself to the sofa.

'I had a kept woman in Maidenhead for a number of years,' he continued, 'with whom I was engaged in an illicit affair. And so' – Cranbrook took a step toward her – 'who am I to condemn you?'

'Oh, Charles,' said Cecilia, jumping up and throwing her arms around him. 'Please, please forgive me.'

Holding her by the shoulders and looking in her eyes, he said, 'I shall marry you. But on one condition: you must never, *never* see that man Gully again.'

Chapter Eleven

James Gully sat in his parlour at Orwell Lodge watching the rain. Having treated patients suffering from melancholia for decades, he was well aware of the effects of foul weather on the human mind; oppressive, dreary, dull, an anchor on the soul. And yet, he considered, it was far more than the cold, steady rain beading the windows that induced his gloom and ennui. He lowered his eyes to the simple handwritten announcement that had arrived in the morning mail. *Miss Cecilia Henderson*, he read, *will be married to Charles Spencer Cranbrook, Esq. at 11.00 a.m. on Saturday, 7 December, 1871, All Saints Church, Borough of Kensington, London*. No more, not even the briefest note of regret. Glancing at the handwriting, clearly not Cecilia's, he picked up the envelope and studied the return address on the flap: *Mrs Jane Clark, The Priory, Balham*. What a damnably thoughtless way to inform him that he was losing the only woman he had truly loved. 'Humbug,' he muttered, tossing the note on the carpet. Rising from his chair, he walked to the window, gazed out at a passing carriage on the rain-slick street, and then moved to his writing-desk. Taking a sheet of paper from the drawer, he dipped his pen in the inkwell and wrote:

15 October 1871
Orwell Lodge, Balham
My dear Mrs Clark
I am in receipt of your note concerning the marriage of Miss Henderson. Please advise your employer that while I appreciate having been notified, I cannot congratulate her on what I regard as an ill-conceived and potentially ruinous union. She may rest assured, however, that I have no intention of attending the nuptials.

Furthermore, it is my considered judgement that you have greatly influenced, I daresay manipulated, Miss Henderson in this matter for reasons as to which I may only speculate, though I am cognizant of the relationship that has existed between you and the family of the

154

groom. *I believe you have acted at least in part out of a desire to cause me pain, and it may give you some satisfaction to know that in this you have succeeded admirably. As I fear there are certain persons, perhaps including yourself, who are motivated in this matter by avarice and Miss Henderson's fortune, rest assured that I, as her one time guardian, will do all in my power to ensure she is protected. I remain*

Yr obedient servant
J. M. Gully

With a smile of grim satisfaction, Gully lifted the page, blew softly on the drying ink and then carefully folded it in an envelope. After addressing it and affixing a stamp, he donned his top hat and ulster, slipped the letter in his pocket and headed out in the rain to post it.

Cecilia stood by the casement window in the drawing-room, gazing out on the lawn, littered with fallen leaves, and the green fields and woods of Tooting Bec Common in bright sunshine. Wearing a long-sleeved white batiste blouse, buttoned up to her neck, with a forest green wool skirt, she turned toward Mrs Clark, who was seated in an armchair with a thick ledger open in her lap. 'Where were we?' said Cecilia, fingering the brooch on a gold pin at her bosom.

'Your expenditure,' said Mrs Clark, 'over the past month, of which, as you know, I maintain careful accounts–'

'Yes, I know.'

'Exceeded your income. You must cut back.'

'Oh, really?' said Cecilia with a short laugh.

155

'My income is merely the amount I instruct my banker to deposit in the account, dear Mrs Clark. I shall simply instruct them to increase the allowance. An extra fifty pounds should suffice, don't you think?'

'You must learn to practise thrift,' said Mrs Clark with a frown, as she closed the ledger and put it aside. 'Your profligate spending will one day get you in trouble.'

'In trouble? With whom?'

'With your husband.' Mrs Clark rose from her chair and approached Cecilia. 'Mr Cranbrook,' she said, 'strikes me as a man who'll take a hard line when it comes to the household budget.'

'Well, it's my money,' said Cecilia with a flippant air, 'and I shall spend it as I please.'

'Not after you're married,' countered Mrs Clark. 'Then it shall be *his* money.'

A concerned look clouded Cecilia's face. 'His money?' she repeated. 'Charles will control *my* income, what *I* can spend?'

'Under the law,' said Mrs Clark, 'a married woman is a slave to her husband.'

'I shall see about *that,*' said Cecilia. 'I'm certain Mr Jenkins at Coutts can refer me to someone in the City for advice on such matters. Before the wedding.'

Seated in a second-storey outer office overlooking the Strand, Cecilia studied the stacks of documents crammed into the shelves of the floor-to-ceiling bookcases. How, she wondered, as she waited for her appointment with the solicitor, could anyone keep track of his cases, if that was the proper term, amid such hopeless clutter? After the lapse of another five minutes, the oak door beneath the transom opened with a creak, and the lawyer's wizened secretary appeared. 'You may come in, miss,' he said, holding open the door and beckoning with a crooked finger. With a pretty smile at the white-haired gentleman, who stood no taller than she, Cecilia entered a dim, narrow passageway that led to the solicitor's office. Edmund Thistlewaythe, an attorney highly recommended by the bankers at Coutts, was a portly, apple-checked gentleman of the old school, whose attire – black frockcoat, embroidered crimson waistcoat, and old-fashioned knickerbockers with stockings that reached his knees – was unchanged since his days at Cambridge in the 1820s. 'Come in, come in, my dear Miss Henderson,' he said with a smile, gesturing to a red leather armchair before his mahogany desk, which, in contrast to the outer office, was free of papers except for a writing tablet and pen. Cecilia sat, gazing beyond the desk at the arched windows with their view of the Georgian buildings lining the busy thoroughfare.

'Very well,' said Thistlewaythe once he was seated at his desk, 'I understand from Mr Jenkins that you're engaged to be married.'

'That's right,' said Cecilia, 'to Mr Charles Cranbrook, a barrister at Gray's Inn.'

'Why, congratulations, Miss Henderson. How may I be of assistance?'

Thinking that Thistlewaythe's genial manner was as different as could be imagined from the severe Throckmorton, she said, 'At the death of my first husband, I inherited a large fortune–'

'So I was advised by Mr Jenkins.'

'And, as I am soon to remarry, I desire to understand my legal rights in respect of my property.'

'I see.' Folding his hands on the desk, Thistlewaythe said, 'Has not your father advised you regarding this matter?'

'No.'

'Well, then, as a general rule, under the common law a married woman's rights are governed by the doctrine of coverture. Whereas a single woman is a feme sole, a married woman is a feme covert.'

'And the difference...?'

'In marriage,' said Thistlewaythe, 'in the eyes of the law, husband and wife become one.' Reaching for a thick volume from a nearby shelf, he leafed through its pages and said, 'As Blackstone put it: "By marriage, the husband and wife are one person in law: that is, the very being or legal existence of the woman is incorporated or consolidated into that of the husband, under whose wing, protection, and cover she performs everything".' Closing the volume and returning it to the shelf, Thistlewaythe explained, 'All property theretofore owned by his wife is his, all income belongs to him, all rights to enter into contracts, etc may be exercised exclusively by him.'

'I see,' said Cecilia with a frown.

'Under the law of coverture,' the solicitor continued, 'even if a married woman should be employed, her salary or wages would belong to her husband.' Cecilia shook her head with a dismayed expression. 'However,' said Thistlewaythe, inter-

158

locking his chubby fingers, 'conceding the patent unfairness of this doctrine, as applied to women of property, and under considerable pressure from the fathers of wealthy daughters, including certain lords, Parliament in its wisdom recently enacted a statute: The Married Women's Property Act of 1870.'

'Ah.' said Cecilia, brightening, loosening her grip on the edge of her pocket.

'Among other things,' continued Thistlewaythe, 'the Act permits married women, under certain limited circumstances, to retain ownership of property inherited from next of kin prior to marriage.'

'And these circumstances?' said Cecilia, leaning forward in her chair.

'Require an agreement between husband and wife, a so-called prenuptial agreement, which must be ratified by the court before the marriage is entered into.'

'Well, then,' said Cecilia. 'I must have such an agreement. I presume you will prepare it?'

'I would naturally be pleased to do so. You remarked, Miss Henderson, that your fiancé is a barrister?' She nodded. 'I should caution you,' he continued, 'that he may strongly object to this arrangement and insist on his rights under common law. The statute, you see, is only recently enacted and not well accepted, especially by men such as your future husband, trained in the law.'

'That may be, Mr Thistlewaythe,' said Cecilia, rising from her chair with a great rustle of taffeta, 'but I shall insist on it.'

Having heard the sounds of the door-knocker and muffled men's voices in the entrance hall, Cecilia was aware that Charles had arrived, but preferred to make him wait. With a glance out of the bedroom window into the cold, dark evening, where a sharp wind was shaking the trees, she drew the heavy curtains and walked to her boudoir. Seated on a cushion, she picked up her silver-handled mirror and studied her face, the smooth skin of her rouged cheeks, her glossy red lips and her eyes, pale blue with long lashes. Awareness of her sensuous beauty buoyed her confidence, she reflected with a smile, and tonight she would need as much confidence as she could muster. Putting the mirror aside, she opened a vial of French perfume and applied a droplet to her wrists and the nape of her neck. Satisfied, she rose and walked to the stairs.

Charles Cranbrook was warming himself before the fire blazing in the drawing-room, wearing as usual a black wool cutaway and stiff Piccadilly collar but with polished black boots that nearly reached his knees. Turning toward Cecilia when she appeared at the foot of the staircase, he smiled faintly and remained where he was standing with his hands clasped behind his back. As she walked up, he reached for her hands and bent down to kiss her. 'Mmm,' he said, 'what a charming fragrance.'

'Do you like it?' she asked. 'It's from Paris.' Cranbrook nodded, thinking that all of her fine things – the expensive gown and very elaborate matching shoes just visible below the hem, white satin encrusted with gems – were from Paris. 'Do you have a drink?' she asked.

'No, but I would like one. Wretched night out.'

With a good English butler's exquisite sense of timing, Sawyers shimmered into the room and said, 'Sir?'

'Whisky and soda,' said Cranbrook, rubbing his hands together.

'Champagne,' said Cecilia. After they were seated before the fire with their drinks and the usual, ice-breaking small talk about the weather and Charles's pedestrian affairs, Cecilia put her glass aside and said, 'Only three more weeks till we're married. I can scarcely believe it.'

'Yes, darling,' he said, placing a hand on her knee. 'You shall be mine, and no more tiptoeing about after dark.'

Placing her hand on his, she said, 'Charles ... when I was married before, to the captain, I had no property.' Cranbrook's eyes narrowed slightly. 'And my husband, as it happened, was very well-to-do. And so when he passed away, I inherited, well, a large fortune.' Cranbrook looked at her keenly, as he might a witness he was about to cross-examine. 'Which, of course,' she continued, 'is my property. And as we are shortly to be married–'

'Once we are married,' Cranbrook interrupted, 'your property shall be *my* property. Your income shall be *my* income. That is the law.'

Undeterred, Cecilia gave him a coquettish smile and said, 'That is the *common* law. According to my solicitor.'

'What!' said Cran brook, quickly taking his hand from her knee as though he'd touched a hot

161

stove. 'You've retained a solicitor?'

'Yes,' said Cecilia calmly. 'On the advice of my bankers. A certain Mr Thistlewaythe, very highly respected. Who advises me that under a recent Act of Parliament, intended to protect the property rights of married women, I am entitled to retain my inheritance.'

His dark eyes flashing with anger, Cranbrook rose from the settee and began pacing before the fire. 'Solicitor,' he muttered. 'Act of Parliament.' Suddenly halting, he shook his fist and said, 'I'll not stand for this impudence. The woman I marry shall respect the rights of her husband, under English common law! Do you suppose,' he asked sneeringly, 'that I would live in a house which is not *mine*, with furnishings which are not *mine*, or dine on china which is not *mine?* We shall be married, Cecilia, in the old-fashioned way, and *I* shall be lord and master of the household!'

Having anticipated such an outburst, Cecilia, clutching the fabric at her throat, said, 'Very well. But I insist you discuss the matter with Mr Thistlewaythe. He has prepared an agreement for our signature. Which must be approved by the court.'

Cranbrook glared at her, having utterly underestimated her intelligence and cunning. 'The matter will be moot,' he said after a moment, 'if I break off the engagement.'

'That is your prerogative,' said Cecilia, holding him in her steady gaze. 'But I would prefer that you meet my solicitor.'

'Very well,' said Cranbrook. He reached for his glass and downed his drink. 'I haven't much appetite for dinner,' he concluded, 'and shall be on my way.'

As the nuptials loomed, Cranbrook wasted little time arranging an appointment with the distinguished solicitor, who was regarded at the Inns of Court in very high esteem. Cursing himself for failing to consider the advice Cecilia was likely to receive from the shrewd bankers at Courts, who preferred, above all other clients, a wealthy widow, he lowered his head and clutched his top hat as he made his way along the crowded pavement in the sharp November wind. With a glance at the handsome brick edifice in the heart of the Temple Bar, he entered the marble lobby, consulted the clerk, and made his way up the stairs to the second-storey law office. Opening the frosted glass door, with 'G. Edmund Thistlewaythe, Esq.' stencilled in gold, he was received by the elderly secretary who invited him to wait in the cluttered anteroom, assuring him that the lawyer would see him shortly. Shown into the spacious office with its view of the Strand, Cranbrook strode toward Thistlewaythe, who rose from his chair with a smile and extended his hand.

'I congratulate you, sir,' said the solicitor, shaking Cranbrook's hand, 'on your forthcoming marriage.'

'Damn your congratulations,' said Cranbrook, releasing the older gentleman's hand. 'I've come to see about the money.'

'Very well,' said the solicitor equably, lowering himself in his leather chair. 'I would suggest we begin with this.' He handed a blue-backed legal document across the desk.

Cranbrook clenched and unclenched his teeth with lips tightly closed as he perused the prenuptial agreement, which provided that *all property heretofore inherited by the party of the first part, and all income derived therefrom, shall remain the property of said party of the first part following, and notwithstanding, her marriage to the party of the second part,* with only the stipulation that Cecilia provide for the *nurture and support* of any children *who may issue from the aforesaid marriage.*

'Rubbish,' said Cranbrook, tossing the document on the desk with a glare. 'I'd never consent to such an arrangement.'

'The recently enacted marriage statute,' said Thistlewaythe, folding his hands on his smooth desk, 'was intended for just such a situation as this. In fact, it fits Miss Henderson like a glove: a widow who has inherited a *vast* fortune from her late husband and who requires the protection of the law from a possibly unscrupulous suitor.'

'I shall be going,' said Cranbrook, beginning to rise.

'Of course it's possible,' said Thistlewaythe, 'I am mistaken about your interest in Miss Henderson's property.' Cranbrook returned to his chair, eying the solicitor coldly. 'Your stepfather, as I understand it, is a very wealthy man who may possibly have provided you with substantial property and income.' Cranbrook responded with a thin smile. 'Or possibly not.'

'My affairs are none of your business.'

'As I thought.' Thistlewaythe removed another document from his desk drawer and slipped on his reading glasses. 'This,' he said, 'is Miss Henderson's latest statement of account from Courts. It may interest you to know, Mr Cranbrook,' he continued, holding up the document for closer inspection, 'that Miss Henderson's portfolio comes to some seven hundred and seventy thousand pounds, invested in the highest quality railway and industrial shares and bonds.'

'Oh,' said Cranbrook, aware that Cecilia had property but never imagining a fortune of such magnitude.

'As I see it, my good man,' said Thistlewaythe in an avuncular tone, 'you have a choice: walk away from this marriage, or consent to some arrangement with respect to the ownership and disposition of Miss Henderson's property. Of course, my client would prefer the marriage, which has its obvious advantages.' With a smile, he returned the document to the desk drawer.

'Well,' said Cranbrook, thoughtfully rubbing his chin, 'I suppose I might consider a compromise.'

After an hour of at times heated negotiations, Thistlewaythe rose and reached across the desk to shake Cranbrook's hand. 'I shall provide you with drafts of the documents to effectuate our understanding, hopefully by the morrow, Miss Henderson's retention of her inheritance but with a lease in your favour of The Priory and its contents at a nominal consideration and a codicil to Miss Henderson's will, naming you as her sole heir.'

'Very well.' Cranbrook turned to go.

'And Mr Cranbrook,' said Thistlewaythe.

'Yes?'

'Miss Henderson strikes me as a vain and headstrong woman. You would do well not to attempt to rein in her extravagant tastes.'

And you would do well, considered Cranbrook, to mind your own business. 'Good day, sir,' he said and walked to the door.

Jane Clark was exhausted by the assorted tasks that fell upon her with the approach of the wedding, as Cecilia had no one else to see to them – trips into the city to meet the vicar, the florist, the endless dressmaker visits, the musicians, the photographer, and, most tiresome of all, Sir Richard Henderson at his imposing house in Belgravia, where she succeeded in securing an understanding that the mother and father of the bride would, after all, attend the ceremony and the reception afterward, to be held at The Priory. Resting her chin on her fist, she studied her notes in the light of the lamp on her small desk beneath the stairs.

'Excuse me, ma'am,' interrupted the maid.

'What is it,' said Mrs Clark testily.

'Mr Cranbrook desires a word with you.'

'Where is Miss Henderson?'

'Resting in her room, ma'am.'

'Very well,' said Mrs Clark, pushing back her chair. 'Do not disturb her.' She walked to the small, seldom used library at the back of the house, where she found Charles Cranbrook examining the leather-bound volumes in the floor-to-ceiling bookshelves, selected by Cecilia strictly for their decorative value. 'You wished to see me?'

she said.

'Yes,' said Cranbrook, looking at her in his usual accusatory way. 'I'm bloody well fed up with these anonymous letters.'

'You've received another?'

Cranbrook nodded and said, 'Where's Cecilia?'

'In her room.'

He reached into his breast pocket for an envelope, which he handed to Mrs Clark. 'Read it,' he said.

Briefly examining the envelope, she extracted a single sheet and quickly scanned the brief note. 'It is obvious,' she read aloud, 'that you are marrying Miss Henderson purely for her money–'

'A vile slander,' said Cranbrook.

'I'm certain Gully sent it,' said Mrs Clark. 'The old wretch.' She folded the letter in the envelope and handed it to Cranbrook. 'And I'd advise you to burn it, lest poor Cissie should discover it.'

'If that old fool ever comes round,' said Cranbrook, stuffing the envelope in his pocket, 'I'll ... well, he'll rue the day.'

The day of the wedding dawned clear and cold, with a cobalt sky and heavy frost on The Priory lawn and adjoining common. In preparation for the reception, the household staff were scurrying about, and the entrance hall and drawing-room overflowed with hothouse flowers, the perfume of which filled every room save the kitchen, where the aroma of baking bread commingled with roasting goose and savoury pie. The proprietor of the mansion, however, was not at home, having taken rooms for herself and Mrs Clark at the

Duke of Wellington Hotel in Kensington. As the bride was a widow, the wedding party was small by the standards of London high society, consisting principally of extended family, the more influential friends of both Sir Harry and Sir Richard, and a number of Charles's associates from the Bar and his days at Magdalen College. The bishop presided, however, as the wealthy fathers of bride and groom had generously tithed over the years, and Cecilia, wearing an exquisite white satin gown with a stunning diamond tiara in her auburn curls, elicited gasps from many of the women. At the end of the service, bride and groom were ushered, amid a shower of rose petals, into a waiting black landau drawn by white horses for the trip to Balham and the inauguration of their new life together, as the other guests were content to make the brief journey by rail.

Standing by the front parlour window at Orwell Lodge, Dr James Gully consulted his pocket watch and noted the time: half past noon. By now, he bitterly conceded, Cecilia was married; married to a man she did not love, who was interested only in her money and who, he suspected, would subject her to cruel mistreatment. Through his many years of professional observation, Gully was all too familiar with the type, a young man of middle-class origins and modest resources, the stepson of a wealthy but uncharitable upper-class man, who is driven by a ruthless determination to acquire property and respectability in all its trappings. Gully suspected Charles Cranbrook had learned of the circumstances of Cecilia's shame and had used it to secure a bargain: marriage and the restoration of her reputation in return for control of Cecilia's large fortune. And the entire affair orchestrated by the dastardly Mrs Clark.

'A dirty business,' muttered Gully, 'and likely to lead to ruin.'

Hearing hoofbeats on the cobblestones, he peered out the window as an impressive carriage drawn by a matched pair of white horses with ribbons on their manes and jingling bells strung around their necks passed along Bedford Hill Road. Through the carriage's glass window, Gully could clearly make out Charles Cranbrook, wearing the expression of a proud and ruthless man who at last possessed the resources to match his ambitions.

Chapter Twelve

In the beginning Cecilia's marriage appeared to have achieved its dual objectives: the restoration of her sullied reputation and the establishment of Charles Cranbrook as lord and master of her impressive Balham mansion. Indeed, within weeks of the ceremony the newlywed couple hosted a lavish Christmas banquet for thirty-one guests, including the Mayor of Streatham, serving an array of roasted duck, pheasant, and partridge, fine French wines, and assorted cakes and pies. Even more satisfying was Cecilia's rapprochement with her father and mother, who, after years of estrangement, had been plainly impressed by her choice of a husband and the grandness of The Priory. Outwardly, little had changed in the couple's quotidian routines, with Charles departing by eight on the train to the Temple and returning in time for dinner after his customary stop for drinks at Boodle's or White's. Cecilia occupied her time as before, riding horseback on the common and increasingly with excursions into the city to the dressmaker's, often accompanied by Mrs Clark. And, for the first time since her arrival at Balham, an occasional invitation to lunch or tea.

Charles also appeared content in the marriage, writing letters to Cecilia while away at Sessions, quoting Keats and Shelley and declaring that, *I have never felt such happiness as when I hold you in my arms.* The seldom used library at the back of The Priory was converted to his study, a masculine sanctuary where he could work undisturbed on his briefs, enjoy an after-dinner pipe and brandy, and indulge his passion for history and poetry. Within days of the wedding Cranbrook had made it clear to the large Priory staff, consisting of the butler, three maids, the cook, two gardeners, and coachman, that he was ruler of the household, issuing brusque commands and treating them with cold condescension. Mrs Jane Clark, however, remained by unspoken convention outside the scope of Cranbrook's authority.

On a dreary cold and wet January morning, Cecilia, accustomed to sleeping late and descending for breakfast after Charles had departed for the train, was surprised to discover that he was still in his study. Taking a final cup of tea, she was further surprised to find that the door was firmly shut. She knocked, said 'Charles?' and turned the knob.

Seated at his leather-tooled desk with a robe over his usual business attire, he looked up with an annoyed expression and said, 'What is it? Can't you see I'm working?'

Standing in the partly opened doorway, Cecilia observed the large book of accounts – Mrs Clark's ledger – open on the desk next to a stack of bills, invoices, and receipts. 'Are you ill?' she said.

'Of course not,' he snapped. 'With the miserable weather I decided to stay home and try to make some sense out of *this*.' He smacked his hand on the ledger.

'That belongs to Mrs Clark...'

'She's your bookkeeper, is she? Well, a fine job she's done managing your affairs.'

'I manage my own affairs. Jane merely–'

'See here,' said Cranbrook, turning to the ledger. 'During the months of November and December alone, a total of nine hundred and seventy six pounds expended under the heading *Cecilia – Personal*. Nearly *a thousand pounds!* And on what? Dressmakers, milliners, jewellers, florists, God knows what else. Look here. It lists *pair of leather and silk boots, eleven quid!*'

'There was the wedding,' said Cecilia, conscious of a flush of anger on her face, her fingers moving furtively to the edge of her cuff. 'I need to look my best, my position–'

'And look what we're spending on the household.' Turning the page, Cranbrook ran a finger down a long column of penciled figures. 'Some-

171

thing like eighty-five pounds a month.'

'I know what it costs to manage this house,' said Cecilia sharply. 'And I can well afford it. It's my money and I shall spend it as I please.'

'Oh, no,' said Cranbrook, rising from his desk and walking over to toss a lump of coal on the grate. 'As your husband I insist on managing our affairs with some semblance of economy, or it's just a matter of time before we're facing the poorhouse.'

'Oh, pshaw.'

'Beginning with one of the gardeners, and perhaps your maid Fanny.' Cranbrook paced before the fire with his hands behind his back.

'What?'

'How can you possibly justify *two* gardeners? And *three* maids?'

'I understand,' said Cecilia with her hands on her hips, 'that you are accustomed to living in modest circumstances. Well, I am not. I refuse to sacrifice the luxuries I regard as necessities, merely because of your misplaced notion of *economy*. I forbid you to dismiss the gardener or the maid,' she concluded, angrily closing the ledger.

'Forbid me? We shall see about that.' He pounded his fist on the desk so violently that Cecilia's teacup was knocked onto the carpet. As she watched with her hand at her lips, Cranbrook stripped off his robe and stormed from the room, slamming the door behind him.

'I warned you,' said Mrs Clark, who sat in the chair by the window in Cecilia's oak-panelled bedroom and idly glanced at the boxes piled on the floor, the latest delivery of parcels from some of London's finest shops. As it was mid-morning and Cranbrook had long since departed for work, she spoke without fear of being overheard.

'You didn't,' said Cecilia, seated before the mirror in her boudoir with her back to Mrs Clark. 'You merely said that a woman's income belongs to her husband after marriage. Well, I consulted a solicitor and arranged otherwise. Charles has no control over *my* income.'

'And yet,' said Mrs Clark, putting aside a sheaf of bills and rising from the chair to approach Cecilia, 'he's dismissed poor Fanny and one of the gardeners, despite your protests.' Cecilia gazed at Mrs Clark's reflection in the mirror. 'And,' she continued, 'I overheard him telling Griffiths he intends to dispose of the gelding.'

'What?' said Cecilia as she spun around. 'Sell the gelding?'

Mrs Clark nodded and said, 'He complained about paying the bills—'

'You pay the bills.'

'Not any more, Cissie. Mr Cranbrook, as he insists I address him, has taken over that task. And he has a very sharp pencil when it comes to totting up the figures.' Looking Cecilia in the eye, Mrs Clark, gently taking Cecilia's hand and moving it from her cuff, said, 'You must curtail your spending, no matter the size of your income, or there will be hell to pay.'

It was dark and the grandfather clock in the hall had chimed eight times when the front door swung open, admitting Charles Cranbrook amid a shower of swirling snowflakes. Stripping off his gloves and long coat, he hung them on the stand, along with his hat, and strode into the drawing-room, where Cecilia was seated before a brightly burning fire. 'You're late,' she said, putting aside her wineglass.

'The judge refused to recess the trial before six,' said Cranbrook, walking up to the fire to warm his hands. 'And then with the weather the train was a good hour late leaving Victoria.'

'Your drink, sir,' said Sawyers, holding out a salver.

'Thanks,' said Cranbrook, reaching for his glass and taking a sip of diluted Scotch.

'Tell the cook,' said Cecilia, 'we'll be ready for dinner as soon as Mr Cranbrook has finished his drink.'

'Yes, ma'am.'

'We're having a delicious soup, leek and potato,' said Cecilia to Charles, 'and your favourite roast beef and Yorkshire pudding. And then early to bed on this wintry night.'

'Good,' said Cranbrook with something like a smile. He gave Cecilia a brief, wolfish look and then took a large swallow of whisky.

Following dinner at the long dining-room table, during which Charles chiefly discussed the trial in progress, a typical commercial dispute about which Cecilia feigned interest as she enjoyed several glasses of wine, he abruptly stood up, tossed his napkin on the table, and said, 'Come along, darling. Time for bed.'

In her previous marriage, and throughout her long affair with Dr Gully, Cecilia was accustomed

174

to choosing the circumstances for love-making, the time of day and month and only when it suited her mood, on the unspoken assumption that her partner would acquiesce. And though intercourse with the inebriated Richard Castello seldom, if ever, gave satisfaction to either party, she had discovered with the gifted doctor that it was the source of ineffable pleasure, the conferring or withholding of which by a woman exerted powerful control over a man, a lesson as old as Eve. But since she had first slept with Charles Cranbrook, Cecilia discovered to her dismay that the tables had turned.

The word 'rape' was never spoken in the presence of a girl or young woman of the English upper classes, and so as a child in Adelaide Cecilia had been baffled when a mixed-race serving girl informed her that another of the servants had been sentenced to prison for rape. Consulting the dictionary, she read that it meant 'sexual intercourse forced on a woman against her will', which both disgusted and frightened her. Now, in her first month of marriage to Charles she was beginning to believe that rape was the prerogative of a husband under English law. This night, sleepy with wine, she fervently desired it would be otherwise, standing barefoot in her boudoir in her broderie Anglaise bodice and knee-length knickers. Approaching her silently from behind as she brushed out her hair, Charles slipped his hands around her waist and softly kissed the nape of her neck. 'Not now,' she murmured. Suddenly spinning her around, he seized the tops of her bodice and tore it apart.

'There,' he said with a leer, admiring her bare breasts. He suddenly kissed her hard on the mouth as he fondled her nipples.

Breaking away, she said, 'Please, don't,' conscious of his nakedness beneath his silk dressing-gown.

Undeterred, Cranbrook lifted her in his strong arms, carried her to the bedroom and lowered her on the bed. Not bothering with the covers, he violently pulled down her underwear, threw off his robe, and straddled her, forcing his way into her with animal intensity. Thankfully for Cecilia, he was done within minutes, panting as he lay next to her immobile form. Without a word, she rose and went to her bath, anxious to wash away every trace of him and hopefully avoid another pregnancy.

'You wanted a word with me, sir?' said Griffiths, standing in the entrance to Charles Cranbrook's study.

'Come in,' said Cranbrook, seated at his desk in shirtsleeves and a silk brocaded waistcoat. Ill at ease in his muddied riding boots, Griffiths clumsily sat in a chair facing his employer.

'Pity about the carriage,' said Cranbrook, folding his hands in front of him.

'Aye,' said Griffiths with a nod. 'A turrible accident. Thankfully, the missus warn't injured.'

'She might have been killed,' said Cranbrook with a menacing glare. 'And a very fine carriage is now a shambles.'

Griffiths hung his head and muttered, 'Sorry, sir.'

'Sorry? I'm paying you to take care of my wife and belongings, and you go crashing into a wine-cart on Bond Street!'

'It warn't my fault, sir. The driver of the cart came flyin' round the corner and before I could get out of the way, he–'

'That's enough,' interrupted Cranbrook, raising a hand. 'I'm discharging you.'

'What?' said Griffiths, looking up at Cranbrook with a startled expression.

'You're sacked. I'll expect you out of the coach-house in a fortnight.'

'But, sir,' said Griffiths, rising from his chair. 'It ain't right. I swear, it was the fault of the other driver.'

'That's what they always say,' said Cranbrook. 'Now, you may go.'

Glaring at Cranbrook, a flush spread over Griffith's face. 'It *ain't right*,' he repeated. 'The wife's expectin' a baby in two months. I'll take this up with the missus.'

'Do as you please,' said Cranbrook, rising from his chair. 'It won't do any good. And if you're not out of the coachhouse in a fortnight, I'll have you evicted.'

Cecilia remained sequestered in her boudoir with the door latched until at least a half-hour had passed since her husband had dressed for dinner and descended the stairs. Brooding with anger since her talk with Griffiths, she'd refused to discuss the matter with Mrs Clark and exchanged only a brief, hateful look with Cranbrook when she passed him in the upstairs passageway. Choos-

177

ing a dark red dress that matched her mood, she emerged from the boudoir and started down the stairs to confront him. Seated in an armchair with his pipe and newspaper, Cranbrook affected an air of indifference as Cecilia entered the gas-lit drawing-room.

'Sawyers,' she called out in a loud voice.

'Yes, ma'am,' said the butler, who appeared after a moment.

'Bring me a glass of brandy.'

Cranbrook shot her a curious look over the top of his newspaper.

'I suppose Sawyers will be next on the chopping block,' said Cecilia with her hands on her hips. Cranbrook sucked on his pipe, expelled a cloud of aromatic smoke, and then carefully folded the paper and put it aside. The butler reappeared, served Cecilia her drink, and withdrew. Taking a sip, she said, 'How dare you sack Griffiths without consulting me?'

'He was negligent,' replied Cranbrook, 'and cost me fifty quid in repair bills.'

Cecilia was unable to stop herself from rubbing her wrist gently along the soft silk of her cuff. 'First it was Fanny and Rance, the gardener,' she said with flashing eyes, 'and now my very own groom! And Griffiths claims you blamed the accident on *him!*' Cranbrook met this accusation with a smirk. 'Well,' she continued, 'I've reinstated him. And I demand you give him an apology.'

'You demand?' said Cranbrook, leaping up from his chair. 'An apology? Griffiths is *sacked,* and there's no more to be said about it.'

'I won't stand for it!' said Cecilia with a stamp

178

of her foot.

Walking up to within a foot of her, Cranbrook waved his pipe in her face and said, 'I'm master of this house, and you had better get used to it. If I'm not satisfied with the stableman, I shall sack the stableman, or the cook, or the laundress...'

'You beast!'

'Or even your dear friend Mrs Clark–'

'Liar!'

'If it suits me.'

'Never!'

'Hah!' said Cranbrook, turning away.

Taking a swallow of brandy, Cecilia threw the glass against the marble fireplace and ran from the room, nearly colliding with Jane Clark, standing in the shadows at the foot of the staircase.

Mrs Clark tapped lightly on the door to the study and, hearing a muffled response, turned the knob and let herself in. Charles Cranbrook was seated at his desk with an unlit pipe clenched in his teeth, holding a sheet of paper. 'Yes, Mr Cranbrook,' she said, eyeing him coldly. 'You wished to see me?'

'Yes,' he said sourly, removing the pipe. 'It's another of these infernal letters. God damn that miserable wretch Gully.'

'Are you certain it's from Gully?'

'Of course it's Gully. Accusing me of marrying Cecilia for her money. Threatening to expose me.'

'May I see it?' Cranbrook pushed the sheet of paper across his desk. Quickly scanning it, Mrs Clark said, 'I don't recognize the handwriting. I'm almost certain it's not the doctor's.'

'Not the doctor's?' exclaimed Cranbrook, rising from his chair and aggressively leaning across the desk. 'You don't mean to say there's more than one lunatic behind these anonymous libels?'

Sitting in a chair facing the desk, Mrs Clark gazed impassively at Cranbrook and said, 'There's certainly more than one person with a motive to punish poor Cissie for her ill-judged affair.'

'Punish Cecilia?'

'Yes,' continued Mrs Clark calmly, 'by attempting to destroy her marriage. Judging from the penmanship, I wouldn't be surprised if the author is a woman.'

'Rubbish,' said Cranbrook, beginning to pace behind his desk. 'It's that blasted Gully.'

'Such as Throckmorton's spinster sister,' said Mrs Clark, handing Cranbrook the letter.

'It's Gully, all right,' said Cranbrook, pointing a finger at Mrs Clark, 'and you're merely trying to protect Cecilia by saying otherwise. Well, by God, I won't have it! She can go back to that old bugger, as far as I'm concerned.' Tossing the letter on the desk, he stormed from the room.

After a moment Mrs Clark rose and followed him to the hall, watching as he threw open the door and strode quickly down the gravel drive. 'Wait!' she called out, hurrying after him. He turned and stood with his hands on his hips. 'Where are you going?' she asked.

'I'm leaving,' he said. 'I know what's up between Gully and that wicked Cecilia.'

'You're mistaken,' said Mrs Clark. 'I'm sure of it.' Cranbrook glared at her. 'You mustn't blame Cecilia for the actions of some jealous fool.'

Cranbrook considered, his ardour dimmed by her cold logic and the even colder February wind. 'Oh, all right,' he said after a moment. 'But I'll never rest until I see Gully's coffin going across Tooting Bec Common.'

Cecilia climbed down from the hansom into the cold, steady rain, paid the driver a generous tip, and hurried into the house. Hanging her hat and coat, she walked into the drawing-room, craving a cup of hot tea. Anticipating her wishes, Mrs Clark appeared, holding a tray with a teapot, cups, saucers, and milk jug. Lowering it to the butler's table, she looked Cecilia in the eye and said, 'Well? What did the doctor say?'

'Just as I thought,' said Cecilia, bending down to pour herself a cup of tea. 'I'm expecting.'

'Oh dear.'

'Charles will be thrilled. Perhaps it will take his mind off household economy.' She took a sip of tea and said, 'Would you be a dear, Jane, and go to the telegraph office? I want to announce the news to my parents and advise them I'm coming to Buscot Park for a visit.'

'All right. When will you be leaving?'

'On Saturday next. I'd go sooner but I have a fitting in Mayfair on Tuesday for my new wardrobe.'

Cecilia's telegram elicited a prompt reply from her father, advising that they were delighted to learn she was expecting and would welcome her visit. Charles, too, expressed his satisfaction and for a time behaved decently toward her, even with a modicum of cheerfulness. Within a week, however, he reverted to his former demeanour, glaring at her across the dinner table, responding to her small talk in monosyllables, and spending as much time as possible away with male companions at his clubs. When the day came for her departure, Charles, having dismissed Griffiths, offered to drive Cecilia to the Balham railway station in the carriage. 'As you wish,' said Cecilia, 'though I'm sure Mrs Clark–'

'No, I'll drive.' Cranbrook helped his wife into the carriage, stowed her luggage, and climbed onto the driver's seat. Within a few minutes they entered Balham on Bedford Hill Road. Passing by Orwell Lodge, he abruptly halted the mare with a jerk on the reins, turned to Cecilia, and sneeringly remarked, 'Do you see anyone familiar? Old man Gully, perhaps?'

Restraining the impulse to slap him, Cecilia said, 'Why must you torment me? I'm not always talking about *your* other woman.'

Cranbrook glowered at her, lifted his whip, and for a moment looked as if he might strike her, sending her fingers to her cuff in furious rubbing. Snapping the whip at the horse's ears, he started off with a creak of wheels. Arriving at the station, Cranbrook turned back to Cecilia and said, 'How long will you be away?'

'I was planning to stay a week,' said Cecilia as she climbed down. 'But I despise you, Charles, and am leaving for good!' Watching as a porter hefted her luggage, Cranbrook curled his lip and said, 'Convey my regards to your father and mother.' With that, he snapped his whip and drove away, leaving Cecilia alone on the pavement with a forlorn expression and her hand at her belly.

Despite tearful entreaties, Sir Richard Henderson, who had never forgiven his daughter for her shameful affair with Gully, insisted that she return to her husband after staying a week at Buscot Park. 'At all events,' he said over breakfast in a sunlit alcove, 'your mother and I are departing on Saturday for a month-long excursion to Italy. Your place is with Charles, especially as you've been blessed with a child.'

'But I hate him, Father. He's cruel to me...'

'As I recall you saying about Richard.'

'But it's true!' Suffering from morning sickness, she bolted from the alcove to her upstairs bed. Recovered after a brief rest, she rose and found an envelope on the dresser, addressed to her in her husband's distinctive hand. Tearing it open, she quickly scanned his note, declaring that *he missed her dreadfully* and imploring her to return home. Tossing it on the dresser with a sigh, she rang for the upstairs maid to assist her in packing her bags.

'She's coming home,' said Charles Cranbrook, waving a sheet of paper. 'Arriving tomorrow afternoon.'

'I expect she hadn't any say in the matter,' said Mrs Clark, seated in a chair facing Cranbrook's desk. 'Poor woman.'

'She's bearing my child,' said Cranbrook with out-thrust chin. 'My son. Charles the Second,' he added with a smile. 'I knew she'd come back.'

'Cecilia is acting under duress,' said Mrs Clark. 'You must treat her with decency.'

Cranbrook's eyes narrowed as he stared across the desk at the petite woman clad in black. 'It's not Mrs Cranbrook I desired to discuss with you. I'm sorry to say it, madam, but I've made up my mind to dispense with your services.' She glared back at him, though the news of her dismissal hardly surprised her. 'However,' said Cranbrook, steepling his fingers at his chin, 'you shall have ample time to look for another position, as you've served me well, urging my suit with Cecilia.'

'Thank you, sir.'

'I'm aware you have children in school.' She nodded. 'Perhaps debts to pay.' She responded with an expression so cold, so intense, that he was forced to look away. 'Naturally,' he continued after a moment, 'I will provide you with good references. Now, if you will excuse me.' With a final inscrutable look, Mrs Clark rose from her chair and walked slowly from the room.

For the first few days after Cecilia's return from Buscot Park it seemed to her that relations with Charles had improved; he made no mention of household economy nor of Dr Gully and treated her with some consideration, if not warmth, during their times together in the evening. Neither he nor Mrs Clark made any mention of the impending termination of Mrs Clark's employment. Returning to The Priory on Saturday afternoon, however, after his usual lunch and chess match at Boodle's, Charles accosted Cecilia in the drawing-room, scolding her for refusing to eat properly and her excessive consumption of wine, as the cook, no admirer of Cecilia, had informed him that she routinely drank several glasses with lunch and a full bottle with dinner. 'It's my child you're carrying,' he said, pointing his finger. 'My son.'

'How can you know it's a boy?'

'I know it is. And by God I don't intend to see something happen to him because you're an ill-nourished inebriate–'

'Oh, stop it!'

'–and a conceited fool who cares more about her figure than her unborn child's health.'

Bursting into tears, Cecilia hurried up the stairs, locked the door to her room and threw herself on the bed. She must have dozed, because the light in the room had grown dim when she sleepily rubbed her eyes and sat up. Rising from bed, she gasped at the blotches of bright, red blood staining the sheet. Throwing open the door, she called to the upstairs maid, 'Mary Ann! Send for Mrs Clark at once!'

Chapter Thirteen

Jane Clark stood at Cecilia's bedroom window and watched Dr Harrison, a physician from nearby Streatham carrying a black medical bag, as he walked down the flagstones to his waiting horse and buggy. Turning toward the bed, she studied Cecilia, propped up on pillows under fresh linen

185

with her eyes closed. Silently approaching her bedside, she took Cecilia's limp hand, cold to the touch, and leaned down to kiss her pale cheek. 'There, there,' she murmured as Cecilia stirred. 'Try to sleep.'

Opening her eyes, Cecilia said, 'Did the doctor speak to Charles?'

Mrs Clark shook her head. 'I merely advised Charles that you were not feeling well and instructed the doctor not to disturb him.'

Cecilia nodded and said, 'Does the doctor know that I–?'

'No,' said Mrs Clark, 'I said nothing about it. But of course you understand why you may never be able to bear a child.'

Brushing a tear from the corner of her eye, Cecilia said, 'Yes. Under the circumstances, it's just as well.' Despite her shock at the loss of the baby, Cecilia's dominant emotion was relief. 'Now,' she said, 'you must inform Charles.'

Mrs Clark found Cranbrook in his study, sucking on his pipe and reworking a legal brief at his desk. 'What is it,' he said gruffly, giving her a look of frosty annoyance as she stood in the doorway.

'It's Mrs Cranbrook.'

'Is she ill?'

'No. She's miscarried.'

'What!' said Cranbrook, jumping up from his chair. 'Lost the child?' Mrs Clark nodded. 'Damn,' said Cranbrook under his breath. 'I knew she wasn't taking proper care of herself. I warned her! Damn her selfishness and stupidity!' he said with a shake of his fist.

'It's important that she rest,' said Mrs Clark

calmly. 'She's lost blood and is very weak.' Cranbrook glared at her. 'And she requests that I stay with her at night until she's recovered.'

'Oh, she does?' said Cranbrook. 'And where will I sleep?'

'She suggests the spare bedroom at the top of the stairs.'

'Very well,' said Cranbrook with a malevolent glare. 'You may go now.'

Following a light supper of consommé and toast, served to her in bed, Cecilia had the strength to rise and enjoy a long, indolent soak in her clawfoot bathtub. Emerging from her bath enfolded by a large towel, she encountered Mary Ann turning down her bed.

'Do you need anything, ma'am?' said the maid.

'Yes,' said Cecilia. 'A glass of sherry.' After donning her nightgown and brushing out her hair, seated on the cushion in her boudoir as she drank her wine, Cecilia entered the bedroom, where she found Mrs Clark in a chair at the foot of the bed, wearing a robe with her dark hair down on her shoulders.

'I'll tuck you in,' said Mrs Clark, rising from her chair as Cecilia walked to the bed and slipped under the covers. Checking to make sure the door was firmly shut, Mrs Clark pulled the coverlet up to Cecilia's chin, bent down and gently kissed her. Then, with a tender look, she doused the gaslights and returned to her chair in the darkness.

After a week had passed, during which Mrs Clark shared Cecilia's bed at night and Charles Cranbrook had virtually no contact with his wife, Cecilia dressed before nine on a Sunday morning in the hope of encountering him over breakfast. Pausing at the top of the stairs, she glanced through the partly open door into the small guest bedroom, listening to the church bells in the village and observing a water pitcher and glass on a bedside table and Charles's riding boots at the foot of the neatly made single bed, a room, she reflected, she had never entered. Descending the stairs, she found her husband at the dining-room table.

'Hallo,' he said, looking up from his newspaper and plate of eggs and kippers. 'Looking hale and hearty.'

'I'm better,' she said. 'Much better.' She rang a small silver bell to summon the kitchen maid, who appeared after a moment and said, 'Yes, ma'am?'

'I'll join Mr Cranbrook for breakfast. An omelette with bacon.'

Taking a piece of toast from the rack, Cranbrook smeared it with marmalade, took a bite and a sip of tea as he reverted to his newspaper. After a few minutes of silence, the maid reappeared, served Cecilia her eggs and bacon and poured her a cup of tea from the pot. Cecilia stirred in milk and sugar and sampled the omelette. 'What's this?' she asked, picking up a folded sheet at Cranbrook's elbow.

'A letter from my stepfather,' said Cranbrook, snatching it away from her. 'Taking me to task for speculating in the stock market.'

'How much did you lose?'

188

'None of your business, nor his. I intend to send him a shirty reply.'

'Charles,' said Cecilia after eating a few bites.

'Yes,' said Cranbrook, continuing to read his paper.

'I'm going on holiday to Worthing.'

'What? To Worthing?'

'Yes. Mrs Clark is there now, looking for suitable lodgings. The doctor says it will do me good.'

'Nonsense,' said Cranbrook, tossing his napkin on the table. 'There's nothing the matter with you.'

'But why should you object? It's only with Mrs Clark, for at most a week.'

'Because of the blasted expense.' He glared at her. 'We're piling up debts, and all you can think to do is spend, spend, spend.'

'That's grossly unfair,' said Cecilia, pushing back from the table. 'The doctor says I need rest.'

'You can rest here,' said Cranbrook, rising from his chair, 'and spare the expense of a *holiday* with dear Mrs Clark. And let this serve notice I intend to expel *that* woman from your bedchamber.'

'You vile creature!' said Cecilia. 'I should never have married you!'

'You'll learn to obey me!' said Cranbrook. He suddenly lunged and slapped her hard across the face.

'Ooh,' cried Cecilia as she crumpled to the floor, where she lay cradling her head in her arms, moaning. For a moment Cranbrook stared down at her, his mouth curled into a disdainful frown, before tramping noisily from the room.

'The holiday to Worthing is scotched,' said Cecilia, reclining on the *chaise* in her bedroom in an embroidered blue silk robe.

'We're not going?' said Mrs Clark, just returned from the Balham station. 'Why, I've arranged a room for us at a seaside hotel.'

'Charles forbids it.'

Mrs Clark took a step closer, a look of disbelief in her eyes. 'Cissie – what happened to your face?'

Running her tongue over her swollen lip, she said, 'He hit me.'

'My God.'

'Knocked me to the floor.' Tears welled in her red-rimmed eyes. 'Oh, Janie, I've got to find a way out of this marriage.'

'I don't see how,' said Mrs Clark, walking over and stroking Cecilia's hair. 'Unless something were to happen to that wicked brute.'

'Well, he's gone into town to his club. Staying the night.'

'You should dress,' said Mrs Clark. 'And then we'll take the carriage on a nice drive through the common.'

The following day Charles Cranbrook arrived home unusually early. That morning he had suffered a severe attack of nausea on his way from his room at the club to his office, becoming violently ill on the pavement, but had recovered sufficiently to continue to work and even consume a brandy over lunch at White's with his law partner Edward Hope, celebrating a minor courtroom victory. Arriving at The Priory, Cranbrook changed into his riding coat and boots and instructed Mac-

190

Donald, the gardener, who, after Griffiths' dismissal was also responsible for looking after the stable, to saddle the gelding.

'He's already been exercised, sir,' objected MacDonald.

'I'll be back in twenty minutes,' said Cranbrook as he swung into the saddle.

Over an hour had passed, however, when Cranbrook rode unsteadily into the paddock. 'Are you all right, sir?' said MacDonald, taking the reins.

Cranbrook, visibly shaken, slowly climbed from the horse, whose haunches were dark with lather. 'As we were leaving the common,' he said, 'Cremorne bolted. Ran for four miles, all the way to Mitcham, before I could stop him.' With a wince he began walking painfully toward the house.

Cecilia found him an hour later, collapsed in a chair in his study, deathly pale with a dazed expression, still wearing his riding boots. 'Cremorne ran off with me,' he muttered as Cecilia gave him a concerned look.

'I'll have Sawyers help you with your boots,' she said, 'and then draw you a bath. You look unwell.'

'I was sick this morning,' he said. 'But then I felt better and had lunch with Hope at White's.' When the time came for his bath, Cranbrook was too weak or too ill to climb the stairs, and so was helped to his feet and half-carried upstairs by the butler, who steered him to the small guest room and laid him on the bed. After an hour's rest, he'd regained enough strength to make his way downstairs, where he found Cecilia having supper with Mrs Clark in the dining-room, mutton chops

191

with French green beans, accompanied by a decanter of sherry.

'Are you better?' said Cecilia, reaching for the bell to summon the maid.

'I suppose,' said Cranbrook, wearily slumping in a chair.

'Bring Mr Cranbrook a plate,' Cecilia instructed the maid when she appeared after a moment. 'Wine?' she asked Cranbrook.

'Yes. I'll have a glass of claret.'

Cecilia refilled her glass, briefly exchanged looks with Mrs Clark, and then continued eating in silence. The maid returned with a plate and glass of red wine for her master, who summoned the strength to carve a few bites of mutton and consume a portion of his vegetables. Mrs Clark, having finished her supper, seemed to be watching him, which caused him to avert his eyes. After the lapse of five minutes of awkward silence, Cecilia downed the last of her sherry, rose from the table and said, 'I'm going upstairs to undress.' Cranbrook wordlessly looked up at her.

'Good evening,' said Mrs Clark, as she rose from her chair. 'Rest well.'

Cecilia, wearing a robe over her nightgown, stood before the mirror over her dressing-table, brushing out her hair. Seeing Mrs Clark's reflection in the glass, she turned and said, 'Janie – send for Mary Ann and ask her to bring me a glass of Madeira.' Mrs Clark, still fully dressed, walked to the staircase, pausing to glance into the empty guest bedroom before descending. Avoiding the dining-room, she delivered the request to the maid and returned to Cecilia's bedroom. Mary Ann, locating the bottle of Madeira in the butler's pantry, poured a glass and walked to the stairs where she encountered Charles Cranbrook with his hand on the banister. 'Pardon me, sir,' she said as she hurried past him, aware of his strong disapproval of his wife's habit of drinking after dinner. Too weak to object, Cranbrook slowly made his way upstairs.

After delivering the wine, Mary Ann tidied up her mistress's boudoir, careful to properly hang the dresses and fold the many robes and bed jackets, and then entered the bedroom, where she found Cecilia under the covers, evidently asleep, and Mrs Clark in her chair at the foot of the bed, knitting by the light of a candle. Bidding her goodnight, Mary Ann left the room, gently closed the door, and started down the stairs. Halfway down, she heard footfalls and looked back as the door to the spare bedroom swung open and Cranbrook, clad only in his nightshirt, staggered out. 'Cecilia!' he shouted, clutching his throat. 'Cecilia! Hot water!' As Cranbrook stumbled back into his room, the maid hurried up the stairs and knocked on Cecilia's door. Hearing no answer, she turned the knob and peered into the darkened room, lit only by the coals burning on the grate. Cecilia was sleeping, but Mrs Clark, fully dressed, remained in her chair at the foot of the bed. 'What is it?' she stage-whispered.

'Come quick!' said Mary Ann. 'It's Mr Cranbrook. He's ill!'

Mrs Clark rose and hurried to the spare bedroom with the maid following. The door was ajar and, though the room was dark, Mrs Clark could see and hear Cranbrook leaning out the window with his hands on the sill, violently retching. He turned toward her with a wild look and again shouted, 'Water!' Attempting to stand, his knees gave way, and he collapsed on the floor, unconscious. Kneeling beside him, Mrs Clark looked back at the maid, frozen in the doorway, and said, 'Turn on the lights!' She turned Cranbrook on his side and placed her hand on his chest, detecting a faint, irregular heartbeat. When the gaslights flickered on she briefly studied his pale face and listened to his laboured breathing. 'Go downstairs,' she calmly instructed the maid, 'and fetch hot water and some dry mustard.'

'Yes, ma'am.'

'Be quick about it.'

After some minutes, Mary Ann returned with a water pitcher and small bowl, which she lowered with trembling hands to the carpet beside Cranbrook's still form. Mrs Clark, kneeling beside him, poured hot water from the pitcher into the bowl, which contained powdered mustard, and stirred the mixture with her finger. Lifting the back of Cranbrook's head, she managed to pour some of the concoction down his throat, which caused him immediately to vomit. 'Ooh,' said Mary Ann, turning away. After trying unsuccessfully to shake him awake, Mrs Clark looked up at Mary Ann and said, 'Find Sawyers and tell him to send for Dr Harrison in Streatham. Tell him Mr Cranbrook is deathly ill and that the doctor must come at once!'

Mary Ann started down the stairs, hesitated,

194

and changed her mind, thinking the master's dying and no one's awakened his wife to tell her! Bursting into Cecilia's room, she ran up to the bed and said, 'Wake up, ma'am! It's Mr Cranbrook!'

'What!' exclaimed Cecilia, disoriented from a wine-induced deep slumber. 'Charles?' She sprang from the bed and raced to the spare bedroom. 'What is it?' she screamed at Mrs Clark, who was still kneeling beside Charles's prostrate form. His eyes were shut and nightshirt soiled with vomit and the yellow mustard solution.

'He's alive, but barely,' said Mrs Clark. 'He must have swallowed chloroform; I smelt it on his breath. See the bottle there.' Cecilia glanced at a medicine bottle on the mantel containing a small quantity of green liquid. 'I've sent Sawyers for Dr Harrison,' added Mrs Clark.

'Dr Harrison?' said Cecilia. 'Too far. We must get someone local.' She ran from the room, shouting 'Sawyers!' from the top of the stairs. Hurrying down, she found the front door partly open and a lamp burning in the passage. 'Sawyers!' she called.

'Yes, ma'am.' The butler, clad in a dressing-gown, appeared from the pantry.

'Has someone gone for Dr Harrison?'

'Yes, ma'am. I sent MacDonald.'

'We must get a doctor from Balham. Doctor Moore is only ten minutes away.'

'I'll get cracking.'

It was well past midnight when the carriage bringing Dr Harrison from Streatham turned into The Priory drive. Taking his black bag, he hurried to the entrance, ablaze with lights, and up the staircase. Cecilia was sequestered in her bedroom with Mrs Clark, and Mary Ann was with Sawyers in the kitchen brewing coffee, leaving Dr Moore, a short, thin man with grey hair and a neatly trimmed beard, alone with Cranbrook, who lay motionless on the bed, wearing a clean nightshirt. Taking his stethoscope from the bag, Dr Harrison listened to Cranbrook's weak heartbeat and then opened his eyes and peered at his dilated pupils.

'Well,' he said, turning to Dr Moore. 'What do you make of it?'

'In my judgement,' said Moore, 'he's been poisoned. According to the women who found him, he was craving water and vomiting violently before collapsing and losing consciousness.'

'Poison,' said Harrison, gazing down on Cranbrook's spectral pallor, his skin cold and clammy to the touch.

'One of the women insists he swallowed chloroform,' said Moore, pointing to the almost empty bottle. 'But I doubt it. No one could choke the stuff down.'

'Unconscious,' said Harrison, 'violently ill, pulse weak but racing. I doubt he'll live till morning.' Summoning Cecilia, accompanied by Mrs Clark, to the sickroom, Dr Harrison asked if she could provide an explanation for her husband's symptoms.

'Why, I suppose,' she said, 'he's suffered a heart attack. He went for a ride this afternoon, and his horse bolted. It left him weak and unwell. And Charles's prone to fits of fainting, and was worried about stocks and shares.'

'Your husband is gravely ill,' said the doctor. 'I'm afraid he's dying, and not from consuming chloroform, nor a heart attack. The symptoms are those of an irritant poison, such as arsenic.'

'Arsenic?' said Cecilia, holding a hand to her mouth. 'Oh, my God.' Taking Harrison's arm, she said, 'Charles's cousin is Royes Bell, a Harley Street surgeon, whose partner is the eminent Dr Johnson. If Charles could be dying, I wish to send for them.'

'Of course,' said both doctors in unison.

By the time Dr Johnson, a kindly looking older gentleman who served as Vice-President of the Royal College of Physicians, and his young colleague Dr Bell, entered the sickroom, the grandfather clock in the hall had struck three times. Cecilia sat on the bed beside the still form of her husband, stroking his damp hair; Mrs Clark occupied a chair in the corner, and the other servants were keeping a vigil in the kitchen. Doctor Johnson briefly examined Cranbrook and then conferred with his colleagues in the upstairs passageway. Returning to the room, he said to Cecilia, 'I concur with Dr Moore's diagnosis. Your husband has been poisoned and is unlikely to survive the night.'

Cranbrook, hitherto silent, stirred and his eyelids fluttered open. Giving the physicians a wild, incoherent look, he struggled to get out of bed but was forcibly restrained. 'Charles,' said Dr Bell, hovering over him, 'do you recognize me?'

'Yes,' said Cranbrook in a barely audible voice. 'It's Royes.'

'Charles,' said Bell, 'you've swallowed something. What did you take?'

Looking dazed, Cranbrook blinked uncomprehendingly and then muttered, 'Laudanum. I ... rubbed it on my gums for toothache. I may have swallowed some.'

'Laudanum won't explain your symptoms,' said Dr Johnson. 'You must have taken something else.' Cranbrook shook his head. 'You're in mortal peril,' continued Johnson. 'Good God, man, if you've taken poison you have a moral duty to tell us.'

'No,' said Cranbrook with a groan. 'I've only taken laudanum.' He winced in pain and doubled over.

'Give him a grain of morphia by suppository,' Johnson instructed Bell. 'And an injection of brandy in his bloodstream for his heart.'

'Doctor Johnson.' Mrs Clark stood at his elbow. 'May I have a private word with you?' Stepping out into the passage, she leaned close to him and said, 'I must tell you that Mr Cranbrook *has* poisoned himself. When I found him, he said, "I've taken poison – don't tell Cecilia", before he collapsed.'

'Why didn't you tell someone sooner?' asked Johnson angrily.

'I told Dr Harrison,' she replied calmly.

Summoned to the passageway, Harrison hotly denied Mrs Clark's assertion. 'You merely stated he'd swallowed chloroform,' he said, pointing an accusatory finger. 'That you smelt it on his breath.' The three returned to the bedroom, where Cranbrook had lapsed again into unconsciousness. He lay in his bed, groaning, with Cecilia sitting at his bedside, clutching her arms as the physicians retired downstairs for coffee, and Mrs Clark went to her room to snatch a few hours' rest.

Despite the direst predictions, Cranbrook survived the long night, though it was evident to Cecilia, studying his contorted features and the damp hair at his temples in the dim light of early morning that he had only hours to live unless other, drastic measures were taken. Summoning Mary Ann to sit with him, she went to the writing desk in her room and composed a brief note, an appeal to Sir William Gill, the personal physician to the queen and a close acquaintance of Cecilia's father, to come at once to attend her husband, *who is deathly ill*.

As it happened, the arrival of Dr Gill, the most eminent physician in the land, coincided with that of Sir Harry and Lady Cranbrook, summoned by Cecilia at first light. Quickly advised by Dr Johnson of the circumstances surrounding Cranbrook's collapse and the conclusions drawn by the team of doctors, Gill proceeded to the sickroom. During the course of Gill's examination, Cranbrook briefly regained consciousness, semi-delirious and complaining of excruciating abdominal pain.

'This is not disease,' said Gill, leaning down over Cranbrook. 'You have been poisoned. Pray tell how it happened.'

Sweating profusely, Cranbrook muttered weakly, 'Laudanum.'

'This is more than laudanum,' said Gill. 'If you

199

reveal the name of the poison, we will try an antidote.'

With a groan, Cranbrook closed his eyes and rolled on his side. Shaking their heads, the physicians withdrew and, notwithstanding the tears and fervent prayers of his wife and family, Cranbrook slipped deeper into unconsciousness, writhing in agony, until, at last, as the sun reached its zenith, he took a sharp breath, uttered a long, rasping gargle, shuddered, and was still. Wiping away a tear, Cecilia rose from her bedside chair and walked out into the passage, where Cranbrook's parents were in hushed conversation with young Dr Bell. Cecilia approached Lady Cranbrook, who was weeping, took her hand, and simply said, 'Charles is gone.'

Chapter Fourteen

'Antimony,' said Duncan Cameron, seated in his study by a brightly burning fire with his friend and colleague, James Clifton. 'A most unusual choice of poison.'

'Antimony, you say,' said Clifton, sipping his brandy. 'Never heard of it. This was the stuff that killed Charles Cranbrook?'

'Precisely,' said Cameron. 'As a chemist, I'm well acquainted with it. A brittle, bluish-white metal, highly caustic. When you mix the metal's oxide with cream of tartar, you produce tartar emetic, small, white crystals.' He stroked Smith, the orange cat lying on the sofa beside him, eliciting a purr. 'The autopsy performed on Cranbrook found traces of tartar emetic everywhere, in his mouth, throat, and stomach, but especially in the intestines.'

'Hmmph,' said Clifton, listening to the wind and rain outside the window. 'What does the poison do?'

'In extremely small doses,' said Cameron, 'say one or two grains, it has an emetic effect, inducing vomiting. Three grains can be used as a sedative, resulting in unconsciousness. Any larger dose is invariably fatal. A single grain administered to Smith, for example,' – he patted the cat on the head – 'and he'd be as dead as a doornail.' The cat leapt from the sofa, swishing its ringed tail in the face of the black Scottie dog curled at Cameron's feet. 'The doctor who conducted the autopsy,' continued Cameron, 'Joseph Payne, good man, concluded that Cranbrook ingested between thirty and forty grains, over *ten times* the lethal dose. It completely destroyed the poor fellow's digestive tract, turning his bowels to shredded pulp.'

'How ghastly.' Clifton rose from his chair and walked to the trolley to pour an inch of brandy. 'Do I presume,' he said as he returned to his chair by the fire, 'that the mother of the deceased has engaged your services in order to cast doubt on the finding that Cranbrook was murdered?'

'Presume nothing,' said Cameron. 'Establish the facts and follow where they lead you.'

'Yes, but according to the newspaper accounts, the inquest raised the possibility that Cranbrook took his own life. What, then, has the good lady hired you to do?'

'To identify her son's murderer,' said Cameron. 'The inquest chiefly concerned itself with the scandalous affair between Mrs Cranbrook and Dr Gully–'

'Ah, yes. The well-known practitioner of hydrotherapy.'

'And by all accounts rather carelessly reached the conclusion that Cranbrook was murdered, without identifying a suspect, and leaving open the possibility of suicide.'

'But certainly suicide is a plausible explanation.'

'While there are many men, Clifton,' said Cameron, uncrossing his long legs and leaning forward in his chair, 'who desire to end their lives, there are very few, if any, who desire to torture themselves in the process. I can assure you, my good fellow, that death by a massive dose of tartar emetic is torture of the most horrific kind, considering how many painless methods exist for self-annihilation.'

'O-ho!' said Clifton. 'I take your point. This should prove a fascinating case. How may I assist?'

'I intend to begin,' said Cameron, 'with a precise reconstruction of the twenty-four hours before Cranbrook's collapse. Meanwhile, I should like you to interview the witnesses questioned by Scotland Yard.'

'Very well,' said Clifton, tossing back the last of his brandy. 'I shall start in the morning.'

The following day, bright and sunny after the storms that had swept across southern England in the night, Duncan Cameron slipped on his bowler and departed from his flat on Beaufort Gardens in Knightsbridge. With his leather case under his arm, he walked to Pont Street and climbed aboard the omnibus for the short trip to Victoria Station. Seated in the swaying railway compartment, he reread his précis of the lengthy report of the coroner's inquest conducted two months following Charles Cranbrook's death, shaking his head at the coroner's court's obsessive preoccupation with the illicit love affair between Cecilia Cranbrook and Dr James Gully. Arriving at Balham Station, Cameron made his way to the Bedford Hotel, site of the inquest, and then walked to 21 Bedford Hill Road. 'Orwell Lodge,' he murmured as he studied the small house with its neatly tended flowerbeds and window-boxes. Noting the 'To Let' sign in the window, he slipped his watch from his fob pocket, checked the time, and began strolling at a leisurely pace in the direction of Tooting Bec Common, turning onto the gravel drive that led to a large, white, neo-gothic house, by far the most impressive in the vicinity. 'Ah' he said aloud. 'The Priory.' Again consulting his watch, he noted the elapsed time, four minutes thirty-eight seconds, and walked around to the stables behind the house. Finding the stalls empty and neatly swept, and observing that the curtains were drawn in all of the windows of the house, he moved furtively to the kitchen door, removed a tool from his pocket that resembled a penknife and quickly picked the lock.

The house was empty and dark, with slipcovers shrouding the furniture in the drawing-room.

With his shoes creaking on the bare parquet, Cameron moved to the entrance hall and ascended the staircase. He turned the knob and peered into the oak-panelled bedroom on the left, devoid of furnishings, and then went to the small bedroom near the top of the stairs. Quietly opening the door, he found the room as its deceased former occupant had left it; a single bed against the wall by a window, a bedside table with a lamp, a dresser, and two straight-back chairs. According to the testimony of the upstairs maid at the inquest, Cranbrook had staggered from the room in his nightshirt at approximately half past nine and then gone back inside where, moments later she and Mrs Clark had found him leaning out the window, vomiting. Pushing back the curtains, Cameron gazed out of the window, which looked down on the slate roof of the floor below. Closing the curtains, he studied the bed where Cranbrook had died, wondering why he was sleeping there rather than with his wife in the master bedroom. And why the other woman, Mrs Clark, was with the deceased's wife in the bedroom when Cranbrook fell ill. Though neither question had been answered during the inquest, he deduced that something was amiss between husband and wife.

Exiting the mansion, Cameron walked the short distance into town and, as it was only noon, stopped in at the Wheatsheaf, a public house opposite the railway station. Taking a seat at the bar, he ordered a half pint of the local bitter and glanced around the dimly lit room the tables of which were occupied by local regulars. 'I say,' said Cameron to the barman as he paddled the foam from Cameron's glass, 'I don't suppose any of your customers were employed by the late Mr Cranbrook at The Priory?'

Sliding the glass across the scarred oak counter, the barman gave Cameron a curious look and said, 'Well, there's MacDonald.' He nodded toward a table in the back where two men sat with their pints. 'Looked after the old boy's garden.' Everyone in town, Cameron surmised, had paid rapt attention to the massive publicity surrounding the case and would assume he was merely another reporter. 'Thanks,' he said, taking a swallow of beer and leaving a shilling on the bar. Walking to the table in the back with his glass, he said, 'It's MacDonald, isn't it?'

The former gardener looked up at the stranger and said, 'Why, yes.'

'Mind if I join you?' said Cameron pleasantly. 'I'm doing a story...'

'Quite all right,' said MacDonald, sliding over his chair. 'This here is my mate Willoughby.'

'My pleasure,' said Cameron. 'I understand you were employed at The Priory?'

''At's right. The gardener, until we was all let go. And looked after the stables.'

'The stables?' said Cameron. 'I thought this fellow Griffiths–'

'Griffiths was sacked,' said MacDonald with a trace of anger. 'By Mr Cranbrook, rest 'is soul.'

'When was this?'

'Oh, a month or so before the ... the, ah, incident.'

'I see. Did you happen to see Mr Cranbrook on

205

the day he fell ill?'

'I did indeed.' Pausing to take a swallow of beer, MacDonald said, "E came home early and insisted I saddle Cremorne, one of the 'orses.'

'Insisted?'

'Well, I thought it was wrong, as I'd already exercised 'im. But I did as told, and the gelding run off with 'im. All the way to Mitcham Common.' He jerked his thumb over his shoulder. 'And when he got back, 'e's as pale as a ghost and sweatin'. I supposed somethin' was wrong with 'im, but what do I know? I'm just the gardener.'

'He seemed unwell?' said Cameron.

'Oh, yes, sir. Sawyers told me 'e 'ad to carry 'im up the stairs.'

'Sawyers?'

'The butler.'

Cranbrook appeared to be ill, considered Cameron, when he returned from his ride, so ill that he had to be helped upstairs by the butler. Was it possible he'd already been poisoned? 'Well, thank you, my man,' said Cameron, rising from his chair. 'This has been quite useful.' He hurried from the tavern into the bright sunshine, arriving at the station just in time to make the 1.20 to Victoria. Thence he proceeded by omnibus to 87 Theobald's Road, the chambers at Gray's Inn Cranbrook had shared with his law partner, Edward Hope. Admitted by a secretary, Cameron found Hope at his desk in a small, tidy office with a view of the Inn's emerald courtyard. He was a pleasant-looking young man, with sandy blond hair, worn short in the current fashion, wearing a black frockcoat, polka-dot cravat,

206

and dove-grey waistcoat.

'How may I help you, sir,' said Hope somewhat eagerly, as his law practice had flagged since the demise of his partner.

'My name's Cameron. Duncan Cameron. My card.' He handed Hope an engraved calling card.

'Consulting detective,' said Hope as he studied the card.

'Yes. My services have been engaged by Lady Cranbrook.'

'Oh, I see,' said Hope with a startled expression. 'Please sit down.'

'Thank you.' Cameron sat in an armchair. 'Did you see Cranbrook,' he began, 'on the day preceding his death?'

'Why, yes,' said Hope. 'We lunched together at Charles's club. He came into the office that morning, complaining that he'd been ill.'

'This would have been...'

'Monday. He'd spent the previous night at his club. At Boodle's.'

'Where you had your luncheon?'

'No. Our luncheon was at White's.'

'I find it curious,' said Cameron, 'that Cranbrook would have dined at Boodle's.'

'How so?'

'Because members are required to dress for dinner.'

'Charlie kept evening wear at Boodle's, as he often took a room there for the night.'

'Was he at odds with any of the other members?' asked Cameron. 'Someone with a score to settle?'

'Of course not,' said Hope with a dismissive gesture. 'Charlie had no enemies. In any case, he mentioned that he'd been sick on his way to the office. But he was feeling better over our luncheon. In fact, I'd say he was fine.'

'After your luncheon,' said Cameron, 'did he return to work?'

'No. He said he was going to Balham, at something like half past two. It was the last time I ever saw him.'

'In your judgement, Mr Hope, was Cranbrook a contented man?'

'I would say so. He seemed happily married, and to a beautiful woman. In fact, he was extremely proud of the property in Balham. He continued to enjoy his other pastimes, playing chess and lawn tennis, for example.'

'Was he in any sort of trouble, financial difficulties, for example, that might explain his taking his life?'

'Why, no. It's quite unthinkable that Charles could have committed suicide.'

'I see.'

'He did mention, however,' said Hope, leaning closer to Cameron, 'that his stepfather was vexing him over some losses he'd incurred in the stock market.'

'But he was a wealthy man,' suggested Cameron.

'Charles?' said Hope with a short laugh. 'His stepfather is as rich as Croesus, as I'm sure you know, but Charlie had to work for a living. Law's a respectable profession, certainly, but not likely to make one rich.'

'Thank you very much,' said Cameron, rising. 'You've been very helpful.'

'Not at all,' said Hope, standing and reaching across the desk to shake his visitor's hand. As Cameron turned to go, Hope said, 'I say, Mr Cameron...'

'Yes?'

'Do you have any idea who might have done this?'

'None whatsoever.'

Returning to his flat on Beaufort Gardens, Cameron whistled an air as he gazed up at the bright green canopy of the plane trees. He advised his dour Scottish housekeeper that he desired a pot of Orange Pekoe, and then retired to his study with Angus, his Scottie. Tossing his jacket over the back of a chair, he sat at his desk with a fresh writing pad and sharpened pencil. The encounter with MacDonald at the pub had been fortuitous, he considered, and the interview with Cranbrook's partner Hope had yielded interesting details. Once his cup of tea, unsweetened and with milk, was at his elbow, he composed a succinct account of the day's findings: the distance from Gully's lodgings to The Priory, the arrangement of the upstairs bedrooms, the fact that Cranbrook slept in a separate room from his wife, that he spent the night before the crime at his club in town, complained of being ill in the morning, returned early to The Priory, where a riding incident left him shaken and unwell to the point that that he had to be helped upstairs by the butler, and that he'd sacked the stableman within a month before he was poisoned. And, Cameron considered after taking a sip of tea, that Cranbrook did *not* possess wealth and was distressed over losses in the stock market shortly before his death. Quite an interesting picture, he reflected, as he put his pencil aside and reached down to scratch the dog's ears.

Next morning, as Cameron did not expect Clifton's return from his travels until later in the day, he decided to pay a call on Detective Chief Inspector Cox at Scotland Yard. Donning a heather-mixture tweed cap and his ulster, as the day was cold with dense, swirling fog, Cameron travelled by hansom cab to Trafalgar Square, where he instructed the driver to turn on White-hall and again on Whitehall Place, arriving at 10.00 a.m. at the former medieval palace that housed the London Metropolitan Police. He was well acquainted with Scotland Yard, and vice-versa, though he had not previously met Chief Inspector Cox, a high-ranking official he suspected had been assigned to the case due to the elevated social station of both the deceased and his widow. The inspector was seated at his desk in a cramped second-floor office with a view of the courtyard when Cameron was shown in, his long coat draped over his arm.

'How do you do,' said Cameron, reaching out to take Cox's hand. 'I appreciate your seeing me.'

'The famous crime detective Duncan Cameron,' said Cox, fixing him in his gaze. 'To what do I owe this honour?'

'My services,' said Cameron as he sat in a chair facing the desk, 'have been engaged by Lady Cranbrook. I understand you oversaw the investigation into her son's death.'

'Correct,' said Cox. A large man, he had a prominent forehead and long side-whiskers that joined a walrus-like moustache. 'Unfortunate affair.'

'I was hoping,' said Cameron, casually crossing his leg over his knee, 'that you might share your findings with me.'

'I presume,' said Cox, resting his elbows on his cluttered desk, 'you've read the report of the coroner's inquest?'

'I have, though in my opinion it sheds very little light on the case.'

'I quite agree. One would have thought Dr Gully was on trial for adultery. My investigation revealed that Cranbrook was poisoned with tartar emetic, either by his own hand or by an assailant.'

'A rather odd choice of poison, wouldn't you agree?'

'Antimony?' said Cox. 'Highly lethal, at even the smallest doses, and readily available from a chemist.'

'Yes,' said Cameron, 'but quite difficult to administer. If mixed with food it has a highly noxious odour and taste, and if added to wine, it turns cloudy. It is, however, soluble in water, in which it is tasteless.'

'Well,' said Cox, drumming his fingers on the desktop, 'my men did a thorough search of the premises and failed to find a trace of the poison. As for the murder hypothesis, there was certainly ample opportunity, some seven or eight persons who had access to the deceased's person on or about the time of the alleged poisoning, but what's wanting is *motive*. Such a crime is obviously premeditated, carefully planned in advance.'

'Obviously.'

'I personally interviewed all the key witnesses and am convinced none of them had a motive for seeing Mr Cranbrook dead.'

'Not Dr Gully?' said Cameron, flicking a bit of ash from his sleeve.

'Oh, Gully was jealous, no doubt,' said Cox, leaning forward. 'But it is inconceivable to me that such a kindly old gentleman was in any way implicated. And, therefore,' he concluded in a self-satisfied way, 'we are left with the hypothesis of suicide. And here we have *evidence*.'

'I see.'

'First, the statement of Mrs Clark that Cranbrook confided he had poisoned himself, and second, the expert opinion of Dr Gill, who examined Cranbrook and questioned him in the hours following his poisoning.'

'Yes,' said Cameron, 'but according to the report, one of the other physicians challenged Mrs Clark's assertion.'

'That may be,' said Cox, spreading his large hands on his desk, 'but I repose great confidence in the opinion of Dr Gill, the leading medical doctor in the city who, after all, spared the prince consort from death by typhus. Doctor Gill is convinced Cranbrook poisoned himself, as Cranbrook expressed no surprise or shock when he was told he'd ingested a lethal dose of poison.'

'Well,' said Cameron, rising from his chair, 'it's apparent you've conducted the investigation with the usual thoroughness and professionalism of the Metropolitan Police. I'm much obliged to you for sharing your conclusions.' With a quick shake of the chief inspector's hand, Cameron turned and let himself out. Donning his coat and hat in the foyer, he walked the short distance from Whitehall Place to the Embankment in fog so thick he nearly collided with a nurse pushing a pram. Strolling beside the indistinct river with his hands clasped behind his back, Cameron reflected on his interview with the pompous police inspector who, in the usual fashion of Scotland Yard, had clumsily bungled the investigation, failing to interview key witnesses such as the doctors who'd attended the dying man, dismissing Gully as a suspect out of hand, and making no effort to identify others who might have had a motive. Nor, he considered as he stopped to listen to the boom of the foghorn of a ship gliding past on the water, to determine the origin of the poison used to murder Cranbrook. All in all, the circumstances surrounding the death of Charles Cranbrook were as murky as the London fog and as disagreeable as the stench of bilge emanating from the Thames. Approaching the ghostly silhouette of Waterloo Bridge, Cameron decided to duck into Gordon's Wine Bar for some toasted cheese and a glass of claret before returning to Beaufort Gardens and his much anticipated conversation with James Clifton.

Clifton's travels had taken him first by rail to Malvern for a scheduled appointment with Dr James Gully, thence to Oxfordshire to interview

Cecilia Cranbrook at her family's country estate, and lastly to Birmingham to meet Mrs Jane Clark at the home of her sister, returning on the afternoon express to London's Paddington Station. Clifton's arrival at Cameron's flat coincided with the Scottish housekeeper's serving tea, accompanied by squares of shortbread, still warm from the oven, strawberry jam, and cucumber sandwiches. Clifton, a large man with an appetite to match, greedily helped himself to a plate as Cameron lounged on the sofa in his study, casually spinning the empty chambers of a long-barrelled Colt .45 revolver.

'The Americans,' he said, 'have produced by far the finest sidearm. Not surprising, considering the frequency with which they resort to it.'

'Frightfully violent race, the Americans,' said Clifton, between bites of shortbread.

'My dear Clifton,' said Cameron, sitting upright and laying aside the revolver. 'Pray describe your interviews.'

Wiping crumbs from his lips with a napkin, Clifton said, 'I'll save the best for last. Let me begin with Mrs Cranbrook. A poor, miserable woman, though quite pretty, who couldn't control her tears, though I detected little fondness for her deceased husband. You see, Cameron' – Clifton paused for a sip of tea – 'the lady was entirely undone by the coroner's inquest and all that was written in the Press about her affair with Gully. She struck me as, well, almost indifferent to the fact that Cranbrook had been killed and without any notion as to why, or by whom, he'd been poisoned.'

'Go on,' said Cameron, sampling a square of shortbread.

'Mrs Clark, on the other hand,' said Clifton, 'was as cold as ice. Her statements to me matched almost precisely the testimony she gave at the inquest. How she found Cranbrook, her attempts to revive him with a mixture of hot water and mustard–'

'A mixture,' interrupted Cameron, 'widely used to induce vomiting. As a means of rescuing one from poisoning. Interesting.'

'Quite. Let me see.' He consulted his extensive handwritten notes. 'She confirms that she told Mrs Cranbrook and the doctors that she smelt chloroform on Cranbrook's breath, but insists Cranbrook admitted to poisoning himself. Says relations between the deceased and his wife were "cordial" and insists Gully no longer had anything to do with Cecilia. Bridles at the suggestion Cranbrook's death was anything other than suicide.'

'And the best?' said Cameron, reaching for a cucumber sandwich. 'You saved for last?'

'Do you mind?' said Clifton, taking the last of the shortbread. 'My interview with Dr Gully. A very impressive individual. Freely admits that he was in love with Cecilia, though he owns it was an error of judgement for a man his age. Extremely bitter about the sensational newspaper reportage of the affair. But here's the interesting bit. Gully is certain Cecilia was the victim of maltreatment at the hands of her husband, perhaps violence. Convinced that Cranbrook married her strictly for money.'

'Would you say,' said Cameron, reaching for his

215

teacup, 'that Gully, in love with the beautiful creature who is suffering at the hands of an abusive, avaricious husband, might have resorted to murder?'

'Perhaps. But even more intriguing, Cameron, is the fact that Gully maintained contact with Mrs Clark.'

Chapter Fifteen

Duncan Cameron sat at the round table in his dining alcove, the bay window of which looked out on the leafy esplanade of Beaufort Gardens, enjoying his customary breakfast of two eggs, boiled precisely for four and one-half minutes, crisp bacon, and dry toast. Reaching for the china pot, he poured a second cup of black coffee, Jamaican Blue Mountain, for which he'd acquired a fondness during his travels in the West Indies. He observed a man wearing a bowler hat glide past the window on a bicycle, followed after a moment by the large form of James Clifton with a thick parcel under his arm.

'Hallo, Cameron,' said Clifton upon entering the alcove after a few moments.

'I see you brought the newspapers,' said Cameron.

'Just as you specified,' said Clifton, taking the chair opposite and unwrapping the parcel. *The Times,* the *Evening Standard,* and *The Pictorial World,* all from the week of the coroner's inquest.'

The Scottish housekeeper, a small woman wearing an apron, with her grey hair in a bun, appeared, wordlessly placed a cup and saucer before Clifton, and poured him coffee.

'May I have a look?' said Cameron, reaching for one of the newspapers. Studying its columns, he said, 'Here's what the *Evening Standard* had to say about Cecilia: *She was a miserable woman, who indulged in a disgraceful connection.*'

'*The Times*,' said Clifton, folding over another newspaper, 'was even less kind. *She was an adulteress and an inebriate*,' he read aloud, '*selfish and self-willed, a bad daughter and worse wife*. The Press showed far more interest in her affair with Gully than the poisoning of her husband.'

'What is curious to me,' said Cameron as he thoughtfully nibbled a piece of toast, 'is not that the doctor had a love affair with one of his patients, a beautiful, highly impressionable young lady, but that he would have ended it. Neither was married?'

'Cecilia's first husband, from whom she inherited her fortune,' replied Clifton, 'died while still in his twenties, after the couple separated. Gully, on the other hand, is married. His wife, however, is quite elderly and reportedly confined to an insane asylum. He claims not to have seen her for thirty years. But surely, Cameron, you're not suggesting the affair was anything less than a gross indecency–'

'While it may be perfectly acceptable,' said Cameron equably, 'especially among the upper classes, for a married man to keep a mistress, it is unpardonable for a young woman, even an unmarried one, to engage in a dalliance with an older man. I have no doubt that it was Gully who enticed her into the relationship.'

'How so?'

'I've been reading his writings, published for the most part in medical journals. Besides advocating homeopathic medicine, Gully is an outspoken supporter of the rights of women. Argues they should be given the suffrage, for instance.'

'Good heavens.'

'And moreover, attributes the malady of hysteria, so prevalent among affluent, middle-aged women, to what he describes as a want of sexual gratification in their marriages.' At this, Clifton visibly reddened. 'Not quite an adherent of the free love movement,' concluded Cameron, 'but a believer that women, like men, should actually derive pleasure from sexual intercourse.'

'Cameron!' said Clifton with a look of exaggerated reproach. 'What about Mrs McNab?'

'Don't worry,' said Cameron. 'She's as deaf as a post. And so I return to my question. Why would Gully have ended the affair?'

'Well,' said Clifton, after taking a sip of coffee, 'he didn't say. He intimated that Mrs Clark exerted an increasingly strong influence over Cecilia. I detected that Gully distinctly disliked the woman. Perhaps she persuaded Cecilia to end the affair and marry Cranbrook.'

'And yet,' said Cameron, 'Gully had dealings with Mrs Clark shortly before Cranbrook was poisoned.'

'He made it plain,' said Clifton, 'that she approached him one morning at Balham railway

218

station to ask a favour: to procure medication for Mrs Cranbrook that might help her sleep. Says he obliged her with a solution composed chiefly of laurel water which he delivered, at Mrs Clark's instruction, to her lodger in Notting Hill.'

'Very well,' said Cameron, pushing back from the table. 'You are to seek out this lodger and ascertain what became of this so-called laurel water while I shall interview two very important witnesses neglected by the police: Miss Mary Ann Stokes and Dr Royes Bell.'

Cameron had little difficulty locating Miss Stokes, the former upstairs maid at The Priory, who had found another position in the vicinity and lived with her mother in a modest cottage in nearby Streatham. Arriving at the house at the hour of six on a pleasant summer evening, he rapped his knuckles on the door and, after a moment, was greeted by Mary Ann's mother, a thin woman of indeterminate age wearing a bonnet and shawl who, after hearing Cameron's explanation of the purpose of his visit, consented to the interview with her daughter in the parlour while she eavesdropped from the adjoining kitchen.

'How long,' began Cameron, once they were situated in the snug room with a pot of tea, 'were you employed in the Cranbrook residence?'

Speaking so softly that Cameron was obliged to lean forward, Mary Ann said, 'I was engaged by the missus directly after she moved into The Priory. Before she was married to Mr Cranbrook.'

'Were you treated well?'

'By the missus, you mean?' Cameron nodded.

219

'Yes, very well, though Mrs Clark could be a bit harsh.' Relaxing a bit, Mary Ann explained, 'Mrs Clark supervised the household. That is, until Mr Cranbrook come along.'

'Would you say they were happily married?' asked Cameron.

Mary Ann frowned and bit her lower lip. 'I suppose I may speak openly,' she said, 'as I'm no longer in service and in view of what happened.' Cameron nodded encouragingly. 'I've been engaged to a number of households,' she continued, 'and never have I witnessed such quarrelling. Mr Cranbrook was, well, very angry with the missus for the way she managed the household. Before the marriage we'd been a contented lot. But afterward, oh my. First it was Fanny, one of the parlourmaids, he got rid of, and then Rance, one of the gardeners. And next when he sacked Griffiths, well, what a scene!'

'Do you know if Mr Cranbrook physically harmed his wife?'

'He once struck her in the face,' said Mary Ann. 'Knocked her to the floor in the dining-room, or so I was told.'

'Did he threaten to sack the other servants?'

'Sawyers and the cook had a wager as to who would be next. Of course, it was only a matter of time before Mrs Clark was dismissed.'

'Do you know this?' asked Cameron.

'She wouldn't own up to it,' replied Mary Ann. 'But Sawyers overheard Mr Cranbrook telling her.'

'But she was very close to Mrs Cranbrook, was she not?'

'Oh, yes, sir, indeed. After she lost the baby, Mrs Clark–'

'Mrs Cranbrook had a miscarriage?'

'Yes,' said Mary Ann with a nod. 'And afterward Mrs Clark moved into her bedroom, and Mr Cranbrook took the spare room at the top of the stairs.'

'Did Mrs Clark share Mrs Cranbrook's bed?'

Mary Ann briefly looked down and then said, 'Yes, sir.'

'I've read your testimony before the coroner's inquest,' said Cameron. 'How you first observed Mr Cranbrook in distress, summoned Mrs Clark, and assisted her attempts to revive him.'

'Yes.'

'You were present with Mrs Clark in his room when he collapsed?' asked Cameron. Mary Ann nodded. 'Did he say anything to Mrs Clark to the effect that he had poisoned himself, instructing her not to tell his wife?'

'No. Never.'

'Might he have confided this to her when you went downstairs to fetch the water and mustard?'

'Impossible,' said Mary Ann emphatically. 'He was unconscious when I left the room, and unconscious when I returned. He never spoke a word after calling out for hot water, until the doctors arrived, that is.'

'Very, well,' said Cameron, rising from his chair. 'This has been most illuminating.'

The following day Cameron was obliged to wait for over an hour at Dr Bell's Harley Street clinic, as the surgeon was delayed in completing his rounds at St. Bart's. Anticipating the contingency, Cameron had brought along a copy of Trollope's *Phineas Finn,* which enabled him to ignore the curious assortment of Londoners, some heavily bandaged, crowded into the clinic's waiting-room. At length Dr Bell appeared, and learning that the detective was waiting to see him, immediately summoned Cameron to his small, window-less office, the walls of which were adorned with a number of diplomas and certificates.

'So you've been hired by Aunt Margaret,' said Royes Bell, gazing at the brief letter of introduction Cameron handed him. Cameron nodded. 'Charles,' said Bell, 'was not only my cousin but my good friend. What can I do to help you find his murderer?'

'The esteemed Dr Gill is convinced your cousin took his own life.'

'That's absurd,' said Bell. 'I was with Charles days before his death, and he was his usual chipper self, with everything to live for.'

'After you arrived at The Priory,' said Cameron, 'as I understand it, accompanied by Dr Johnson, did Cranbrook briefly regain consciousness?'

'Yes,' said Bell. 'Charlie recognized me and I put the question to him: "What have you swallowed?" "Laudanum", he said. He added that he'd taken it to relieve a toothache and may have swallowed some. Dr Johnson pressed him, but he insisted he'd taken nothing but laudanum.'

'Mrs Clark,' said Cameron, 'has testified that she informed Dr Johnson that Cranbrook confided to her that he'd poisoned himself–'

'A damnable lie–'

'Why should the woman have lied?'

'Obviously, to deflect suspicion from herself.'

'That's mere conjecture,' said Cameron. 'I'm interested in facts.'

'Well,' said Bell hotly, 'here's a fact for you. When Dr Harrison first arrived on the scene, Mrs Clark told him Charles had swallowed chloroform, that she'd smelt it on his breath. Never said a word about Charles having poisoned himself. When she later told Dr Johnson her tale, she insisted she'd informed Dr Harrison, who vehemently denied it. I heard all of this with my own ears, and it caused me to conduct my own investigation.'

'I see,' said Cameron calmly. 'And what did you discover?'

'A small quantity of chloroform on the mantelpiece, together with a half-empty vial of laudanum. I went to the kitchen and had the cook provide me with samples of what Charles had eaten and drunk at dinner – mutton, green beans, and some burgundy wine, no trace of anything suspicious.'

'So Cranbrook was feeling well enough to have dinner?'

'I was told,' said Bell, 'that he joined his wife and Mrs Clark for supper and then retired to bed, at which point he became violently ill.'

'I see,' said Cameron. 'And what else did you learn?'

'I interviewed all the staff, the butler, cook, maids, the gardener, all of whom stated they knew of no reason why Charles would poison himself, nor why anyone else should do so. And lastly, I questioned Cecilia.'

'And?'

'Cecilia feared that Charles had suffered a heart attack, that he'd been worried about "stocks and shares", something like that, but that Mrs Clark had told her his illness was the result of swallowing chloroform. I thereupon searched her bedroom and boudoir and found only a large number of homeopathic and patent medicines, rosewater, and the like.'

'Anything else?'

'I searched Mrs Clark's room as well as the stables and greenhouse and found no evidence of poison of any kind.'

'Very thorough, I must say,' said Cameron. 'If only the Metropolitan Police had been half so efficient.' He rose from his chair.

'Mr Cameron,' said Bell, seated behind his desk. 'I know of your reputation. Do you agree with me that Charles Cranbrook was murdered?'

'Yes,' said Cameron with a nod. 'I do.'

'Do you have a hypothesis?'

'Not yet,' said Cameron. 'But I'm beginning to believe there were a number of people who may have been happy to see him go.'

With the privacy afforded by the etched-glass partition separating their booth from the adjoining one, Duncan Cameron and James Clifton were satisfied they could speak freely in the upstairs salon at Wilton's, the fashionable St James's seafood restaurant. Waiting somewhat impatiently as the waiter de-boned and served their sautéed

Dover sole, Cameron sipped his wine and said, 'As you were saying, the rooms are within a block of Notting Hill.'

'Quite right,' said Clifton, tucking his napkin into his shirt collar. 'A shabby little house on Lancaster Street, divided into flats.' He paused to sample the sole.

'And the lodger?' said Cameron.

'There are several tenants. The lodger in question is a cove by the name of Harmsworth, a Yorkshireman with an accent so pronounced I could scarcely make him out. At all events, he confirmed that Gully delivered a bottle to him, with instructions that it was to be given to Mrs Clark.'

'Did he know Gully by name?'

'No, but when I described him, he said, "That's the chap".' Clifton paused to butter a crusty French roll and take a swallow of wine. 'But here's the interesting part,' he continued between bites. 'When I asked him if he knew what the bottle contained, he exclaimed, "Cor blimey!"'

'Shh,' said Cameron, leaning across the table.

'Sorry,' said Clifton in a low voice. "Poison", he said. "Are you sure?" I asked. "Poison", he repeated. "It said so on the label, with a skull and crossbones".'

'Hmm,' said Cameron, rubbing his chin. 'A laurel water mixture certainly would not have been labelled as poison.'

'Well, Cameron,' said Clifton proudly, 'I think we've cracked it. I say...' He flagged down a passing waiter. 'Would you pour us another glass?'

After the waiter had poured more wine,

Cameron said, 'Oh, you do?'

'It's simple, my good Cameron. Here you have Gully, consumed with jealousy, conspiring with Mrs Clark, who doubtless detests Cranbrook for his ill treatment of Cecilia. Gully, a physician, supplies her with poison, and *voilà!*'

'You're suggesting the little woman was capable of cold-blooded murder,' said Cameron, 'simply because she *disliked* her victim? And that the renowned Dr Gully would freely admit to a private detective that he met the woman and agreed to supply her with a suspicious substance, a fact which never surfaced in the police investigation or the inquest? And what became of the mysterious bottle Gully delivered to this Harmsworth fellow?'

'It seems to have disappeared,' said Clifton with a frown. 'Harmsworth says he never gave it to Mrs Clark, and it simply vanished.'

'Vanished,' repeated Cameron. 'Well, to sum up, this much we know: Cranbrook, a man with upper-class pretensions but no money of his own, marries an extremely wealthy young widow. He promptly sacks many of the household servants, much to his wife's chagrin, violent quarrels ensue, she suffers a miscarriage, Cranbrook is evicted from her bedroom, and his place is taken by Mrs Clark. Gully, allegedly at Mrs Clark's request, delivers a mysterious bottle to one of her lodgers. When Cranbrook collapses, Mrs Clark tells at least two credible witnesses that she believes he ingested chloroform. Later that night she tells one of the attending physicians that Cranbrook admitted to poisoning himself, an assertion vehemently denied by the first physician to arrive on the scene, and more importantly, by the upstairs maid, who was present in the room at the only time the admission could have been made.'

'Very perplexing,' said Clifton, dabbing at his chin with his napkin.

'And lastly,' said Cameron, 'when repeatedly questioned by the physicians after regaining consciousness, Cranbrook insisted that the only thing he'd swallowed was a bit of laudanum, a vial of which was found on the mantel.'

'Well, where does that leave us?'

'I'll warrant Mrs Clark was lying,' said Cameron, 'about Cranbrook admitting to poisoning himself. The question is why. Oh, and there's one other intriguing fact.' Cameron leaned across the table and lowered his voice. 'According to Mary Ann, the upstairs maid, Cranbrook informed Mrs Clark he intended to sack her, something she chose *not* to disclose to Cecilia.'

'Very curious,' said Clifton.

'If we're to get to the bottom of this,' said Cameron, 'we must have a more perfect understanding of the relationship between Cecilia and Mrs Clark, and why the affair between Gully and Cecilia came to an end. I intend to question them myself. Meanwhile, Clifton, I should like you to pay a visit to Balham and see what tidbits you can turn up.'

Chapter Sixteen

Several days passed before Duncan Cameron received a reply to the telegram he'd sent Sir Richard Henderson, requesting permission to interview his daughter Cecilia as a part of his investigation into the death of Charles Cranbrook *undertaken at the behest of Lady Cranbrook*. Henderson readily acceded to the request, though he cautioned that *Cecilia may be of little help, as she is in poor health,* inviting Cameron to come to Buscot Park and stay the night. In the meantime, Cameron dispatched James Clifton to Balham with instructions to mingle freely with the locals and keep his ear to the ground.

Departing from Paddington on the mid-morning train, Cameron gazed out on the sunlit late-summer countryside, admiring the honey-coloured stone cottages, the occasional manor house, the fields of blue and yellow wildflowers, and cattle, as Shakespeare described them, resting under the canopy of an ancient oak. For a while he read his Trollope, and then put the novel aside and turned to the volume he'd borrowed from the library of the Royal College of Physicians, detailing the prescribed uses of poisons in the treatment of certain ailments. Continuing to believe that antimony, or tartar emetic, was a very odd choice of poison with which to commit murder, Cameron was curious about who, in the course of lawful behaviour, might be possessed of it. The passage in the textbook devoted to anti-mony was extremely brief, describing its use to induce vomiting and as a sedative but cautioning that even a tiny overdose could lead to death. One final comment, however, caught Cameron's attention: 'In veterinary medicine, tartar emetic is sometimes used in worming horses and other large animals.' Closing the volume with a snap, he turned his gaze to the window, noting his reflection in the glass as the train slowed per-ceptibly at the approach to Swindon Station.

From the Cotswold village, Cameron travelled by rented carriage to the town of Faringdon, an hour's journey, and thence along a country lane bordered with hedgerows through splendid countryside to the elaborate stone gate that marked the entrance to Buscot Park, one of the finest country houses in Oxfordshire, if not all of England. Situated on a slight rise in the heart of 3000 acres of rolling parkland, the palatial eighteenth-century house had been designed by the noted architect James Darley and con-structed of native limestone in the Palladian style. Cameron counted seven chimneys on the steeply pitched slate roof as the carriage came to a halt on the gravel drive. A liveried footman unloaded Cameron's valise and then escorted him up the stairs where another servant led him to the drawing-room. Sir Richard Henderson rose from his chair as Cameron entered the richly appointed room, with eighteen-foot ceilings, elaborate mouldings, and walls painted pale blue. His tread creaking on the old parquet, Cameron approached Sir Richard with outstretched hand and said, 'Good day, sir. You have a magnificent home.'

'Thank you, Mr Cameron,' said Henderson with obvious pride. Though knighted, his fortune had been self-made in the mining industry and his pretensions were those of the *nouveau riche*. 'Shall we sit, or do you prefer to rest in your room after your travels?'

'Let's sit,' said Cameron agreeably, 'though a glass of water would be much appreciated.'

'Sawyers,' said Henderson, 'bring us water.' Turning back to Cameron, who sat in the chair beside him, he said, 'Terrible, this business about Charles Cranbrook. Dead at the age of thirty after only four months' marriage.'

'Do you believe he took his own life?' asked Cameron.

'Do you?'

'No.' Both men waited for the butler to serve glasses of water from a tray. 'Nor,' said Cameron after the butler retired, 'does my client, Lady Cranbrook.'

Henderson shook his head with a grimace. 'Well,' he said, 'I doubt Cecilia will be of much assistance to you. She's devastated after all she's endured.'

'Was there trouble in the marriage?' asked Cameron, after taking a sip of water.

Henderson hesitated for a moment and then said, 'Yes. Cecilia came home for a visit and seemed quite unhappy. Insisted she could not go back to Charles, which, of course, was out of the question.'

'When was this?'

'In midwinter. My God, the poor girl can't seem to find her place in a marriage. Virtually the same thing happened before, with Captain Castello.'

'What, if I may ask,' said Cameron, 'was the cause of Castello's premature death?'

'Drink,' said Henderson. 'Simple as that. Drank himself to death. This was after his estrangement from Cecilia. He left her a fortune, however, much to my surprise and, frankly, dismay.'

'Dismay?'

Henderson nodded and said, 'The inheritance of sizeable wealth by an eligible young woman can be a curse, attracting unscrupulous men like iron filings to a magnet.'

'Was Cranbrook such a man?'

'I'm not sure.'

'Father...'

Both men turned in their chairs to observe Cecilia, wearing a blue silk tea-gown and matching slippers, standing in the entrance to the room.

'Yes, dear?' said Henderson as both men rose from their chairs.

'Are you ready for me?'

'It would be best,' said Cameron in an aside to Cecilia's father, 'if I were to question her alone.'

'This gentleman,' said Henderson, 'is the private detective Duncan Cameron. I would suggest that you talk to him in the library.' Turning to Cameron, he added, 'Please let Sawyers know if you'd care for tea or something to eat.'

Cameron chose a comfortable leather armchair

231

facing Cecilia, seated on a sofa in the library, redolent of cigar smoke, and filled with book-cases of leather-bound volumes. She clutched a goblet filled with straw-coloured wine, not, sur-mised Cameron, her first of the afternoon. He briefly studied her delicate features, her large, sensual eyes and bow lips, her auburn hair in ringlets; pretty yet wan, with a forlorn expres-sion. The object of desire, he considered, of James Gully, of pathetic indifference to Captain Castello, and of greedy possession by Charles Cranbrook.

Taking a sip of wine, she said softly, 'Where shall we begin?'

'If I'm going to provide any consolation to my client,' replied Cameron, 'in understanding how Charles came to be poisoned, it's essential that you are entirely candid and forthcoming, even if I touch on matters that frankly are embarrassing to you.'

'All right,' said Cecilia with a nod.

'I'd like to begin with your relationship with Dr Gully.'

'If only I'd listened to him,' said Cecilia, sud-denly bursting into tears. Cameron merely looked at her, inviting her to explain. 'He warned me,' she said, wiping away her tears. 'Insisted Charles was only after my money and that marriage was fraught with risk.'

'I see,' said Cameron, holding her in his steady gaze.

'And yet it might have worked,' she continued as if anxious to unburden herself, 'but for the fact that I shared my secret with him. That I had been involved,' she explained, 'in a love affair with James.'

'With Dr Gully.'

'Why not admit it?' she asked, as much to herself as to Cameron. 'It's been spread across every newspaper in London. At all events, I chose to tell him, to afford him the option of ending the engagement, which he chose not to do. But then, within weeks of the wedding it seemed, he was consumed with jealousy. His mind was made up that I still loved James, and nothing I could say or do would alter it.'

'I'm curious,' said Cameron, 'why someone as proper and fastidious as Charles appeared to have been, would have married you, having learned of your affair with a much older married man?'

Cecilia reddened and then finished her wine in a gulp. 'Because,' she said, 'he wanted my money and my household and all its possessions.' She paused and then said, 'And also because he, too, had had an affair.'

'An illicit affair?'

'Yes, with some wench in Maidenhead. Even with a child. And so he said he'd forgive me, which of course was a lie.'

'Which would explain his cruelty.'

'Oh, yes. He was terribly cruel.'

'Striking you and dismissing the household staff?'

'Yes, he struck me in the face and sacked a number of the servants, and threatened to sack the rest.'

'Including Griffiths, the stableman?'

Cecilia nodded and said, 'I must say it made

me furious. Poor Griffiths' wife was expecting a baby. He was very bitter, but Charlie was unrelenting.'

'And what about Mrs Clark? Did he intend to give her notice?'

'What, Jane? Good heavens, no. I would never have allowed it.'

'Why would she have been any different?'

'Jane was no mere employee, sir. She is my dear friend and confidante.'

'Let me return to Dr Gully,' said Cameron. 'Did your affair with him come to an end before meeting Charles Cranbrook?'

'Yes.' Cecilia reached for a silver bell and rang it to summon the butler, who appeared after a moment. 'Bring me another glass of wine, Sawyers, if you please.'

'Why did you end the affair with Gully?' persisted Cameron. 'He'd left his lucrative practice in Malvern, after all, to move to Balham to be near you.'

'Because of scurrilous lies and innuendo spread by a man named Throckmorton and his sister about my relationship to the doctor. Throckmorton was my first husband's solicitor. It was terribly damaging to my reputation, and Jane thought it best I end the affair.'

'Did Mrs Clark dislike Dr Gully?' Cameron paused as the butler returned and served Cecilia another goblet of wine from a salver.

When she and Cameron were alone again, Cecilia said, 'Jane thought it unseemly that I was in love with a man of James's age. He resented her intrusion, but sadly, Jane was right.'

'And,' said Cameron, 'she arranged your introduction to Cranbrook?'

'Yes. Her late husband had been employed by Charles's stepfather in Jamaica.'

'Was there anything else,' said Cameron, 'that influenced your decision to part with Dr Gully?'

Cecilia hesitated and took a swallow of wine. 'No,' she said at length. 'Nothing.'

'I understand,' said Cameron, 'that shortly before your husband's death you suffered a miscarriage.' Cecilia nodded. 'And that afterward, Charles slept in the spare bedroom, where he died, and Mrs Clark shared your bedroom.'

'Yes,' said Cecilia. 'I needed dear Jane at my side.'

'Well,' said Cameron, rising from his chair, 'I very much appreciate your candour, and I'm terribly sorry for all that you've been through.'

'You're not going to ask me about the night Charles was stricken?'

'No.'

'I can't believe that he took his own life,' said Cecilia. 'Nor that anyone could have poisoned him. It must have been an accident.'

'Perhaps,' said Cameron. 'Good afternoon.'

The fact that Sawyers, the butler at Buscot Park, had accompanied Cecilia from The Priory had not escaped Cameron's notice. And so, on the pretext of locating the WC, he accosted Sawyers, portly and bald, and asked if he could describe Charles Cranbrook's condition on the evening before he collapsed.

'Pale and weak,' replied the butler. 'So weak he

had to be helped up the stairs.'

'Would you say he was ill?' enquired Cameron.

'Oh, yes, indeed, sir. Quite ill.'

'Not merely shaken by a ride on a runaway horse?'

'Oh, no, sir.'

'One last thing,' said Cameron. 'According to Mary Ann, the upstairs maid, you overheard Mr Cranbrook speaking privately to Mrs Clark, advising her he intended to give her notice.'

'That is correct.'

'Thank you, my good man,' said Cameron. He returned to the drawing-room where he found Sir Richard Henderson, whom he thanked profusely for his co-operation but informed him that he'd changed his mind and would not be staying for dinner. Departing by the same rented carriage, he reached Swindon before dark, spending the night in a roadside inn and departing on the first train in the morning for London.

A former officer in the Royal Navy, James Clifton was accustomed to spending his leisure hours in public houses, relaxing over a glass of ale or whisky in the company of other similar men. In the day and a half he'd spent in Balham, he'd whiled away hours in the Wheatsheaf opposite the railway station, as well as the village's other two pubs, the Rose and Crown and the Lambeth Arms. Though there had been no shortage of conversation about the celebrated Cranbrook case – everyone, it seemed, had a theory about who'd committed the crime and the motive – he'd thus far encountered no one who possessed any personal knowledge that might shed light on its solution. Seated at a scarred trestle table in the bar of the Rose and Crown, Clifton sipped his pint as the ruddy-faced man seated opposite him expounded his opinion: 'It was the doctor who done it,' he stated emphatically. 'Why, the old blighter's in love with this beautiful young thing, with all the money in the world, and then along comes this lad Cranbrook an' steals her away. Same old story, eh? Slips a bit of poison in his beer, and no one's the wiser.'

Clifton nodded amicably, having listened to dozens of variations on the same theme. He polished off his stout, bid the man good day, and made his way to the bar. 'You don't suppose,' he asked the barman, 'there's somewhere else in the village, apart from the public houses, where a man might go to slake his thirst at the end of the day?'

'Well, you might try the Bedford Hotel,' the man suggested. 'Some chaps prefer the lobby bar with its tiled floor and potted ferns, though I think it's a bit posh.'

'An excellent idea,' said Clifton with a smile. 'I'm much obliged.' He tossed a shilling on the counter and made his way out of the dim, smoky room into the sunlit late-summer evening. Clifton was aware that the Bedford Hotel, located in the centre of town, had been the site of the coroner's inquest. He seemed to recall a lithograph of the proceedings in the hotel ballroom in one of the pictorial newspapers. Entering the fusty lobby, he observed a bevelled glass door opposite the reception desk beneath a sign that said simply 'Bar'. It was just as the man at the Rose and Crown described it, a high-ceilinged room with a black and white tiled floor, large enamelled pots planted with ferns, and gas-lit chandeliers. 'Posh, indeed,' mumbled Clifton to himself as he surveyed the room. Walking up to the long bar, he sat in a cane-back stool and hitched a boot on the brass railing.

'Evening, guv'nor,' said the barman, a plump man with a striped apron and handlebar moustache. 'What'll it be?'

Briefly consulting his watch, Clifton ordered gin with quinine water, a beverage he'd acquired a taste for during his naval service on the Indian subcontinent. Glancing around the room, he counted three tables occupied by other middle-aged men, office workers as opposed to tradesmen, judging from their dress. The man returned with Clifton's drink and then resumed polishing the mahogany counter with a soft cloth. After finishing half his drink, Clifton struck up a conversation with him about the international cricket tournament then in progress, the New Zealand side having bested arch-rival Australia, and then turned to the subject of the Cranbrook coroner's inquest.

'Never in my life,' said the man, 'did I think we'd do so much business, but the lobby was crawling with newspapermen, and believe you me, they drink like fish, at all hours of the day and night.'

'Must have been some spectacle,' commented Clifton, as he thoughtfully sipped his gin. He was vaguely aware that several other men had entered the bar and taken seats at a table behind him. 'Do any of the principal witnesses patronize your establishment?'

'Oh, well, the famous ones, the doctor, for instance, and the severe little woman, I forget the name, are all gone away, but some of the others, you know the ones who worked at the place, come in from time to time.'

'I'm sure they've got a tale to tell,' suggested Clifton.

'Not that I know of,' said the barkeep. 'But I'm off on Wednesdays and Fridays. I heard tell from Higgins, the other barman, that this one fellow, don't know the name, claimed to have worked for Cranbrook and had some very harsh words about him.'

Finishing his drink, Clifton said, 'Oh really? Perhaps I'll drop by tomorrow and see your man Higgins.' Placing several coins on the counter, he slipped from his seat, walked past a nearby table, now empty, and into the hotel lobby. As it was a trifle too early for bed, and too late for the train into London, he decided to take a turn around the block in the cool night air. The dark sky was ringed with lavender as Clifton emerged from the hotel and began strolling the empty pavement. In the distance, a lamplighter stood on his ladder lighting the streetlights. Turning left at the corner, Clifton made his way in the dark shadows cast by buildings on both sides of the narrow street. Conscious of footsteps behind him, he quickened his pace. The footsteps grew louder, and Clifton stopped to look over his shoulder; a fatal error. A man lurking in a nearby doorway leapt out and brought down a cudgel on Clifton's skull with a sickening *thwack*. Clifton groaned loudly, his knees gave way and he crumpled to the ground.

Something of a comic sight, with a large bandage on the back of his head tied under his chin, James Clifton sat in a comfortable armchair in Duncan Cameron's study with his feet up on a stool, nursing a brandy and soda. 'You have no recollection of your assailant?' asked Cameron, holding the orange cat in his lap.

'None whatsoever,' replied Clifton. 'Never saw a thing. Heard something, footsteps, turned to have a look, and then, *smack* and I was out like a light.'

'Judging from the gash on your scalp,' said Cameron, 'he must have used something like this Irish shillelagh.' He held up a sturdy oak staff with a knob on the end and slapped it in his palm. 'Obviously had an accomplice, the man following behind you.' Clifton nodded sourly and took a swallow of his drink. 'What about the men in the bar of the hotel?' asked Cameron. 'Could you identify any of them?'

'Not really. The men I saw were sitting away off. I overheard some fellows at a table behind me, but by the time I left they had gone.'

'Presumably your assailants,' said Cameron. 'There must have been something in your conversation with the bartender that concerned them. Hence the knock on the head.'

'Or else it was merely a cutpurse bent on theft.'

'Except for the fact,' said Cameron, placing his shillelagh on a shelf, 'that you weren't robbed.

No, these men were intending to dissuade you from enquiring further into the singular clue you happened upon.'

'Yes,' agreed Clifton, 'the former servant at The Priory who spoke harshly of Cranbrook with the other barman. Man named Higgins.'

'Whom we shall interview in due course,' said Cameron, 'though it's unsurprising that a man who lost his position would hold a grudge against his employer.' He dropped the cat on the floor and then crossed his long legs. 'On the other hand,' Cameron continued, 'based on my visit to Cecilia Cranbrook, an intriguing picture is beginning to take form.'

'Do you mind?' said Clifton, holding up his empty glass.

'Not at all.' Cameron rose and quickly poured Clifton another brandy. 'What is most striking,' said Cameron as he handed Clifton his drink, 'is the fact that Cecilia was unaware that Cranbrook had advised Mrs Clark he intended to sack her. This is corroborated by two witnesses and yet it was never mentioned during the inquest. Had Cecilia known of Cranbrook's intentions, no doubt she would have been furious, leading to another violent row.'

'Yes,' said Clifton after taking a sip, 'but what's your point?'

'I can only think of one reason,' said Cameron, 'why Mrs Clark would have withheld this from Cecilia. That she intended to murder Cranbrook, and, unaware that Sawyers, the butler, had overheard Cranbrook declare his intention to dismiss her, she withheld the fact, which would otherwise reveal her motive for the crime.'

'Ah,' said Clifton. 'How astute.'

'But I believe she had another, more compelling motive for murder than the mere prospect of losing her position.'

'Pray go on.'

'That of the jealous lover,' said Cameron.

'I'm afraid you've lost me,' said Clifton. 'Jealous lover? Gully, you mean?'

'No. Jane Clark.'

'Lover?' repeated Clifton with a befuddled expression. 'Lover of whom?'

'Why, of Cecilia. I believe it's plausible they were lovers.'

'But two women? How could they possibly...?'

'You're aware of homosexuality between men?' asked Cameron.

'Of course,' said Clifton, reddening. 'In the navy it's referred to as buggery. Punishable by death, or was. But...'

'Well, I'm sorry to shock you, Clifton, but homosexual relations have occurred between women since the days of the ancient Greeks.'

'Good heavens.'

'Here we know for a fact that Mrs Clark was sharing Cecilia's bed. We also know that Cecilia is a sensual, nay promiscuous, young woman. I detected a quite strong emotional attachment, one might even say love, that Cecilia felt for Mrs Clark, whom she refers to as Jane or Janie.' Cameron rose from his chair and began to pace. 'Mrs Clark, Cecilia's lover, observes her cruel mistreatment at the hands of her husband. For his part, Cranbrook, having no money of his own

242

but great pretensions to wealth, would never consent to ending the marriage, or even to a legal separation. Cecilia is trapped. Mrs Clark, a very shrewd woman, resolves to poison him, but must take great care to conceal the fact that Cranbrook intends to sack her, which of course would cast suspicion on her.'

'With poison supplied to her lodger by the old sod Gully,' interjected Clifton.

'And then,' continued Cameron, 'as Cranbrook lies dying, Mrs Clark appears to come to his rescue and contrives this cock-and-bull tale about Cranbrook admitting privately to her that he poisoned himself. *Don't tell Cecilia*. Hah!'

'Brilliant.'

'But now,' concluded Cameron, 'we must connect the little lady to the poison.'

Chapter Seventeen

'I find it implausible,' said Cameron over breakfast, 'that Mrs Clark, on whom suspicion now squarely rests, should have deliberately chosen antimony with which to poison Cranbrook.' They were seated under a vine-entangled pergola in the small garden at the back of Cameron's flat, enclosed by high brick walls covered with pink climbing roses.

Spreading a slice of toast with marmalade, Clifton said, 'I'm not sure I understand what you mean.'

'She would have chosen a more conventional poison,' explained Cameron, 'less difficult to administer, like arsenic, easily combined with food or drink. I suspect she happened upon antimony in the possession of someone else, who presumably had a legitimate use for it.'

'Such as?' said Clifton between mouthfuls of toast.

'The worming of horses, for example,' said Cameron, as he carefully snipped off the end of his soft-boiled egg.

'Curious,' said Clifton as he poured himself more tea. 'Worming of horses.'

'Correct. I should like you to call on all the chemists in the vicinity of Balham and endeavour to ascertain to whom antimony, or tartar emetic, may have been sold for veterinary purposes.'

'Very well.'

'And, as you appear to have recovered from that knock on the head,' said Cameron, 'return to the bar at the hotel and question the other bartender. In the meantime, I intend to travel to Malvern to call on the renowned Dr Gully, an interview I am quite looking forward to.'

Wearing a bowler hat to conceal the bandage on the back of his skull, James Clifton boarded the 4.10 at Victoria, having wired ahead for a room at the Bedford Hotel in Balham. Earlier in the day he'd spent an hour at the public library copying down the names and addresses of all chemists in the area of Balham and Streatham listed in the Directory of Services for Metropolitan London. Arriving at the station during a passing rain shower, he popped open his umbrella and walked the few streets to the hotel, suppressing the urge to glance over his shoulder to see if someone suspicious was following him. He arrived at the hotel at a quarter past five, finding the lobby bar empty except for the barman, a tall, thin man with ginger side-whiskers.

'You must be Higgins,' said Clifton as he pulled up a stool at the bar.

'That's right,' said the bartender with a curious look. 'Do I know you?'

'Clifton's the name. I was here the other evening chatting with your colleague. He happened to mention that you possessed some information concerning one of the former servants at The Priory.'

'Oh, he did, did he?' Higgins ceased polishing a glass and placed it on the shelf behind the bar.

'Yes. A man who'd worked for Charles Cranbrook and had harsh words for him.'

'And what's your angle, mister? Another copper, or newspaperman?'

'I say, Mr Higgins, why don't you bring me a Scotch, and I'd be happy to explain.' Once he had his drink before him, Clifton, with a genial smile, said, 'I'm an assistant to the crime detective Duncan Cameron. Perhaps you've heard of him.' Higgins gave Clifton a sceptical look. 'At all events, we're investigating the, ah, death of Mr Cranbrook. Now what was it, exactly, that this chap had to say about Cranbrook?'

'Well,' said Higgins after a moment, 'one of the men who worked at The Priory was a regular customer of mine.'

245

'Was?'

'I 'aven't laid eyes on him for months. He stopped in one evening, sat by himself at the bar, brooding-like. Had three or more pints. And here's the thing.' Higgins excused himself to wait on two men at the other end of the long bar. Returning to Clifton, he said, 'Mr MacIntosh, the owner of the hotel, dropped by and casually happened to mention Cranbrook – the deceased – by name. Well, this cove perked up and said, "Cranbrook?" I nodded, and he said, "That bloody whore's son." I remember it very well, as the gent turned suddenly so angry.'

'I see,' said Clifton, sipping his drink.

'I said to the bloke, "What about Cranbrook?", something along that line, and he says, "He'll get what's comin' to him. His days are numbered".'

'Those were his exact words?' asked Clifton.

'I would swear on it,' said Higgins. 'I was shocked, actually, but he explained he'd just been sacked by Cranbrook and his wife was expecting a baby. And then he said, and I quote: "I wouldn't want to be in Cranbrook's shoes. He'll be dead within months."'

'Good heavens,' said Clifton. 'Did you report this to the police?'

'They never asked me. Mr MacIntosh said I should keep my mouth shut, and I do as told. But as you enquired...'

'When did this conversation occur?'

'Let me see,' said Higgins, scratching his chin. 'It would have been in February.'

'A final question,' said Clifton. 'Do you recall the gentleman's name?'

'Hmm,' said Higgins, screwing up his face. 'He may have looked after Cranbrook's horses. Oh, yes. Griffiths. George Griffiths. That's the name.'

The late summer day was warm and sunny, and the Malvern Hills were pale blue and ringed with cottony cloud when Duncan Cameron's carriage arrived at the hydro from the railway station. Cameron stood for a moment gazing at the impressive, redbrick Tudor mansion, incongruously connected by the covered bridge to the more conventional Victorian house. Walking up the flagstones to the entrance, he gave the bronze knocker a sharp rap. To the tall, prim woman who answered the door he said, Yes, the doctor was expecting him, as he'd wired ahead. Observing the mostly frumpy women in their plain cotton shifts as he passed through the building, he politely thanked his escort and strode into a large, pleasant office with a view of the rose garden where Dr Gully was awaiting him at his desk.

'Come in, come in,' said Gully cheerfully, rising from his chair and reaching across the desk to shake his visitor's hand. 'The celebrated Mr Cameron.'

'The pleasure is mine, sir,' said Cameron.

'Let's sit,' suggested Gully, walking around his desk.

Cameron chose an armchair facing Gully and began the interview by asking a few knowledgeable questions about the water treatment based on his extensive reading of Gully's writings. 'It would appear,' Cameron observed, 'that business is thriving at the clinic.'

'Business is well enough,' said Gully. 'Most of my patients are firm believers in the salubrious effects of hydrotherapy and consequently are indifferent to the libels that were heaped upon me in the Press.'

'It is true, however,' said Cameron mildly, 'that you were engaged in a love affair with Miss Henderson.'

'I don't deny it,' replied Gully. 'I remain very much in love with her, poor child, though I fear her mind is shattered.'

'Judging from my recent interview at her family estate in Oxfordshire,' said Cameron, 'I would agree that her condition is very fragile. I wonder if you might explain how your affair came to an end?'

'As you are in the employ of Lady Cranbrook,' said Gully, 'and considering your distinguished reputation, I shall be entirely frank. My relationship with Cecilia was exposed by an unscrupulous solicitor and his sister in the most dishonourable fashion, resulting in threats of suits and counter-suits and maltreatment of Cecilia by her village neighbours. Under the circumstances we mutually agreed it would be best if we ceased seeing one another.'

'Would you say that Cecilia was influenced in this decision by Mrs Jane Clark?'

'I would say that she was influenced by Mrs Clark in virtually all decisions.'

'Including her decision to wed Mr Cranbrook?'

'Especially in that disastrous decision. It was Mrs Clark, after all, who made the introduction.'

'Did you dislike Charles Cranbrook?'

'I never met the man,' said Gully with a frown. 'But from everything Cecilia told me about him, and what I've since learned, I considered him a scoundrel.'

'Did you counsel Cecilia that marrying Cranbrook would be a mistake?'

'I most certainly did,' replied Gully. 'It was obvious to me that he was marrying her for her money.'

'Obvious?'

'To someone of my professional experience,' said Gully with a trace of asperity. 'Cranbrook is the stepson of a man of great wealth, travelling in the circle of privilege at the gentlemen's clubs, yet forced to eke out a living as a barrister.'

'I see,' said Cameron. 'Cecilia stated to me that she informed Cranbrook of her affair with you to afford him the opportunity to terminate the engagement.'

'Yes,' said Gully with a nod. 'She sought my advice on the matter. I urged her not to marry the cad but, if she was determined to do so, to share her secret with him, considering the probability that he would learn of it from other sources.'

'And he nevertheless decided to go forward with the wedding.' Gully again nodded glumly. 'Do you know why?' asked Cameron.

For a moment Gully stared into Cameron's expressionless eyes, suspecting that his interrogator knew the answer to his own question. 'Yes,' said Gully, 'I believe I do. There was the money, Cecilia's large fortune, of course, though she made legal arrangements to protect herself to the extent possible. But there was also the matter of Cranbrook's own, shall we say, indiscretion.'

'That he too,' said Cameron, 'had been involved in an illicit affair.'

'Yes,' said Gully. 'Cecilia told me that Cranbrook was willing to forgive her as he had been guilty of the same sin.'

'Do you know the identity of the other woman?'

'No,' said Gully. 'Nor, I believe, does Cecilia. It was merely something in Cranbrook's hazy past.'

'You mentioned that Cecilia was strongly influenced by Mrs Clark,' said Cameron. 'Did you dislike Mrs Clark?'

'Mrs Clark struck me as a cold, hard woman,' replied Gully, 'though there's no doubt she served Cecilia faithfully. I would say that Mrs Clark disliked *me*.'

'Why, then,' said Cameron, 'would you have had dealings with Mrs Clark in the weeks before Cranbrook's poisoning?'

'Oh, the matter I mentioned to your colleague?' said Gully. 'Mrs Clark's request that I provide her with something to help Cecilia sleep?'

'Yes.'

'It seemed a reasonable request, and I complied as a favour to Cecilia, providing her with an innocuous mixture of laurel water and spearmint, which has a soothing effect on the mind.'

'Doesn't it strike you as odd,' said Cameron, 'that you were instructed to deliver this admixture to Mrs Clark's lodger in Notting Hill?'

'I presumed it was for her convenience.'

'It strikes me as singularly inconvenient,' rejoined Cameron, 'as you were a mere five-minutes' walk from Mrs Clark at The Priory. What would you say, Dr Gully, if I were to tell you that Mrs Clark's lodger, a man named Harmsworth, says that the bottle you delivered to him was labelled poison?'

'What?' said Gully, jumping up from his chair. 'That the man's lying! Do you suppose,' he said in a heated tone, wagging a forefinger at Cameron, 'I would have volunteered this information to your colleague if I had a hand in Cranbrook's poisoning?'

'He insists the bottle was labelled poison,' said Cameron evenly. 'Though the bottle has disappeared.'

'Balderdash,' said Gully.

'Can you think of a reason why Mrs Clark might have wanted to murder Cranbrook?' asked Cameron, standing up to look Gully in the eye.

'Cranbrook was of a type,' Gully replied, 'I have seen all too often in my practice. A man who regards his wife as his property, capable of brutal mistreatment. Mrs Clark no doubt witnessed Cecilia's suffering at the hands of Cranbrook. But would this have led her to murder him? I couldn't possibly say.'

'Unless,' suggested Cameron, 'there was the added element of jealousy.' Gully's eyes narrowed. 'Do you suppose,' said Cameron, 'Mrs Clark was in love with Cecilia?'

Gully considered. 'That possibility,' he said, 'has never occurred to me. But Cecilia is a passionate, sensual young woman who'd been awakened to the pleasures of the flesh. But Mrs Clark... I must say, it's an intriguing hypothesis.'

251

Slipping his watch from his pocket, Cameron checked the hour and said, 'You've been very generous with your time, Doctor, and I appreciate your candour.'

'Very well,' said Gully. 'But you must understand that as much as I loathed Charles Cranbrook, I had nothing whatsoever to do with his death.'

Tedious business, considered James Clifton as he trudged along the village pavement, having completed his third interview of the day with a chemist in Streatham. Like the first two, the proprietor maintained records dating back at least a year of all sales of poisonous compounds as required by law. There were only a few instances of the sale of tartar emetic, in each case to a physician with a medical practice in the vicinity. Traversing the green fields and woods of Tooting Bec Common, Clifton decided to reward his exertions with a stop at the Rose and Crown for a pint of the local bitter and a ploughman's. After lunch and a friendly chat with the local patrons, several of whom he remembered from his previous visit, Clifton consulted his notes, looking up the address of the Pickford Apothecary at 17 Elmfield Road, the fourth of five such establishments listed in the directory. After a five-minute stroll, Clifton peered through the half-curtained windows and let himself in. Mr Pickford, the pharmacist, a tall, slender man wearing spectacles and a white coat, stood at the counter with a mortar and pestle. On the shelves behind him was a neat array of jars and bottles of varying colours and sizes, and the small anteroom was redolent of carbolic acid.

'Good afternoon, sir,' said Pickford, looking at Clifton over the rims of his spectacles.

'Howd'ya do,' said Clifton as he approached the counter.

'Toothache?' said Pickford. 'I might suggest laudanum.'

'No, no,' said Clifton agreeably. 'The teeth are just fine, though I'll admit to sore feet what with all the walking. I'm looking for information rather than medicine.'

'I see. What sort of information?'

Clifton produced an engraved card and slid it across the counter. 'We're engaged in an investigation,' he said, with the air of someone sharing a secret.

'Oh, I see,' said Pickford, holding the card up to his face. 'And how may I help you?'

'You maintain records, I presume, of the sale of poisons?'

'I do indeed,' said the chemist. 'A requirement of my licence.' He nodded toward the framed certificate on the wall with its elaborate script and blue seal.

'Over what period of time,' said Clifton, 'do these records exist?'

'As the law requires, the current calendar year and the year preceding.'

'Excellent,' said Clifton. Lowering his voice, he said, 'We – Mr Cameron and I – are interested in knowing to whom you may have dispensed antimony, or tartar emetic, during the twelve months preceding April of this year.'

Pickford rubbed his chin. 'Tartar emetic,' he repeated. 'Rarely dispensed, very rarely. I daresay most physicians aren't familiar with it.'

'What about for veterinary uses?'

'I can't say. Let me consult my records.' Pickford disappeared into a back office from which he returned after several minutes. 'Let me see,' he said, opening a notebook on the counter and running a finger down a line of neat entries, recording the names of the toxic substances, the dates, and the identities of the purchasers. 'Here we are,' he said, looking up. 'Five grams of tartar emetic sold to Dr Davis Witherspoon on 6 June 1871.'

'I see,' said Clifton. 'Any others?' He imagined his query would end in the same result as the preceding three.

'Aha,' said Pickford, turning the page. 'Here's another. Ten grams dispensed to Dr Panghurst at St Luke's Clinic on October 22nd of last year.'

'Is that all?' asked Clifton a bit impatiently.

'I seem to remember another,' said Pickford, 'as it's such an unusual request, frightfully toxic, you know.' Turning another page, he said, 'Yes. Here it is.' He tapped a finger on the page. 'Ten grams of tartar emetic dispensed on 12 December, 1871, to one George Griffiths.'

'What?' said Clifton with a startled expression. 'Griffiths, you say?'

'That's right,' said the chemist. 'With the notation "for veterinary use".'

Seldom in their five-year association had Duncan Cameron seen James Clifton in a state of such

254

excited animation. 'We've cracked this one, Cameron,' said Clifton, smacking a fist into his palm. 'No doubt about it.' Both men were seated in leather club chairs in a quiet corner of the walnut-panelled bar at the Cavendish, Cameron's club in Mayfair.

'Something to drink, gentlemen?' asked the porter at Cameron's elbow.

'A whisky and soda, if you please,' said Cameron.

'Gin and Angostura,' stipulated Clifton. After the man returned with their drinks and withdrew, Clifton's normally expressionless dark eyes shone with excitement. 'The bartender at the Bedford Hotel,' he began as Cameron listened with rapt attention, 'had a vivid recollection of the encounter. The casual mention of Cranbrook's name by the hotel's proprietor prompted an angry outburst, too profane to be repeated in the confines of your club.'

'I see,' said Cameron, sipping his whisky.

'The man explains that Cranbrook sacked him just as his wife is about to deliver a child and goes on to say, "His days are numbered. I wouldn't want to be in his shoes. He'll be dead within months".'

'He is certain?'

'Insists he would swear to it. And lastly, he identified the man as George Griffiths, the stableman at The Priory.'

'Whose dismissal,' said Cameron, 'according to Mary Ann, caused a violent row between Cranbrook and Cecilia.'

'But there's more,' said Clifton in a conspiratorial tone. Inclining his head toward Cameron, he said, 'I interviewed all five chemists in the vicinity of Balham and Streatham, who, as required by law, maintain records of the sale of all poisons. As you might imagine, there were very few of antimony or tartar emetic. In all but one instance, they were to local physicians.' Clifton paused to take a sip of his drink. 'However,' he added importantly, 'a chemist in Balham by the name of Pickford sold ten grams of tartar emetic with the notation "for veterinary use", and the buyer was one George Griffiths.'

Cameron eyed him impassively and asked, 'When did this sale occur?'

'December of last year,' said Clifton. 'The twelfth of December.'

'And when did the barman's conversation with Griffiths take place?'

'In February.' Cameron sat silently, staring into the distance. 'Well?' said Clifton. 'I say, old boy, surely you'd agree we've cracked the case.'

'Griffiths,' said Cameron, thoughtfully stroking his chin. 'The worming of horses. I'll grant you this, Clifton, we may not know the identity of Cranbrook's murderer, but we now know the source of the poison that was used to kill him.'

Clifton gaped at Cameron, unable to think of a word to say, the wind having gone completely out of his once billowing sails.

Chapter Eighteen

Duncan Cameron stared out the bay window at the rain falling in dull grey sheets. He'd waited impatiently for most of the day for a reply to his telegram to the police constable in Balham, which he now held in his hand. George Griffiths was, in fact, well known to the constabulary, with several arrests for public intoxication and a conviction for battery that earned him thirty days in the Balham lock-up. But more importantly, the message concluded: SUBJECT NOW BELIEVED TO BE IN CROYDON. Folding the paper in his pocket, Cameron walked to the desk in his study and removed his Colt .45 from the lower right-hand drawer. After loading it, he slipped it into a holster concealed under his jacket, and then donned his coat and hat, took his umbrella from the stand, and headed out in the rain.

Croydon, a fashionable middle class suburb, was accessible by train from Victoria Station and hence it was late afternoon when Cameron arrived at the station in the centre of town. Griffiths, he reasoned, dismissed from his previous position and with an arrest record, would have difficulty securing employment at a private residence, nor were there many residents of the town wealthy enough to keep their own stables. Enquiring at the railway station, he learned that there were two public livery stables nearby, and it was at the second of these, McDougal's on the Pitlake Road, where Griffiths had been recently employed until dismissed for brawling. 'Considering the time of day,' said the proprietor, 'you'll likely as not find 'im at the public house down the road.' Cameron entered the establishment, with a sign depicting a golden calf over the door, at the hour of seven, hung his coat and dripping hat on the stand and made his way past tables packed with local tradesmen to a cramped space at the end of the bar, as all seats were taken. 'A gill of whisky, if you please,' he said to the barman. Once his drink was in hand, he surveyed the dim, smoky room, filled with the clamour of conversation, observing a small, separate parlour at the rear. After a time, he ordered a second drink, and when the barman slid it across the counter casually said, 'Do you happen to know a man named George Griffiths?'

'Aye,' said the barman, a fellow Scot. 'I do.'

'A regular customer?'

'Aye.'

Fishing in his pocket for change, Cameron slid two coins across the scarred surface and said, 'I don't suppose you could point him out to me?'

Jerking a thumb over his shoulder, the barman smiled and said, 'In the back room, tall fellow with a black beard wearing a wool cap.'

'Thank you, my good man,' said Cameron. Taking his drink he made his way to the low-ceilinged parlour warmed by lumps of coal glowing on an open grate. Two men drinking pints of stout were seated at a table in the corner, one

258

with a black beard wearing a wool cap and the other an exceptionally large man with ill-fitting clothes. Cameron briefly studied the man with the cap, who was handsome in a rakish way, and then walked up and said, 'You're George Griffiths.'

'What's it to you?' he said with a scowl.

'I need a word with you.'

'Bugger off,' said the large man. 'Can't you see we're occupied?'

'It's about the Cranbrook murder,' said Cameron quietly. Both men eyed him warily. Taking an empty chair from a nearby table, Cameron sat down. He took a sip of Scotch and said, 'My name's Cameron. I'm a detective, and I've been hired to investigate the case on behalf of the victim's family–'

'Listen here, mister,' said Griffiths in a low voice. 'I know nothing about it, apart from what I read in the papers. You're wasting your time.'

'My associate was in Balham last week,' said Cameron in a conversational tone, 'having a drink at the Bedford Hotel. Later, while taking a turn in the night air, someone gave him a nasty blow on the back of the head. Might have killed him.' A smile curled the lips of the large man. 'I suspect it was you, Griffiths,' said Cameron, looking him in the eye. 'Trying to stop him from gathering some interesting information from the barman.'

'Sod off, mister,' said Griffiths. 'I've half a mind–'

'Perhaps we should discuss this outside,' suggested Cameron, believing that both men had been drinking for hours and that their reflexes would thus be impaired.

'A capital idea,' said the large man, rubbing his hands. Exiting through a side door, the three men found themselves in a narrow, dark alleyway, with rain dripping from the eaves. Cameron stood with his back to the wall, facing Griffiths and his confederate, who suddenly pulled a short club from his pocket and clumsily lunged at Cameron. Easily sidestepping him, Cameron drew the revolver from his holster, cocked the hammer with an audible *click* and trained it on his would-be assailant.

'I wouldn't, if I were you,' said Cameron. 'Now, drop the billies and put your hands over your heads.' After both men complied, Cameron waved the long barrel of the Colt at Griffiths and said, 'The poison used to murder Cranbrook has been traced to a packet you purchased at the Pickford Apothecary last December.'

The terror in Griffiths' eyes was discernible even in the darkness. 'It wasn't me,' he said hoarsely. 'I swear it...'

'And what's more,' said Cameron, 'the bartender at the Bedford Hotel swears you threatened to kill Cranbrook shortly after he dismissed you from your position as stableman at The Priory. Unless you co-operate with me, Griffiths, you'll be in hot water, very hot indeed, with Scotland Yard.'

Griffiths swallowed hard and then said, 'All right. What do you want me to do?'

'Let's go back inside,' said Cameron, 'and have a little chat by the fire, as though nothing happened.'

Cameron chose a quiet table in the parlour at

the back of the pub, seated alone with Griffiths, whose companion had wisely retreated to the bar in the main room. 'All right,' said Cameron. 'Let's begin with your purchase of the tartar emetic in December.'

'Well,' said Griffiths, holding a fresh pint of stout in both hands, 'I knew it was poison, but I bought it to use on the horses–'

'To worm them,' interjected Cameron.

'That's right,' said Griffiths with a look of surprise. 'Just a few grains mixed in their water does the trick.'

'Where did you keep it?'

'In a cabinet in the stables.'

'Under lock and key?' asked Cameron.

'No, but with a notice that says "danger – deadly poison".'

'You bought the poison in December,' said Cameron. 'Ten grams, a small packet.' Griffiths nodded a little drunkenly. 'And you were sacked by Cranbrook in February, forced to move out of the coach-house, is that right?'

'Right,' muttered Griffiths. 'The effing sod; my wife was almost due.'

'Was anyone else, so far as you know, aware of the packet of poison in the stables?'

Griffiths shook his head and said, 'No one.'

'But after you were sacked,' said Cameron, 'the poison remained where you left it?' Griffiths nodded. 'And so anyone might have come across it by chance,' suggested Cameron. Griffiths nodded again. 'Did you complain of your ill-treatment by Cranbrook to Mrs Clark?' asked Cameron.

'Mrs Clark? No. Never said a word to her. But I told the missus Mr Cranbrook had blamed me for wrecking the coach – it warn't my fault, I assure you – and had give me notice, but it was to no avail – he bein' such a hard man.'

'You never mentioned to Mrs Clark,' said Cameron, 'that you kept poison in the stables?'

'Of course not. Why should I?'

'After leaving The Priory,' said Cameron, 'you moved here with your wife and child?'

'The wife took the baby and moved in with her mother in Lambeth,' said Griffiths, staring into his glass.

'I see. Well, Griffiths, considering the facts, you remain under suspicion.'

'I had nothing to do with it, I swear it.' Griffiths wiped perspiration from his brow and said, 'I'll grant you it didn't grieve me to hear he was a goner, but how was I to get into that house un-noticed, what with all the people about? It was an inside job, no doubt of it.'

'Perhaps,' said Cameron. Abruptly rising from the table, he said, 'Good evening, Griffiths,' and walked quickly from the room.

Having spent the night at a local inn, Cameron took the early train, filled with junior clerks wearing inexpensive business suits and bowler hats commuting into the City, arriving at his flat before ten. After bathing and changing into fresh clothes, he downed a quick cup of tea and a currant scone and ventured out on a long, solitary walk. After the previous day's rain, a heavy fog had settled over the metropolis, obscuring the passing carriages and omnibuses, visible only by their ghostly coach-lamps. He strolled along the pavement, turning at the corner on Walton Street. There was a limit, Cameron knew from long experience, to the powers of deductive reasoning; notwithstanding the most careful examination of the known facts, the solution to the puzzle often lay just beyond the mind's grasp, requiring a spark of imagination, or even a hunch. Walking through the murk, he ignored the shopfronts, forming an image in his mind's eye of his native highlands blanketed with heather on a summer's day, and then allowed his mind to wander, drifting randomly from one fragment to another of his conversations with Cecilia, Dr Gully, and Griffiths. While he was inclined to believe Griffiths, there was something about the man, his appearance or manner, which suggested there was more to the story. Something about the fact that his wife, with newborn child, had left him. Cameron wondered about Cranbrook; by all accounts a polished, well-educated member of the professional classes, outgoing and presumably handsome, and yet deeply disliked by as amiable a soul as Gully and terrifying to Cecilia to the degree that she attempted to run away from him. What was it Gully had said about Cranbrook? Something about his 'hazy past'? Halting at the busy intersection with the Brompton Road, Cameron pondered Cranbrook, and then considered Griffiths, the look in his eyes when Cameron had casually enquired about his wife and child. Thus deep in reflection, Cameron was jolted by collision with a man walking behind him. Aha, thought Cameron as the man mumbled an apology and hurried along the sidewalk. Could that be it? With a quick glance at his watch, he reversed course, tacked across the street, and began walking quickly in the direction of home.

Arriving at his flat, Cameron was greeted as always by Angus, the Scottie, with a vigorously wagging short tail, and by his housekeeper, who tut-tutted when Cameron declined her offer to serve him lunch, declaring that he had 'no time for nourishment when truth is just around the corner', a pronouncement that caused the dour Scotswoman to mutter that her employer 'had gone daft'. Donning a soft wool cap and placing a pair of gloves in his coat pocket, Cameron hurried out the door and walked briskly to the corner, where he hailed a cab to Victoria Station. In Balham, some miles from the centre of London, the fog had lifted when Cameron detrained, and after a brief stop at the Wheatsheaf for a sandwich and half-pint, he continued on foot to The Priory. Noting the sign on the gatepost advertising the property for sale, he approached the house by the gravel drive, having first satisfied himself no one was on the premises. As before, he went first to the stables in the back and with little difficulty located the cabinet to which Griffiths alluded. Turning the latch, he looked in on its empty shelves. On the middle shelf, in plain view, was a small placard on which was crudely scrawled: 'Danger – Deadly Poison.' Cameron closed the cabinet, looked briefly around the neatly swept stalls, and then moved furtively to the door at the back of the house. He had considered the events

264

of the fatal night from the point of view of the victim and of each of the principal witnesses; Cecilia, Mrs Clark, Mary Ann, the butler, and the attending physicians. But not of the murderer, until now.

Putting on his gloves, he took a tool from his pocket and picked the lock on the kitchen door. Nothing had changed from his previous visit. Cameron moved from the kitchen to the dining-room, imagining the night Cranbrook was poisoned, with Cecilia seated at the table with Mrs Clark. Sawyers, the butler, had helped him upstairs and onto his bed earlier in the evening. But then Cranbrook had recovered sufficiently to come downstairs and join his wife and Mrs Clark for supper – mutton and green beans, according to Dr Bell, with a glass of burgundy wine. Whatever may have caused Cranbrook's illness earlier in the day, or his weakness after the riding incident, it was not, Cameron was sure, poisoning with tartar emetic. He walked slowly from the dining-room to the foot of the wide staircase. When Cranbrook had come down to supper, there was no one on the upper floor of the house, as Mary Ann had stated before the inquest court that she had joined the other servants for supper in the kitchen. Lightly touching the banister, Cameron ascended the stairs.

Though the furniture had been removed from the master bedroom, and the door firmly shut, the door to the spare bedroom at the top of the stairs was ajar. Pushing it open, Cameron walked in and surveyed the scene in the weak daylight from the window: the single bed, still made, a dresser, two straight back chairs, and a homely lithograph of children at play over the mantelpiece, where Dr Bell had found a small bottle of chloroform and vial of laudanum. Next to the bed was a nightstand, on which, according to various witnesses, there had been a water pitcher and drinking glass. Cranbrook, according to his friend and cousin, Dr Bell, had long been in the habit of drinking a glass of water just before retiring. Griffiths, Cameron considered, had observed that it would have been highly difficult to enter the house, with its many occupants, unnoticed. Unless – Cameron walked to the window and lifted the sash – the assailant had climbed in through the bedroom window, during the interval when Cranbrook was downstairs having supper. As antimony is soluble in water, and once dissolved leaves no telltale odour or taste, Cameron reasoned it would have been a simple matter to empty the packet of poison from the stable into the water pitcher. Even half of the ten-gram packet would have been twenty times the lethal dose. Having accomplished this in a matter of seconds, the killer left in the same way he or she came – through the window. Cranbrook returns to the bedroom after supper, dresses for bed in his nightshirt, pours his customary glass of water, and downs the deadly potion.

Cameron walked over to the window and leaned out. There was a distance of some eight feet to the pitched slate roof below; Cranbrook's killer could easily have climbed out of the window, dropped to the slate roof, and crawled down to the gutter. The problem would have been getting up from or down to the ground below. Gently closing the window, Cameron took a final look around the small room and then hurried downstairs and out of the kitchen door. He moved stealthily around the house to the spot directly below the window of the spare bedroom on the second floor. Something caught his eye, concealed in the thick shrubbery that bordered the house. Taking a closer look, he discovered a section of lattice, about eight feet long and constructed of sturdy laths. Propping it against the side of the house, he used it to climb up to the roof, just, he surmised, as the killer had done. And there, lying in the gutter, he discovered what his well-honed instincts had suggested he might: the final clue to the identity of Charles Cranbrook's murderer.

'And so,' said James Clifton, relaxing in one of the easy-chairs in Cameron's study with a glass of brandy and soda, 'you've worked it out in your mind?'

'Yes, Clifton,' replied Cameron. The orange cat in his lap purred contentedly.

'I don't suppose you intend to share your theory with me?'

'No,' said Cameron with a slight smile. 'I do not.'

The small black terrier entered the study, sniffed the air, and then bounced up on the sofa beside his master to receive the usual nuzzle of his ears. 'Good boy, Angus,' said Cameron as he gazed into the dog's dark-brown eyes. 'Loyal, faithful, and true. If only more of our race possessed such admirable traits.'

'As opposed to jealousy, deceit, and treachery,' said Clifton after taking a large swallow of brandy.

'Tomorrow,' said Cameron, 'we shall journey to Birmingham to interview Mrs Clark, and the dénouement of this intriguing mystery.'

'Oho,' said Clifton, beaming. 'You've come round to my point of view. Have you made the necessary arrangements?'

'I intend to confront the lady without warning. And, as you've previously visited her, you may show me the way there.'

'Excellent,' said Clifton.

'Mr Cameron,' said the housekeeper, standing in the doorway. 'Your dinner is served.'

Chapter Nineteen

Having worked past midnight at his desk in the study preparing a concise précis of the actions and statements of all material witnesses and suspects in the case, Duncan Cameron slept during most of the three hour trip from London's Paddington to New Street Station in Birmingham, terminus of the London and Birmingham Railway. The one witness Cameron, of course, had not questioned was Mrs Jane Clark, whom he had resolved at the outset of the investigation to interview at the very last. There was the risk that, arriving at the lady's doorstep unannounced, she would refuse to see him, or that she might be away, but Cameron was prepared to trade these risks for the chance of confronting her with the advantage of surprise. While Cameron dozed, James Clifton, seated opposite, occupied himself with the morning newspaper while smoking a mild cigar. At the sound of the train's whistle and slowing speed, he gazed out the window at the factory smokestacks and rows of identical brick houses in the outskirts of the industrial city, only awakening his travelling companion with a shake of the shoulder when the train arrived at the station. Alighting from their carriage, Cameron remarked on the impressive glass and iron arched roof, almost a thousand feet long, before turning toward the exit. As Clifton had previously called on Mrs Clark, who, since Cranbrook's death, had been living at the home of her sister in the Birmingham suburb of Handsworth, he was able to provide the driver of the hired coach with directions for the hour-long journey.

As they passed out of the city centre on the broad thoroughfare of the Soho Road, Cameron silently studied the grim industrial landscape; black smoke belching from numerous factory chimneys, filling the air with a sooty haze that obscured the sun, block after block of dreary working-class tenements, until, reaching a large park with a pretty lake, they entered the semi-rural environs of Handsworth, where yeoman farms competed for space with residential neighbourhoods and commercial establishments, turning at last on Grafton Street and a pleasant double row of small brick cottages. Tapping on the glass, Clifton informed the coachman, 'Number 67, on the left.' Climbing out of the coach, Cameron briefly studied the tidy house, with its neat flower garden in front and ornamental tree, and then walked up the path to the door while Clifton settled up with the driver. Cameron knocked, knocked again and, when the door finally opened, a pale girl, perhaps sixteen, peered out and said, 'Yes? May I help you?'

'Hallo,' said Cameron with a smile. 'We're here to see Mrs Clark.'

'Oh,' said the girl. 'I'm afraid Aunt Jane is not in.'

'My name's Cameron, and this is my friend James Clifton.'

'How do you do,' said Clifton with a slight bow.

'When is your aunt expected?' asked Cameron.

'She had an errand in town,' said the girl. 'Should be home by midday.'

'Perhaps we could wait inside,' suggested Cameron, 'as we've come all the way from London.'

'Oh, I see,' said the girl, holding open the door. 'You can sit in the parlour.'

In due course Mrs Clark returned from her errand, wearing her usual plain black dress with her dark hair tied back with a black ribbon and a basket of fresh fruit and vegetables over her arm. Upon entering the house she immediately observed James Clifton seated in a chair by the fireplace in the parlour. 'Oh,' she said, raising a hand to her mouth and in the process nearly dropping the basket.

Cameron rose from his chair, took a step toward Mrs Clark and said, 'I hope you will pardon our intrusion.' As she gazed at him with narrowed eyes, he added, 'My name's Cameron. Duncan Cameron. And I'm sure you remember my associate, Mr Clifton.'

Clifton bowed slightly and said, 'How do you do, madam.'

'How dare you,' said Mrs Clark, after placing her basket on a chair. 'Barging into my house without invitation—'

'Your niece,' said Cameron equably, 'was kind enough to show us in.'

'That may be, sir, but I shall show you out.'

'If you will spare a few minutes,' said Cameron, unmoving, 'I have a few questions for you. As you know, I've been engaged to investigate the murder of Charles Cranbrook.'

'Murder?' said Mrs Clark with asperity. 'Charles Cranbrook wasn't murdered. He took his own life.'

'I would suggest,' said Cameron, 'that you join us in the parlour and consent to answer my questions.'

'Oh, all right,' she said crossly, 'though it would serve you right if I tossed you out.'

Cameron chose an armchair facing Mrs Clark, who sat alone on the horse-hair sofa, with Clifton seated uncomfortably in a rocking chair next to her. The small room had the air of middle-class respectability, with antimacassars on the arms of the sofa, lithographs depicting scenes of rural life on the walls, and a braided rug before the hearth. Crossing his long legs, Cameron held his palms together in the attitude of prayer and said, 'Let

271

me begin by asking how you came to be employed by Miss Henderson.'

'I answered a notice in the newspaper, shortly after Cecilia ... Miss Henderson moved into The Priory.'

'You may refer to her as Cecilia,' said Cameron, 'as she called you Jane when I recently spoke to her. You were living at the time in London?'

'Yes, at my house in Notting Hill. I needed work as I have two children to bring up, my husband having died prematurely.'

'Your duties at The Priory,' said Cameron, 'were to supervise the household staff.'

'Yes, and to manage the expenses, keep books of account.'

'And provide Cecilia with companionship?'

'I don't deny it. She was new to the neighbourhood and had few friends. I would accompany her on rides on the common or shopping trips into the city.'

'At the time, was Cecilia involved in a relationship with Dr Gully?'

'Yes.'

'An intimate relationship?'

'As you are reputed to be a celebrated detective, sir, I presume you've read the salacious newspaper accounts.'

'*Touché*,' said Cameron with a smile. 'How would you describe your standing with Dr Gully?'

'He seemed a kindly enough old gentleman,' replied Mrs Clark, 'but I considered it wicked of him to pursue a vulnerable young woman like Cecilia, especially with her great wealth, and I cautioned her it could come to ruin.'

'Which it did,' said Cameron. Mrs Clark nodded. 'Would you say,' he asked, 'that the affair was ended by mutual consent?'

'Yes,' said Mrs Clark, 'though the doctor kept his house in Balham, no doubt in the hope of renewing the affair.'

'And after Cecilia's remarriage, do you believe Gully was jealous of her new husband?'

'Oh, extremely jealous. He wrote Mr Cranbrook the most wretched letter, accusing him of marrying her for her money.'

'A single letter?' asked Cameron. 'Or several?'

After the briefest hesitation, Mrs Clark said, 'Only one.'

'I see,' said Cameron. 'And *did* Cranbrook marry Cecilia for her money?'

Mrs Clark stared into Cameron's pale-blue eyes, betraying no emotion. 'Not so far as I know,' she replied after a moment. 'Though Cecilia's habit of extravagant expenditure seemed to vex him.'

'Do you suppose,' said Cameron, adopting a conversational tone, 'that Gully was so consumed with jealousy and unrequited love that he resorted to murdering his rival?'

'Charles Cranbrook was *not* murdered. Nor, in my opinion, was Dr Gully capable of such a thing. Why, he would scarcely harm a fly.'

'I understand there were quarrels in the marriage,' observed Cameron.

'I do not know if you have been married, sir, but in my experience there are always quarrels in a marriage. This was no different.'

'I'm told that Cecilia was particularly distressed over Cranbrook's insistence on sacking Griffiths, the stableman.'

'She disagreed, of course, but naturally Mr Cranbrook was master of the house.'

'Griffiths was extremely angry and bitter, breathing threats against Cranbrook,' said Cameron, 'as his wife was expecting a baby and they were forced to move out of the coach house.'

'If you say so,' said Mrs Clark without emotion.

'Turning to the night Cranbrook was poisoned,' said Cameron. 'You were the first to attend to him.'

'Yes. I did everything in my power to save him.'

'You sent Mary Ann for hot water and dry mustard.' Mrs Clark nodded. 'Which you mixed and administered to the unconscious man, is that so?'

'Yes, it is.'

'Why did you do so?' At this question, the hitherto impassive Clifton gave Cameron a curious look.

'Because he demanded hot water,' replied Mrs Clark.

'Yes, he did. So Mary Ann testified before the court of inquest. But you administered hot water mixed with mustard. A well-known emetic, a method of inducing vomiting, which it succeeded admirably in doing. Why would you have done so, unless you had foreknowledge that Cranbrook had been poisoned?'

'I smelt chloroform on his breath,' Mrs Clark replied without hesitation. 'And he admitted to me he'd taken poison, as I've repeatedly stated. I was merely trying to save him.'

'And when did this admission occur?'

'When Mary Ann went downstairs to fetch the hot water.'

'Mary Ann insists that Cranbrook was unconscious when she left the room and unconscious when she returned a few minutes later.'

'He admitted to me he'd poisoned himself,' said Mrs Clark calmly, 'when we were alone. Instructed me to say nothing about it to Cecilia.'

'I find this a very curious assertion,' said Cameron, leaning forward. 'When you later confided this to Dr Johnson, he demanded to know why you hadn't said something earlier, and you insisted you'd mentioned this vital communication to Dr Harrison, who vehemently denied it. I choose to believe Dr Harrison and am certain, madam, that you were lying then as you are lying now. The question in my mind, is why.'

'I assume you're going to accuse me of murdering Charles Cranbrook.'

Ignoring the comment, Cameron said, 'Not only did you invent this tale about Cranbrook's admission of suicide, you also lied about Cranbrook's treatment of Cecilia and the state of their marriage. As you well know, he abused her cruelly, and the brief marriage was a shambles.' Mrs Clark merely glared at her accuser. 'But of even greater interest to me,' continued Cameron, 'than these mistruths is what you chose *not* to reveal.'

'What do you mean?'

'I have it on the word of two credible witnesses that Cranbrook informed you, some weeks before the murder, that he intended to sack *you*, which you, curiously, never disclosed to Cecilia.'

275

'What of it?'

'I can only think of one reason why you would have kept this extraordinary piece of news from Cecilia, and that is to deflect suspicion from yourself in the eventuality Cranbrook was murdered.'

'Rubbish!' Mrs Clark started to rise from the sofa and then sat down again.

'I happen to believe,' said Cameron, 'that you were in love with Cecilia. And that you despised Cranbrook for his terrible mistreatment of her. You knew she wanted to get out of the marriage. You knew he'd never consent to a separation, as he was wholly dependent on her wealth.' Cameron rose from his chair and stood towering over Mrs Clark. 'And lastly, you knew you were about to lose your position at The Priory, losing your lover to a man you hated, and forced into penury.' Mrs Clark glared at Cameron with eyes as dark as coal. 'And so,' concluded Cameron, 'when Cranbrook was poisoned, you concocted the story that he admitted to killing himself, and then shrewdly you told no one that he intended to dismiss you.'

'All very fanciful,' said Mrs Clark, 'but nothing that would hold up in a court of law.'

'The question is why,' said Cameron, beginning to pace on the rug before the hearth. 'Either because you committed the murder ... or because you were protecting someone else who did.'

'I believe I've heard enough,' said Mrs Clark, rising from the sofa. 'You and your friend may go now. You don't seriously believe that I'm going to admit to these scurrilous accusations...'

'It might have been Cecilia herself,' continued Cameron. 'Or it might have been Dr Gully. Or even Griffiths. Each of them certainly had ample motive to see Cranbrook dead.' He paused and looked her in the eye. 'But it wasn't,' he said flatly. Turning to Clifton, who was paying rapt attention to Cameron's monologue, he said, 'It might interest you to know that Mrs Clark's maiden name was Blackthorn. Jane Blackthorn.'

'What of it?' she said angrily.

'Cranbrook was poisoned with tartar emetic,' said Cameron coolly, 'which Griffiths purchased in December to worm the horses and which he kept in an unlocked cabinet marked deadly poison in the stables. There it remained after Griffiths was sacked. The night Cranbrook was poisoned, his killer slipped into his bedroom through the upstairs window and emptied the packet of tartar emetic into the water pitcher on his night stand.' Cameron paused and stared at Mrs Clark, who was now hanging on his every word. 'As Cranbrook was about to retire to bed,' said Cameron, 'he poured his usual glass of water and drank it. The problem with your having poisoned Cranbrook, my dear lady, is that you were in the company of Cecilia before, during, and after supper right up to the moment he called out for hot water.' She met his steady gaze. 'The killer slipped into Cranbrook's bedroom when he went downstairs for supper. Having poured the poison into the water pitcher, the killer left by the same means – through the open window and down to the roof and on to the lawn. By means of a piece of lattice-work I found concealed in the shrubbery.'

'An interesting speculation,' said Mrs Clark.

'However,' said Cameron with a small, satisfied smile, 'in the process of beating a hasty retreat, something was dropped.' He reached into the inside breast pocket of his jacket and produced a folded handkerchief. 'This,' he said, unfolding it on his palm. 'An ordinary lady's handkerchief, but with the name "Jenny Blackthorn" embroidered in the corner.' He held it out for Mrs Clark's inspection. As he did so, she blanched and her steely reserve dissolved in a flood of tears. 'Your niece, if I'm not mistaken,' concluded Cameron.

'Poor Jenny,' muttered Mrs Clark as she held her face in her hands. 'Poor, poor Jenny.'

'Who, I believe,' said Cameron, 'had been involved in an affair with Cranbrook.' Mrs Clark nodded miserably, wiping the tears from her cheeks. 'By whom she had a child,' said Cameron.

'Yes,' said Mrs Clark softly. 'Little Davy.'

'Jenny murdered Cranbrook,' said Cameron, 'and you, knowing it, tried to protect her.'

'It was the least I could do,' said Mrs Clark, 'after the suffering she'd endured.'

Turning to Clifton, Cameron said, 'Be a good fellow, and go to the kitchen and ask for a pot of tea.' After the lapse of five minutes, an interval passed in silence, the plain girl returned with a tray, teapot, milk jug, cups, and saucers. After serving each of them, she withdrew, and Mrs Clark, now composed, said, 'Charles Cranbrook began his affair with Jenny when the poor girl was in her teens. He put her up in cheap rooms in Maidenhead. All through his law studies at the Temple he treated her as a kept woman, fathering the boy, who's now six.'

'And then,' said Cameron, 'when it suited him, he abandoned her.'

'Yes,' she said, 'but at Jenny's insistence he provided modest support for the boy. That is, until he met Cecilia. Oh, God,' she groaned, unleashing another wave of tears, 'it's all my fault.'

'Pray go on,' said Cameron after a moment.

Wiping her eyes, Mrs Clark said, 'Once Cranbrook realized he was fixed for life, after working out an arrangement with Cecilia's solicitor and setting a date for the wedding, the support for Davy abruptly ended. Nor would Cranbrook answer poor Jenny's letters. He was so heartless. When you asked if there was more than one letter accusing Cranbrook of marrying Cecilia for her money–'

'Yes?'

'There were two. When he showed me the second, I knew it was from Jenny by her handwriting.'

'But what I don't understand,' said Cameron, 'is how Jenny would have known about the poison Griffiths kept in the stables.'

Mrs Clark looked down at the floor and then sadly raised her eyes. 'As you've learned this much,' she said, 'you may as well know it all. After Cranbrook abandoned her and the boy, Jenny – my dead brother's only child – was ruined. And so, to put food on the table, she was reduced to ... she became a fallen woman.'

Cameron grimaced, and Clifton muttered, 'A

terrible shame.'

'And by pure happenstance,' Mrs Clark continued, 'she fell in one night with that rogue Griffiths. This was before he was sacked. He took her back to the stables, where she discovered the poison.'

'How did you learn this?' asked Cameron.

'The poor girl told me one day when I went to see her, taking a cake for the boy. She was beside herself with recriminations for what Cranbrook had done, threatening to take matters into her own hands. I pleaded with her, but how was I to know? And she knew where Cranbrook could be found, knew the house. And so, that night when he collapsed, in my heart of hearts I knew it had to be poor Jenny.'

'I suspect,' said Cameron, looking into Mrs Clark's red-rimmed eyes, 'that someone helped her discover that Cranbrook was sleeping in the spare bedroom.' Mrs Clark looked down at the floor.

Finishing his cup of tea, Cameron rose from his chair and said, 'Well, it is as I suspected from the beginning.'

'What?' said Clifton with an astonished expression. 'From the beginning?'

'Well, not quite the beginning,' said Cameron. 'But from the moment I discovered the obvious defects in your account, madam,' he said, turning to Mrs Clark, 'and learned that Cranbrook had carried on an affair with another woman.'

'I suppose I should thank you,' said Mrs Clark, 'as you've taken a great burden off me.'

'You know I shall have to report this to Scotland Yard,' said Cameron.

Mrs Clark nodded and said, 'Yes, but Jenny's gone away. Taken the boy and fled the country.'

'Aided with funds from her relations, I imagine,' said Cameron.

'I'd never admit to it.'

'Well, madam,' said Cameron, 'we must take our leave, as we have a train to catch.'

'Goodbye, Mr Cameron. I am sorry if I caused you a great deal of trouble.'

Taking her hand, Cameron said, 'You, Mrs Clark, are one of the few actors in this sordid affair who behaved with honour and courage. Clifton, we must be on our way.'

Epilogue

The day following his interview with Mrs Clark, Duncan Cameron paid a call on Detective Chief Inspector Cox at Scotland Yard, whom he presented with the embroidered handkerchief found at the crime scene and provided a succinct account of his theory of the case. 'All very well and good,' commented Cox in a patronizing tone, 'but I maintain this was a case of suicide, not murder.'

'I defer to your judgement,' said Cameron, 'as you are free to investigate the matter further if you choose,' aware that the suspect, whom he was certain had committed the crime, had fled the country. Cameron next called on his client, Lady

Cranbrook, and her husband at their mansion on Palace Green. After exchanging the customary pleasantries, Cameron delivered his devastating findings with as much tact and gentleness as he was able: that their son had indeed been murdered and by someone no one had suspected in the police investigation or the coroner's inquest. A poor young woman in Maidenhead by whom he'd fathered a bastard son, whom he had abandoned as soon as he was engaged to marry the wealthy Miss Henderson. After assuring Lady Cranbrook, who was prostrate with tears, that neither a police investigation nor prosecution of the young woman was likely, and that as a consequence the matter would remain strictly confidential, he bid them good day, patting the substantial cheque in his breast pocket.

In the aftermath of the coroner's inquest, James Gully, curiously, chose to remain at Orwell Lodge, his cottage in Balham. His professional reputation, however, was damaged beyond repair by his merciless cross-examination during the inquest about his scandalous relationship with Cecilia and by the lingering question of his possible guilt in the murder, both of which received extensive coverage in all of the leading newspapers. With the death of his partner, Dr Wilson, his once-thriving practice of the water cure at the hydro in Malvern declined precipitously, though some faithful adherents remained to the end. And so Gully grew old in his cottage, his once brilliant reputation in tatters, his heart broken, the once vigorous outdoorsman frail and alone, attended by his spinster sisters until he died quietly at the age of 75. He never spoke to Cecilia again.

For a time she remained sequestered with her mother and father at Buscot Park, having dismissed the staff and sold most of the furnishings at The Priory by the time of the coroner's inquest. Her prized collection of artworks was sold at auction some months later at Bonham's in London. As her father was deathly ill, and her mother and siblings would have nothing to do with her, Cecilia adopted the assumed name 'Wilson' and purchased a seaside cottage at Southsea, in Hampshire, where she moved in the autumn of 1872, some seven months after Charles Cranbrook's death. Her large fortune still intact, she employed a cook, two maids, a gardener and coachman and spent her days alone, except for the servants, drinking copious amounts of brandy and sherry as she gazed forlornly from her bay window at the ships plying the slate water of the Solent. Cecilia continued this solitary existence, increasingly dependent on alcohol, for another eighteen months, until in the summer of 1874 she received an unannounced visit from an uncle, her mother's Scottish brother, who found her in a drunken stupor, consuming a bottle of brandy a day. Unwilling to heed her uncle's advice to summon a doctor, she was fated to die, perversely, in precisely the same fashion as her first husband, vomiting dark red blood caused by the haematemesis that destroyed the lining of her stomach. Dead at the age of thirty-two, she was buried in an unmarked grave. Under her will, she made generous bequests to Jane Clark's son and daughter and to a granddaughter of James Gully and left the residue of her vast estate in trust to her brothers and sister's descendants.

Mrs Jane Clark, about whose role in the poisoning speculation continued to swirl long after the inquest, bid her sister and niece in Birmingham farewell and, accompanied by her two children, booked passage on a steamer to the West Indies in the autumn of 1872. Arriving at Kingston, Jamaica before Christmas, they proceeded to St. Ann's Bay on the north shore of the island and to Content, one of the largest coffee plantations in the colony, the home of Mrs Margaret Clark, her late husband's aunt. Within two years of their arrival, Margaret Clark died, bequeathing the plantation and her entire estate to her niece Jane, as she and her late husband had no children of their own. That she stood to inherit this large estate had been explained to Jane Clark in a letter she received from her aunt a year before Charles Cranbrook's murder, another of her secrets that certainly would have deflected suspicion from her had she revealed it to the police or coroner's inquest. Hence she raised her family in luxury on Content, returning near the end of her life to England, where she died and was buried in Lewisham, a village south of London, presumably in peace, at the ripe old age of ninety.

The whereabouts of Jenny Blackthorn and Little Davy remained unknown, though it may be safely surmised that they were generously supported by a familial benefactor.

The publishers hope that this book has given you enjoyable reading. Large Print Books are especially designed to be as easy to see and hold as possible. If you wish a complete list of our books please ask at your local library or write directly to:

Magna Large Print Books
Magna House, Long Preston,
Skipton, North Yorkshire.
BD23 4ND

This Large Print Book for the partially sighted, who cannot read normal print, is published under the auspices of

THE ULVERSCROFT FOUNDATION

THE ULVERSCROFT FOUNDATION

... we hope that you have enjoyed this Large Print Book. Please think for a moment about those people who have worse eyesight problems than you ... and are unable to even read or enjoy Large Print, without great difficulty.

You can help them by sending a donation, large or small to:

The Ulverscroft Foundation,
1, The Green, Bradgate Road,
Anstey, Leicestershire, LE7 7FU,
England.

or request a copy of our brochure for more details.

The Foundation will use all your help to assist those people who are handicapped by various sight problems and need special attention.

Thank you very much for your help.